PUP
DETECT

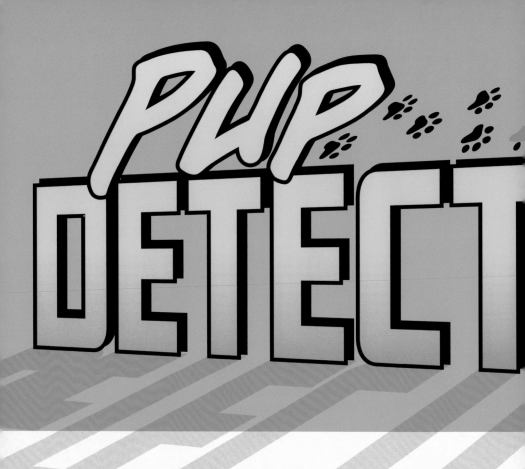

BATTLE OF THE BANDS

Written by **FELIX GUMPAW**
Illustrated by **GLASS HOUSE GRAPHICS**

 LITTLE SIMON
NEW YORK LONDON TORONTO SYDNEY NEW DELHI

LITTLE SIMON
AN IMPRINT OF SIMON & SCHUSTER CHILDREN'S PUBLISHING DIVISION
1230 AVENUE OF THE AMERICAS, NEW YORK, NEW YORK 10020
FIRST LITTLE SIMON EDITION OCTOBER 2022
COPYRIGHT © 2022 BY SIMON & SCHUSTER, INC.
ALL RIGHTS RESERVED, INCLUDING THE RIGHT OF REPRODUCTION IN WHOLE OR IN PART IN ANY FORM. LITTLE SIMON IS A REGISTERED TRADEMARK OF SIMON & SCHUSTER, INC., AND ASSOCIATED COLOPHON IS A TRADEMARK OF SIMON & SCHUSTER, INC. FOR INFORMATION ABOUT SPECIAL DISCOUNTS FOR BULK PURCHASES, PLEASE CONTACT SIMON & SCHUSTER SPECIAL SALES AT 1-866-506-1949 OR BUSINESS@SIMONANDSCHUSTER.COM. ART AND COLORS BY GLASS HOUSE GRAPHICS • LETTERING BY MARCOS MASSAO INOUE • SUPERVISION BY MJ MACEDO/STUPLENDO • ART SERVICES BY GLASS HOUSE GRAPHICS • THE SIMON & SCHUSTER SPEAKERS BUREAU CAN BRING AUTHORS TO YOUR LIVE EVENT. FOR MORE INFORMATION OR TO BOOK AN EVENT CONTACT THE SIMON & SCHUSTER SPEAKERS BUREAU AT 1-866-248-3049 OR VISIT OUR WEBSITE AT WWW.SIMONSPEAKERS.COM.
DESIGNED BY NICHOLAS SCIACCA
MANUFACTURED IN CHINA 0522 SCP
10 9 8 7 6 5 4 3 2 1
LIBRARY OF CONGRESS CATALOGING-IN-PUBLICATION DATA
NAMES: GUMPAW, FELIX, AUTHOR. I GLASS HOUSE GRAPHICS, ILLUSTRATOR.
TITLE: BATTLE OF THE BANDS / BY FELIX GUMPAW ; ILLUSTRATED BY GLASS HOUSE GRAPHICS.
DESCRIPTION: FIRST LITTLE SIMON EDITION. I NEW YORK : LITTLE SIMON, 2022. I SERIES: PUP DETECTIVES ; 8 I AUDIENCE: AGES 5-9. I AUDIENCE: GRADES K-1. I SUMMARY: "THE BATTLE OF THE BANDS IS OFF TO A HAUNTING START WHEN A GHOST TRIES TO SCARE MUSIC AWAY FROM PAWSTON FOREVER!"— PROVIDED BY PUBLISHER. IDENTIFIERS: LCCN 2021053981 (PRINT) I LCCN 2021053982 (EBOOK) I ISBN 9781665912228 (PB) I ISBN 9781665912235 (HC) I ISBN 9781665912242 (EBOOK) SUBJECTS: CYAC: GRAPHIC NOVELS. I MYSTERY AND DETECTIVE STORIES. I DOGS—FICTION. I ANIMALS—FICTION. I BANDS (MUSIC)—FICTION. I CONTESTS—FICTION. I LCGFT: GRAPHIC NOVELS. I DETECTIVE AND MYSTERY FICTION. CLASSIFICATION: LCC PZ7.7.G858 BAT 2022 (PRINT) I LCC PZ7.7.G858 (EBOOK) I DDC 741.5/973—DC23/ENG/20220309
LC RECORD AVAILABLE AT HTTPS://LCCN.LOC.GOV/2021053981
LC EBOOK RECORD AVAILABLE AT HTTPS://LCCN.LOC.GOV/2021053982

CONTENTS

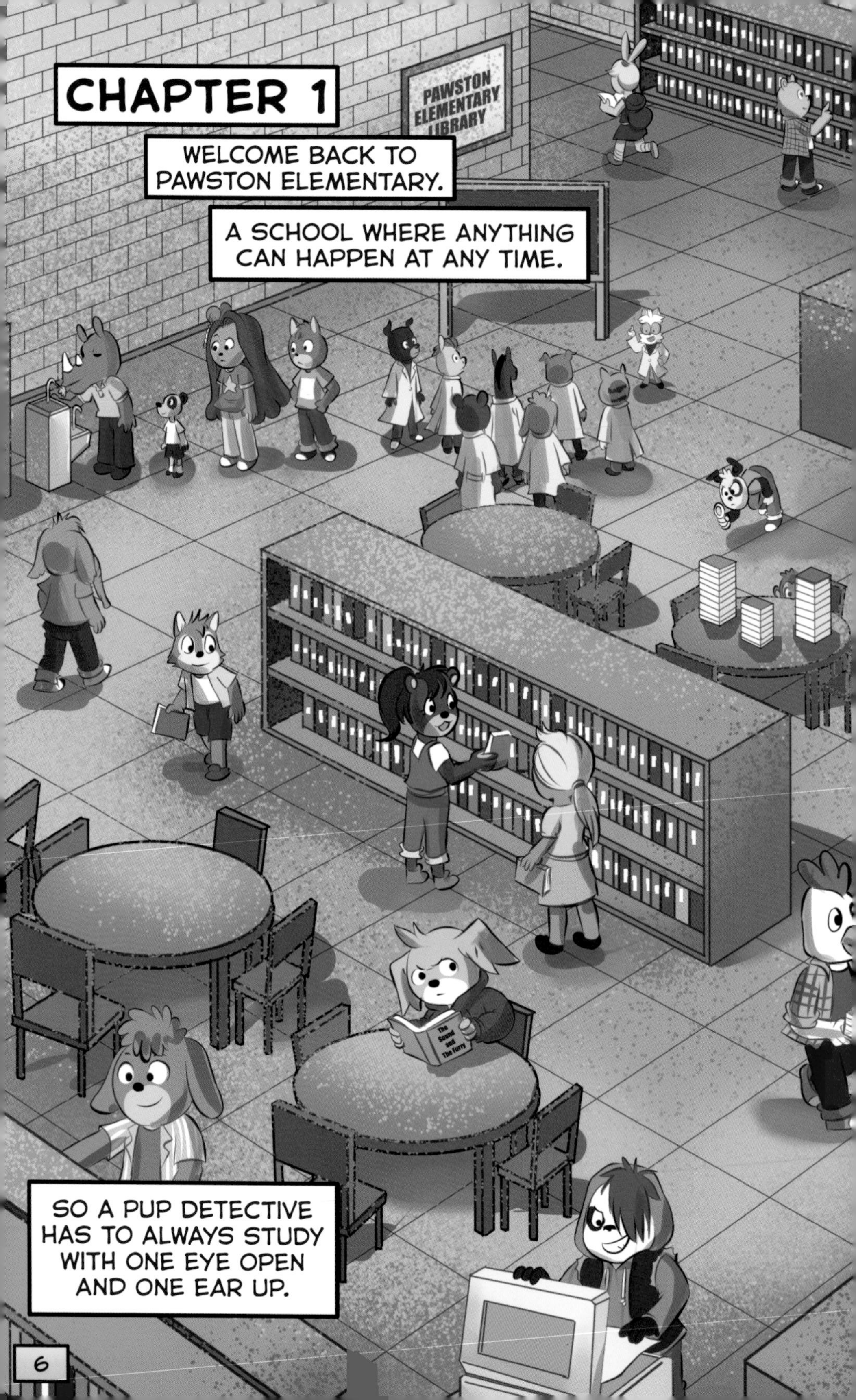
CHAPTER 1
PAWSTON ELEMENTARY LIBRARY
WELCOME BACK TO PAWSTON ELEMENTARY.
A SCHOOL WHERE ANYTHING CAN HAPPEN AT ANY TIME.
The Sound and The Furry
SO A PUP DETECTIVE HAS TO ALWAYS STUDY WITH ONE EYE OPEN AND ONE EAR UP.

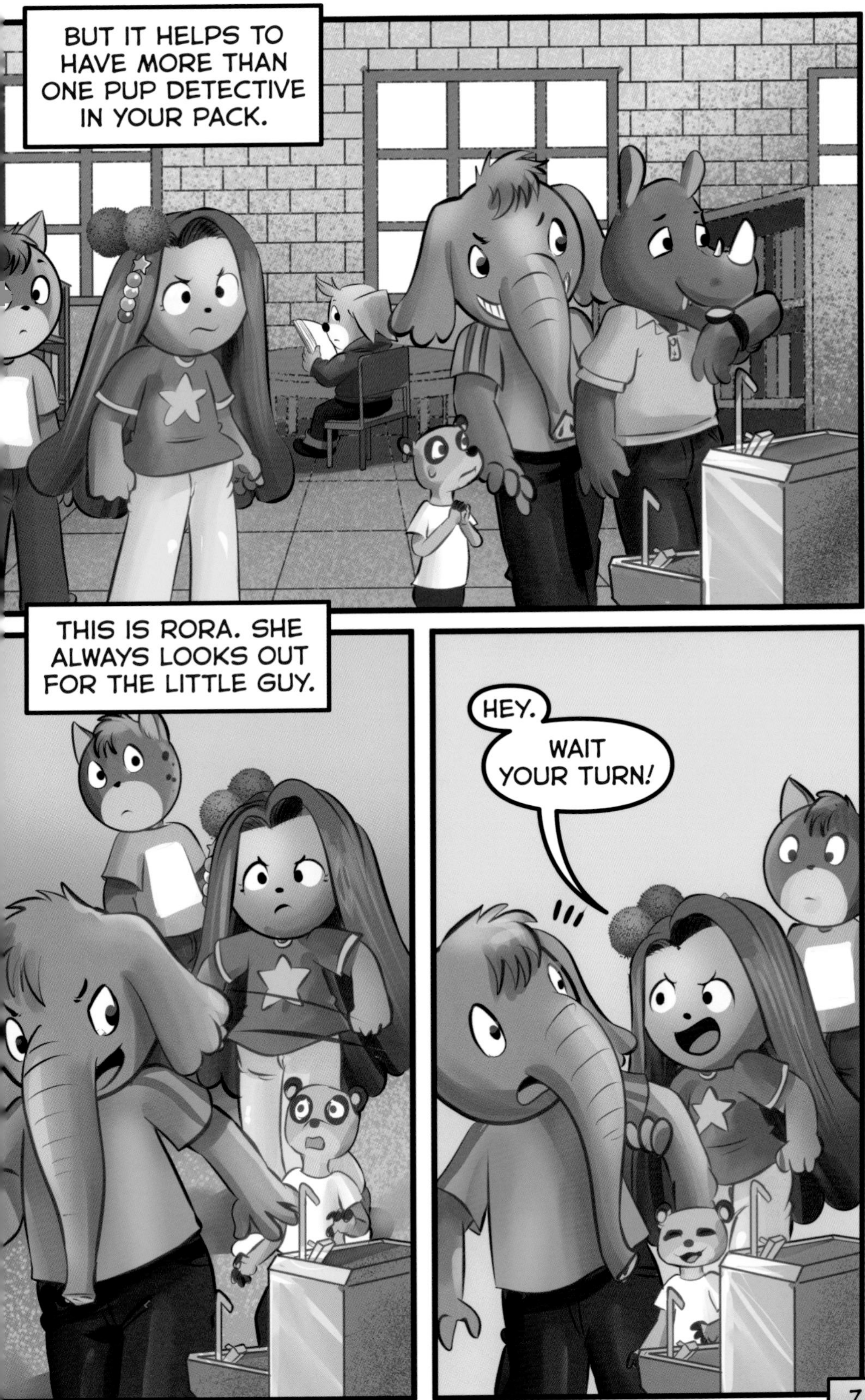
BUT IT HELPS TO HAVE MORE THAN ONE PUP DETECTIVE IN YOUR PACK.
THIS IS RORA. SHE ALWAYS LOOKS OUT FOR THE LITTLE GUY.
HEY.
WAIT YOUR TURN!

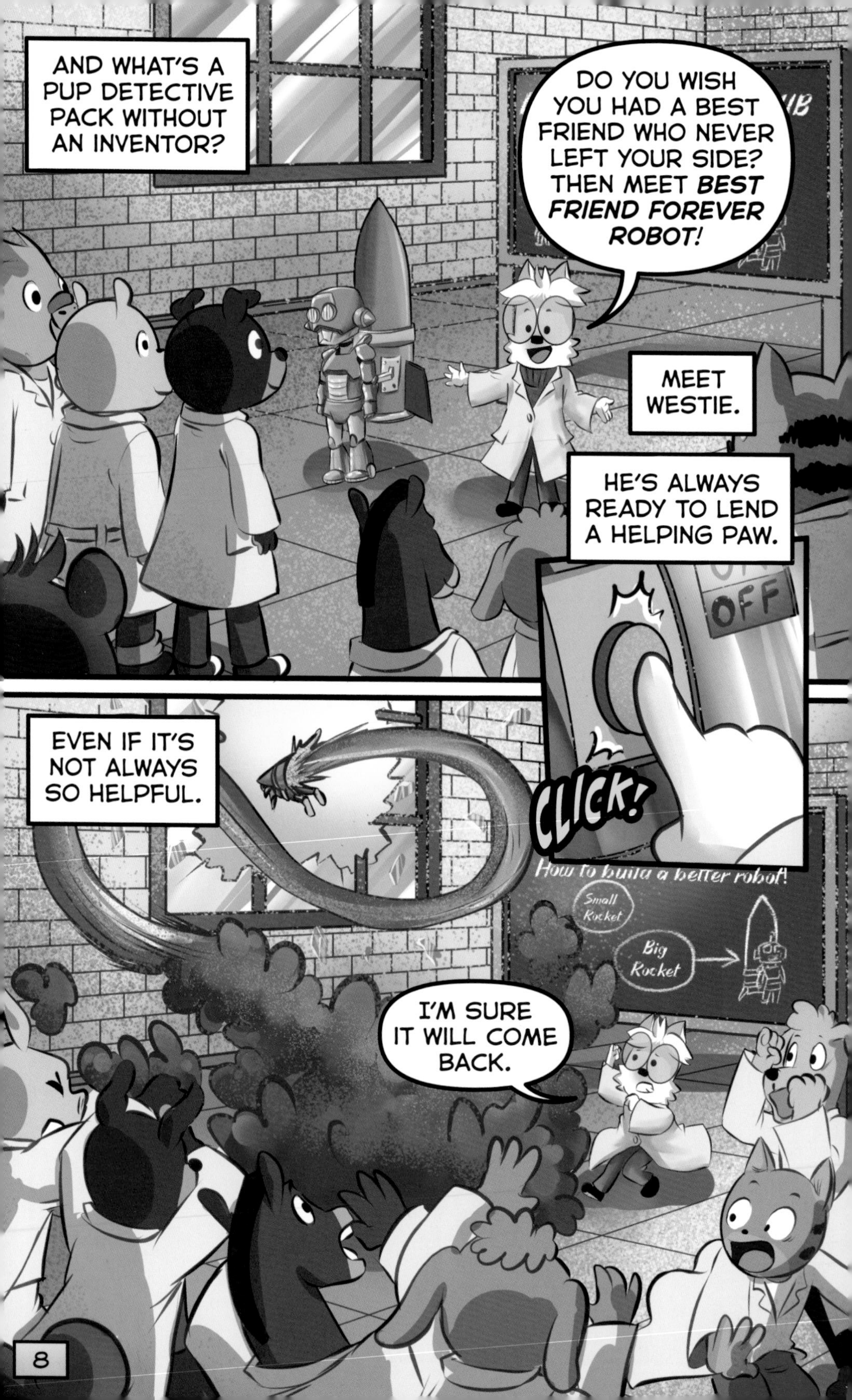
AND WHAT'S A PUP DETECTIVE PACK WITHOUT AN INVENTOR?
DO YOU WISH YOU HAD A BEST FRIEND WHO NEVER LEFT YOUR SIDE? THEN MEET *BEST FRIEND FOREVER ROBOT!*
MEET WESTIE.
HE'S ALWAYS READY TO LEND A HELPING PAW.
OFF
CLICK!
EVEN IF IT'S NOT ALWAYS SO HELPFUL.
How to build a better robot!
Small Rocket
Big Rocket
I'M SURE IT WILL COME BACK.

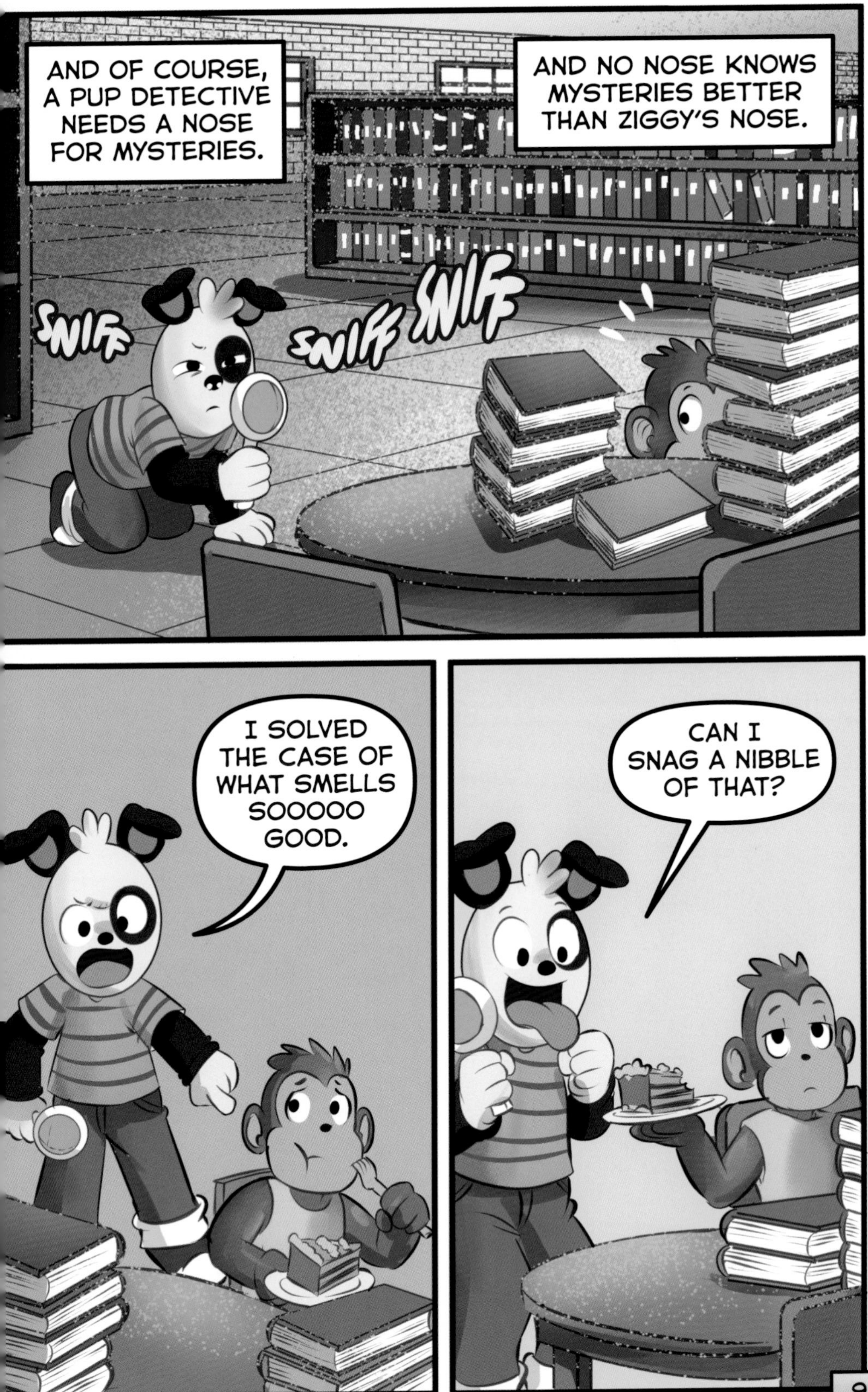
AND OF COURSE, A PUP DETECTIVE NEEDS A NOSE FOR MYSTERIES.
AND NO NOSE KNOWS MYSTERIES BETTER THAN ZIGGY'S NOSE.
SNIFF
SNIFF
SNIFF
I SOLVED THE CASE OF WHAT SMELLS SOOOOO GOOD.
CAN I SNAG A NIBBLE OF THAT?

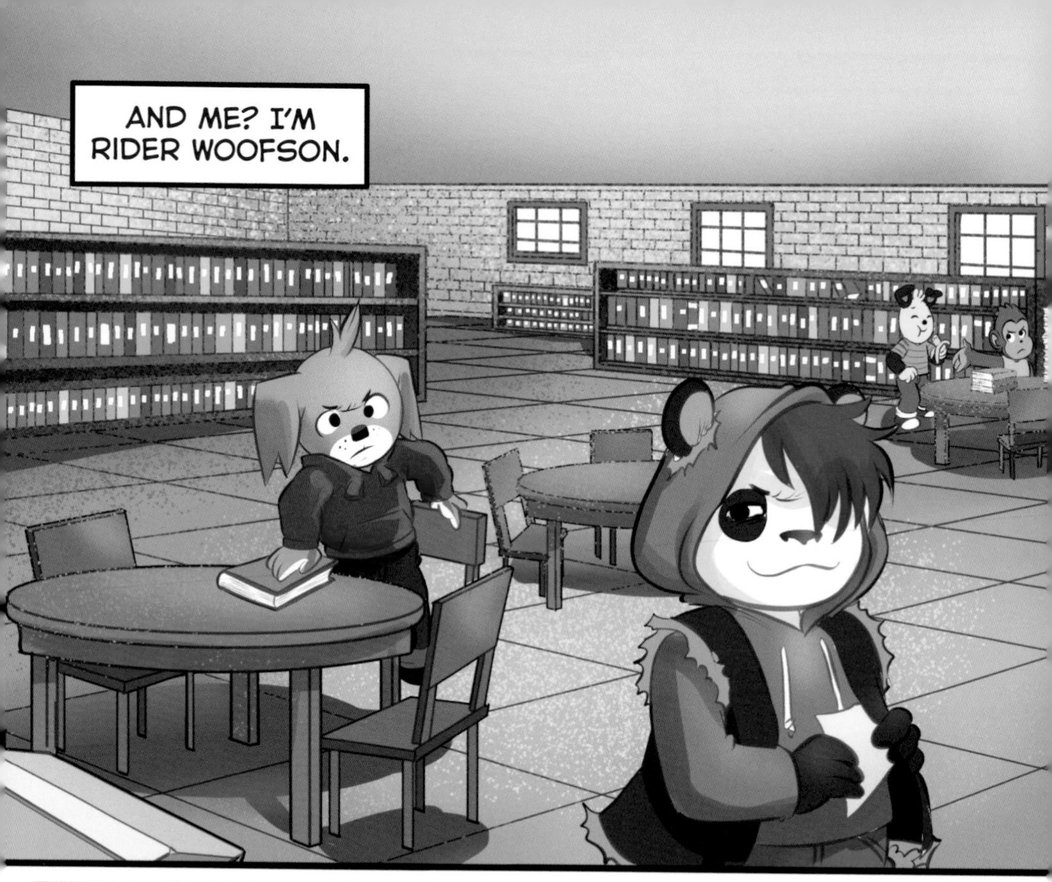
AND ME? I'M RIDER WOOFSON.

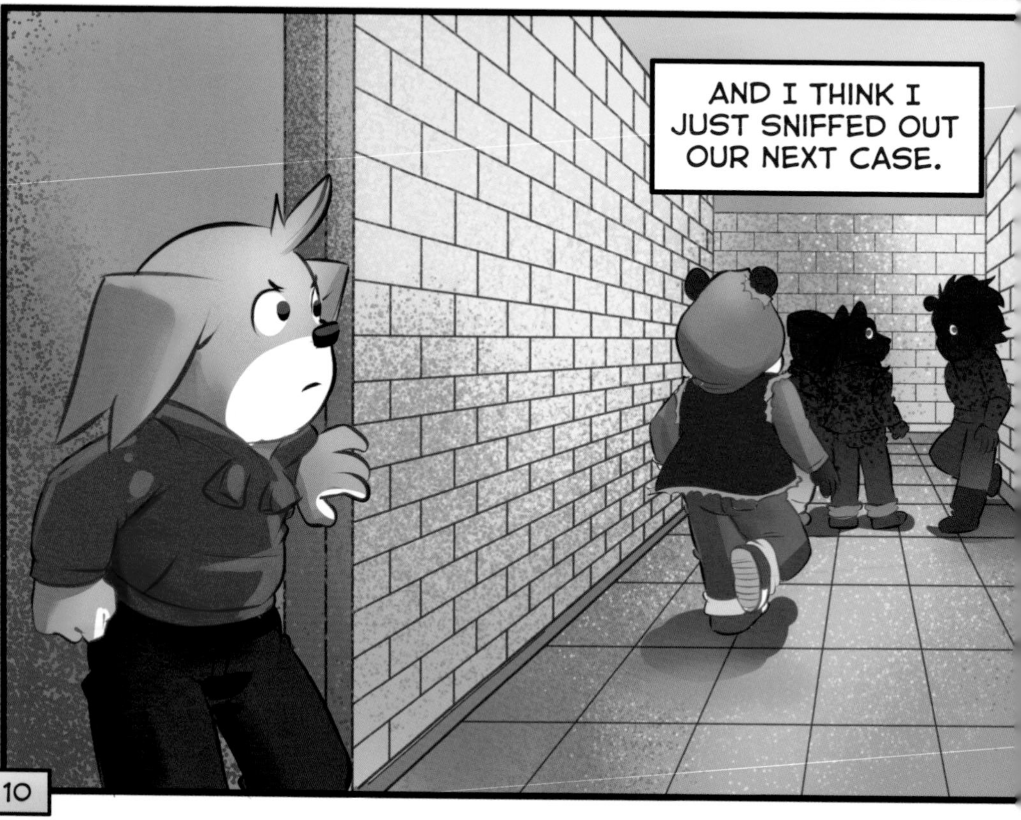
AND I THINK I JUST SNIFFED OUT OUR NEXT CASE.

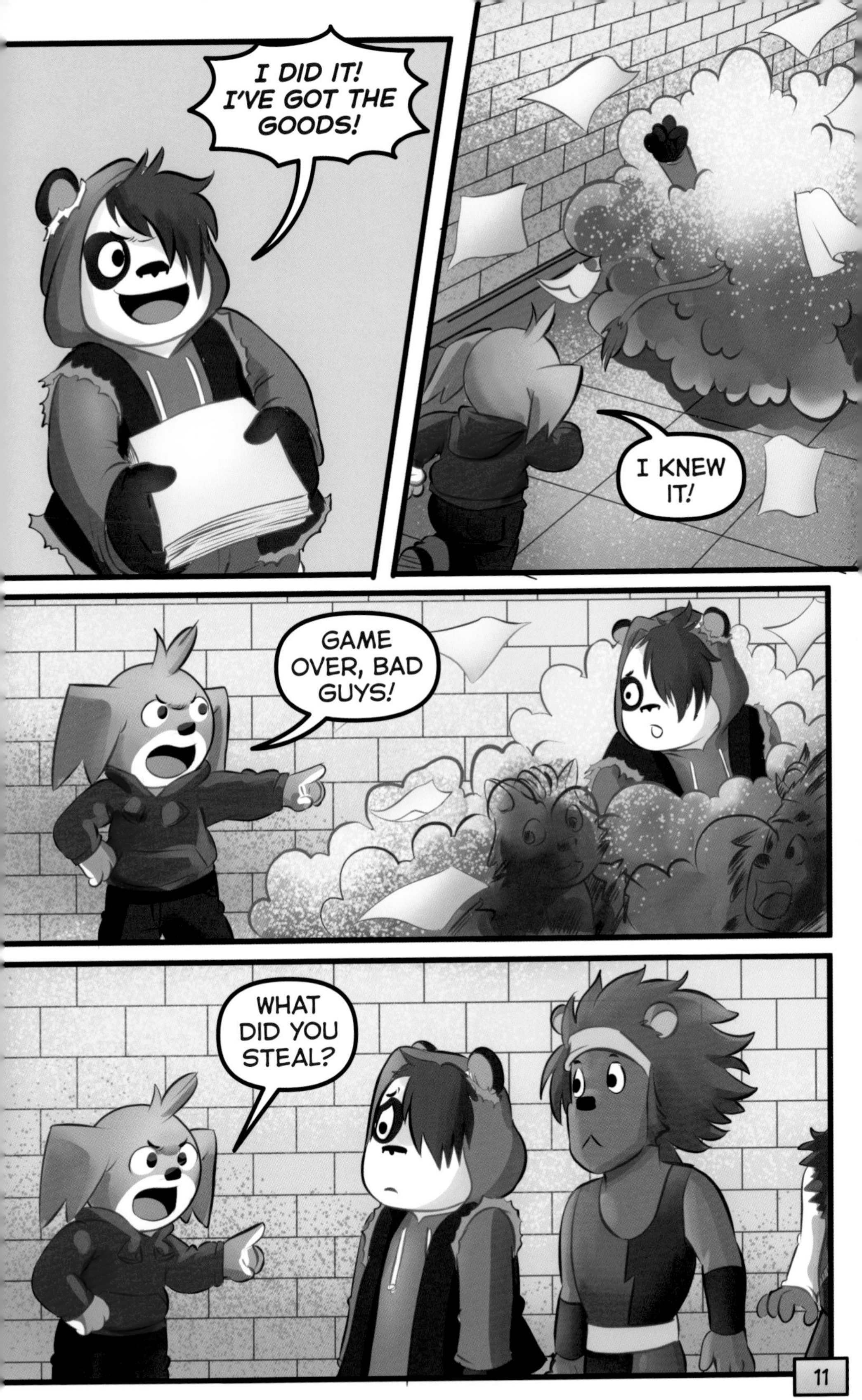
I DID IT! I'VE GOT THE GOODS!
I KNEW IT!
GAME OVER, BAD GUYS!
WHAT DID YOU STEAL?

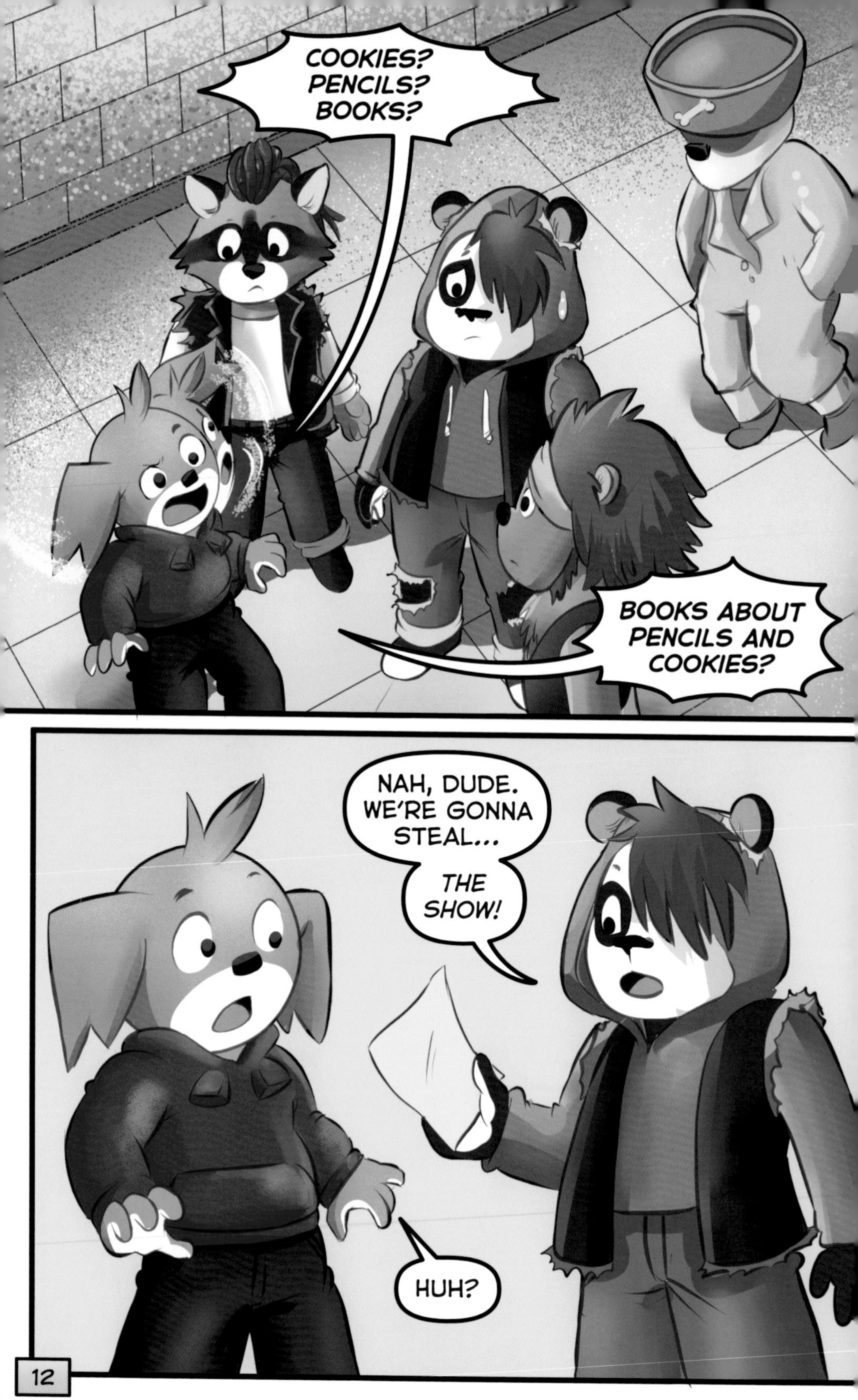
COOKIES? PENCILS? BOOKS?
BOOKS ABOUT PENCILS AND COOKIES?
NAH, DUDE. WE'RE GONNA STEAL...
THE SHOW!
HUH?

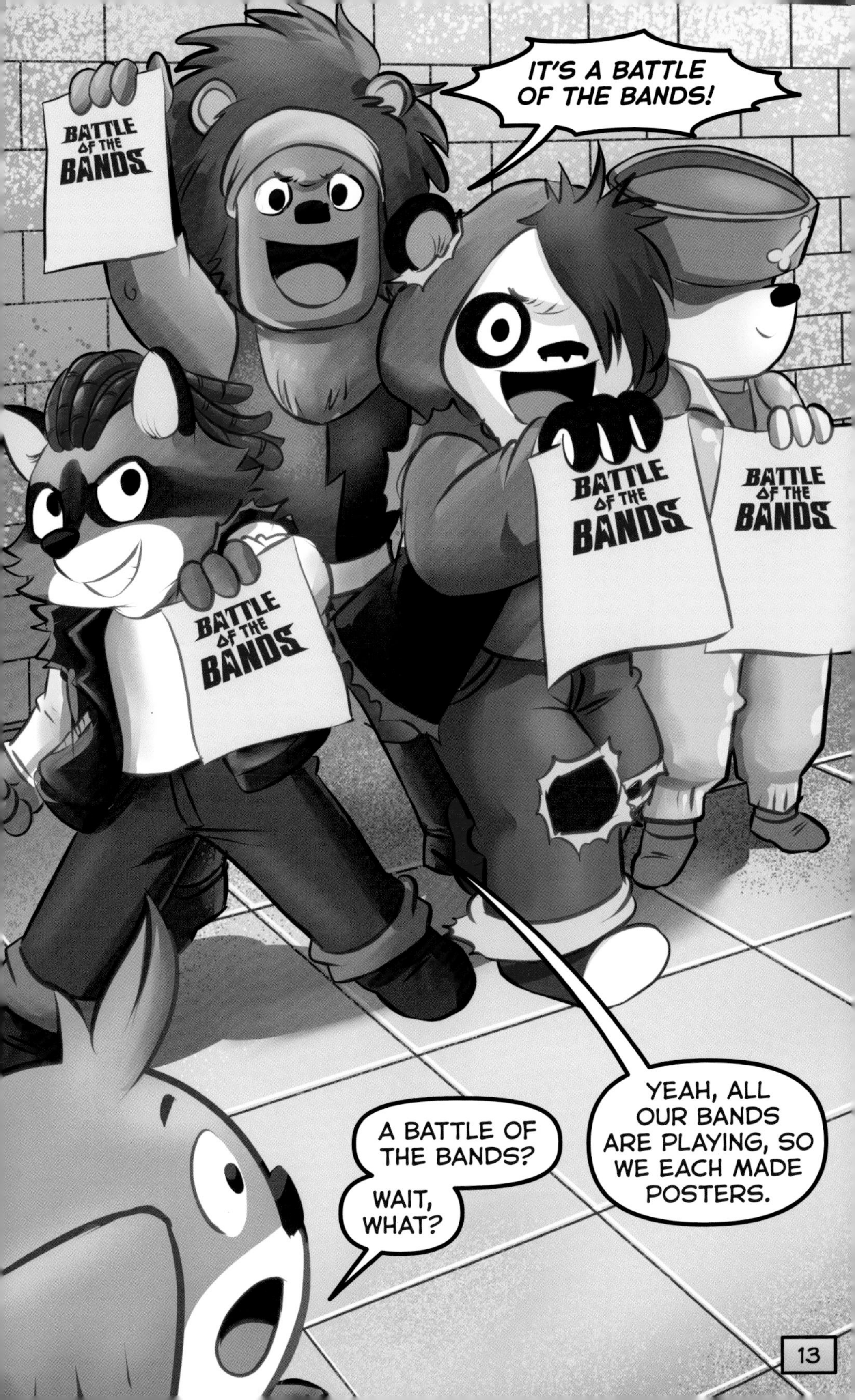
BATTLE OF THE BANDS
IT'S A BATTLE OF THE BANDS!
BATTLE OF THE BANDS
BATTLE OF THE BANDS
BATTLE OF THE BANDS
A BATTLE OF THE BANDS?
WAIT, WHAT?
YEAH, ALL OUR BANDS ARE PLAYING, SO WE EACH MADE POSTERS.

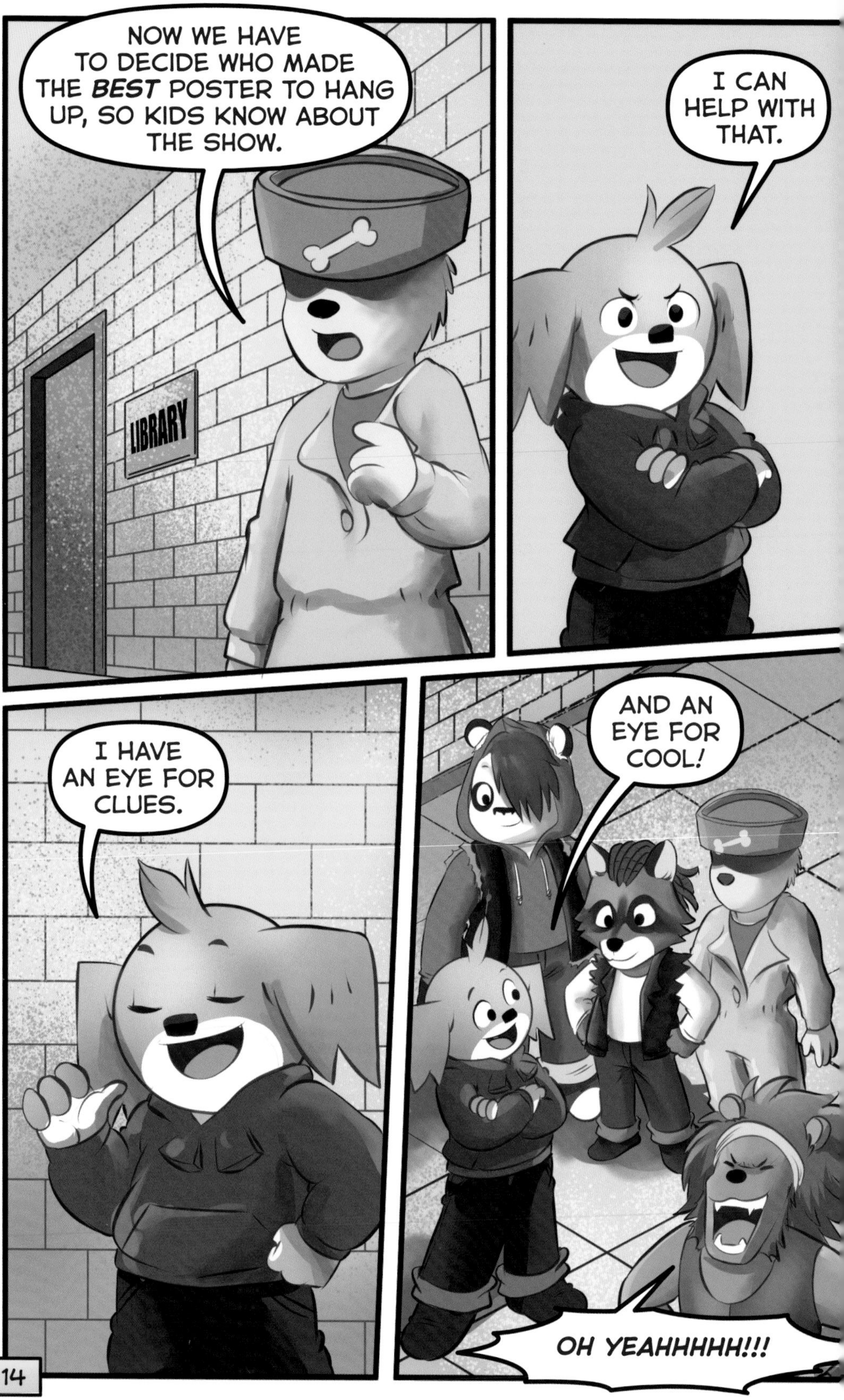
NOW WE HAVE TO DECIDE WHO MADE THE *BEST* POSTER TO HANG UP, SO KIDS KNOW ABOUT THE SHOW.
LIBRARY
I CAN HELP WITH THAT.
I HAVE AN EYE FOR CLUES.
AND AN EYE FOR COOL!
OH YEAHHHHH!!!

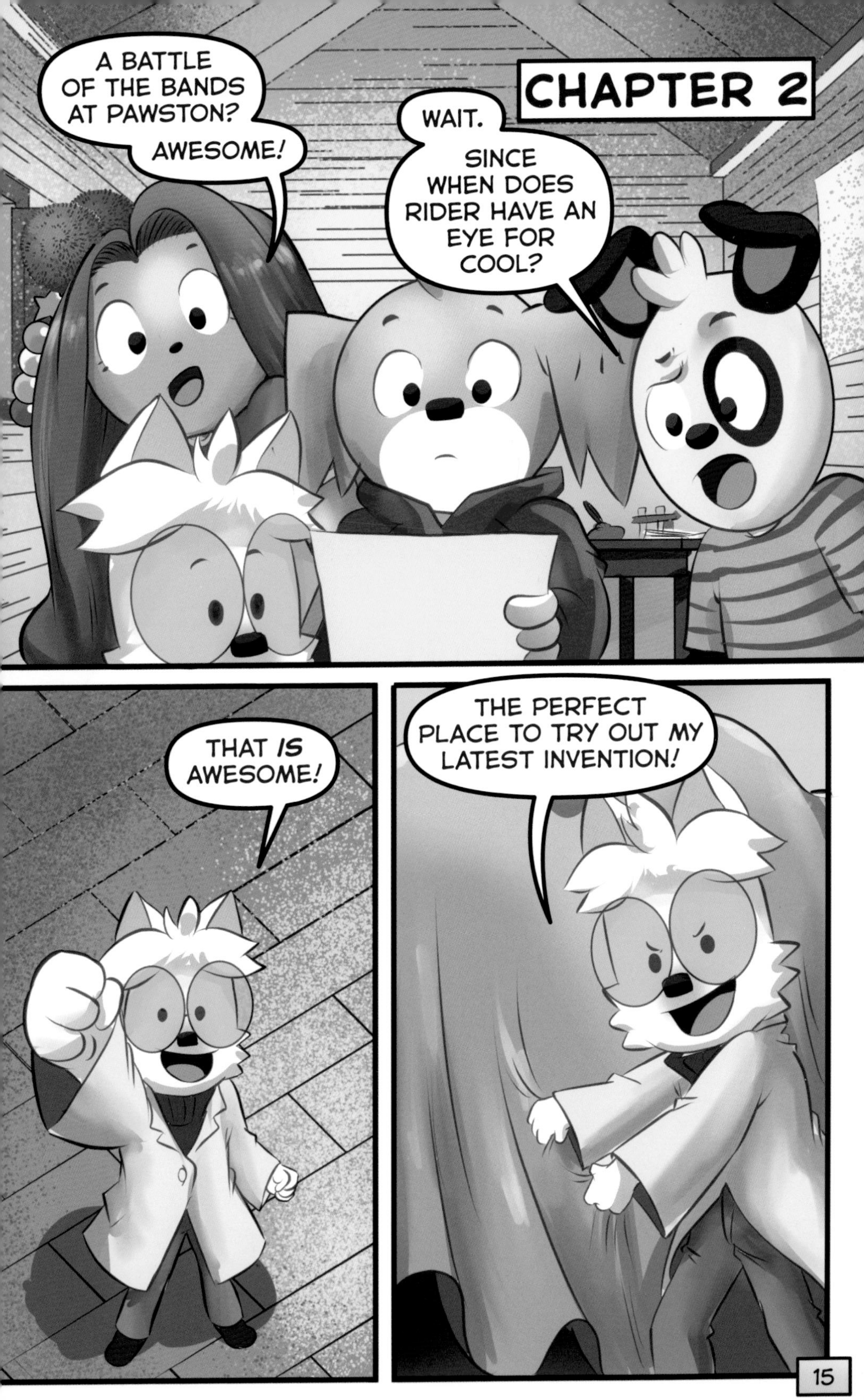
CHAPTER 2
A BATTLE OF THE BANDS AT PAWSTON?
AWESOME!
WAIT.
SINCE WHEN DOES RIDER HAVE AN EYE FOR COOL?
THAT IS AWESOME!
THE PERFECT PLACE TO TRY OUT MY LATEST INVENTION!

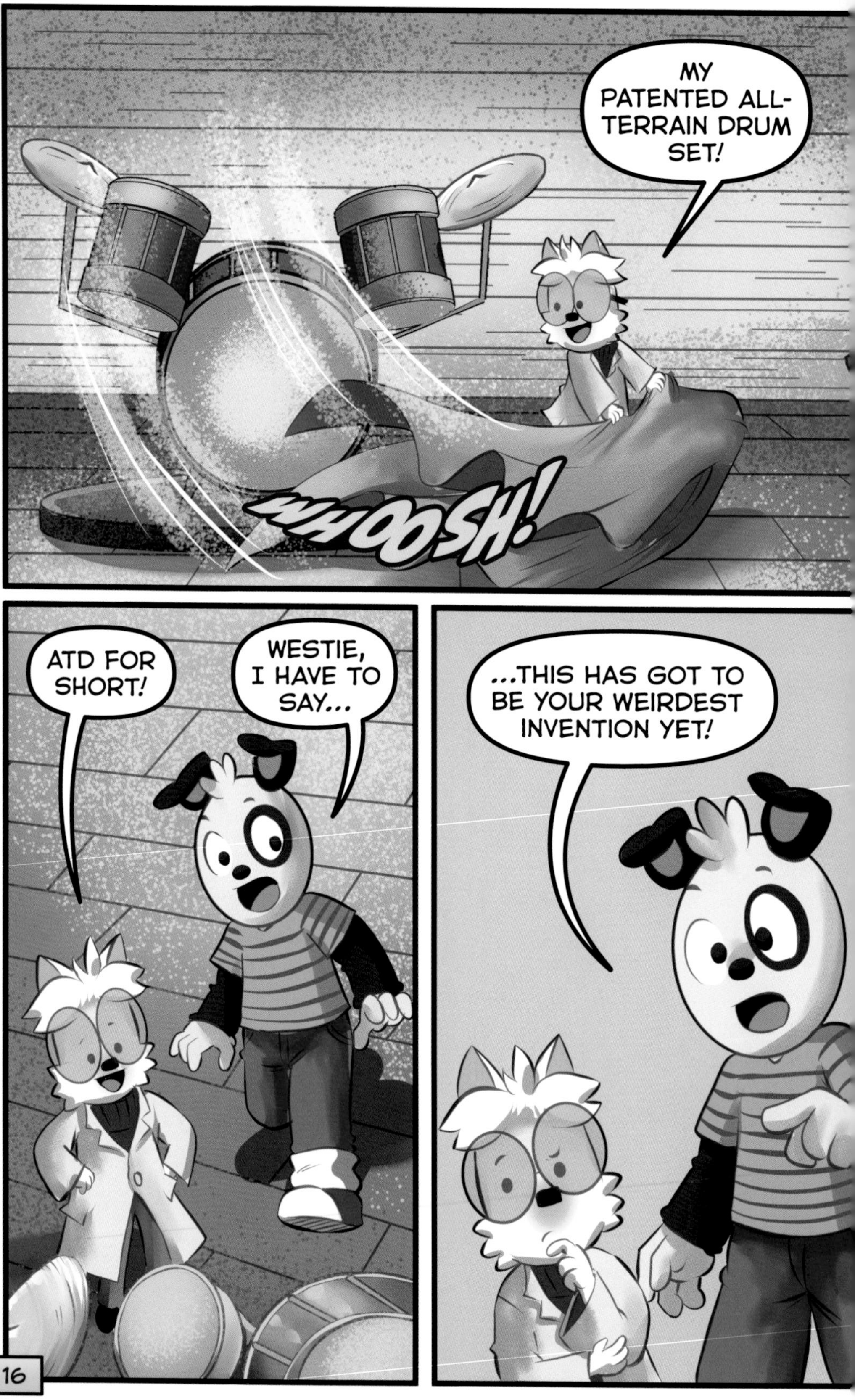

MY PATENTED ALL-TERRAIN DRUM SET!
WHOOSH!
ATD FOR SHORT!
WESTIE, I HAVE TO SAY...
...THIS HAS GOT TO BE YOUR WEIRDEST INVENTION YET!

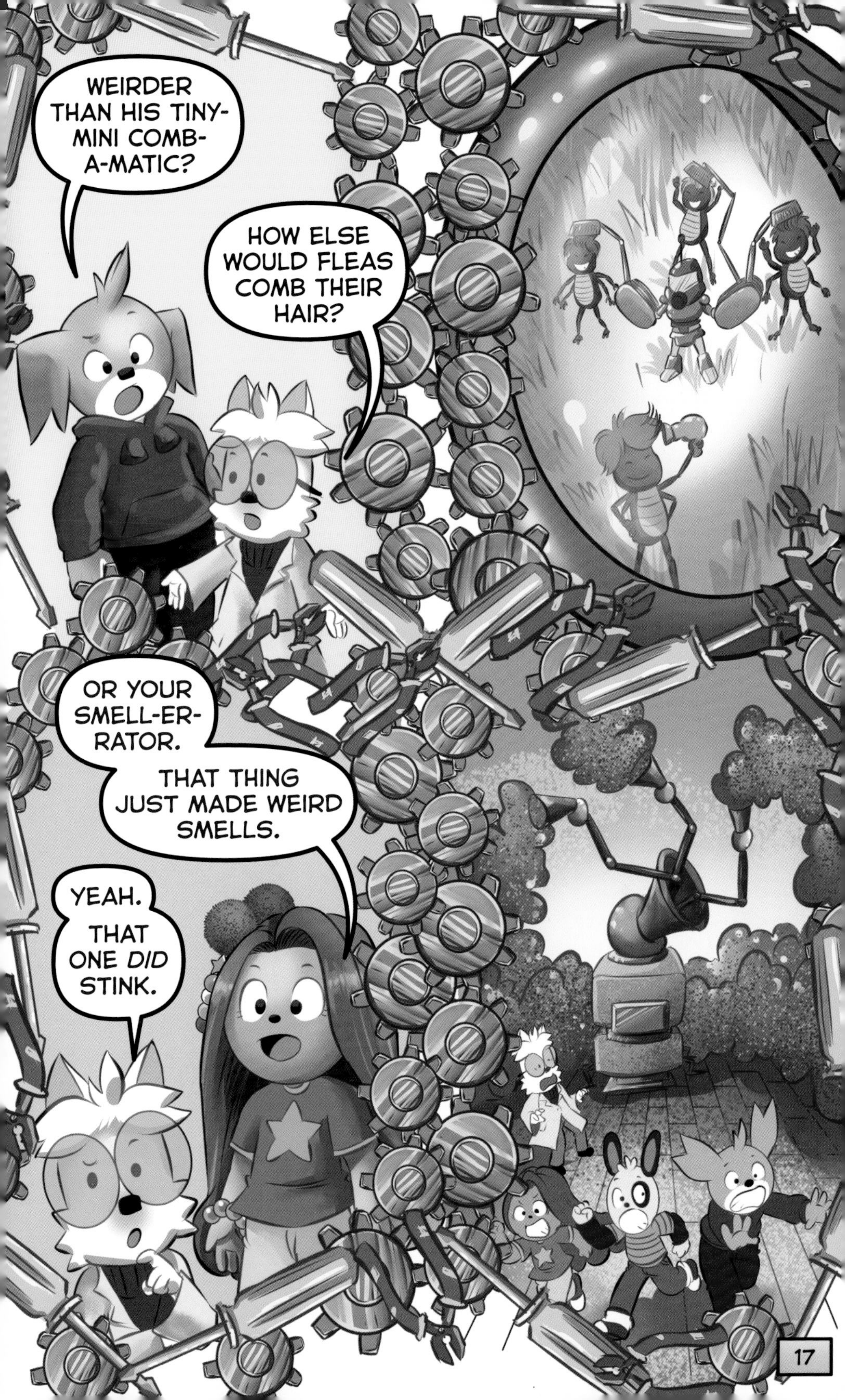
WEIRDER THAN HIS TINY-MINI COMB-A-MATIC?
HOW ELSE WOULD FLEAS COMB THEIR HAIR?
OR YOUR SMELL-ER-RATOR.
THAT THING JUST MADE WEIRD SMELLS.
YEAH.
THAT ONE *DID* STINK.

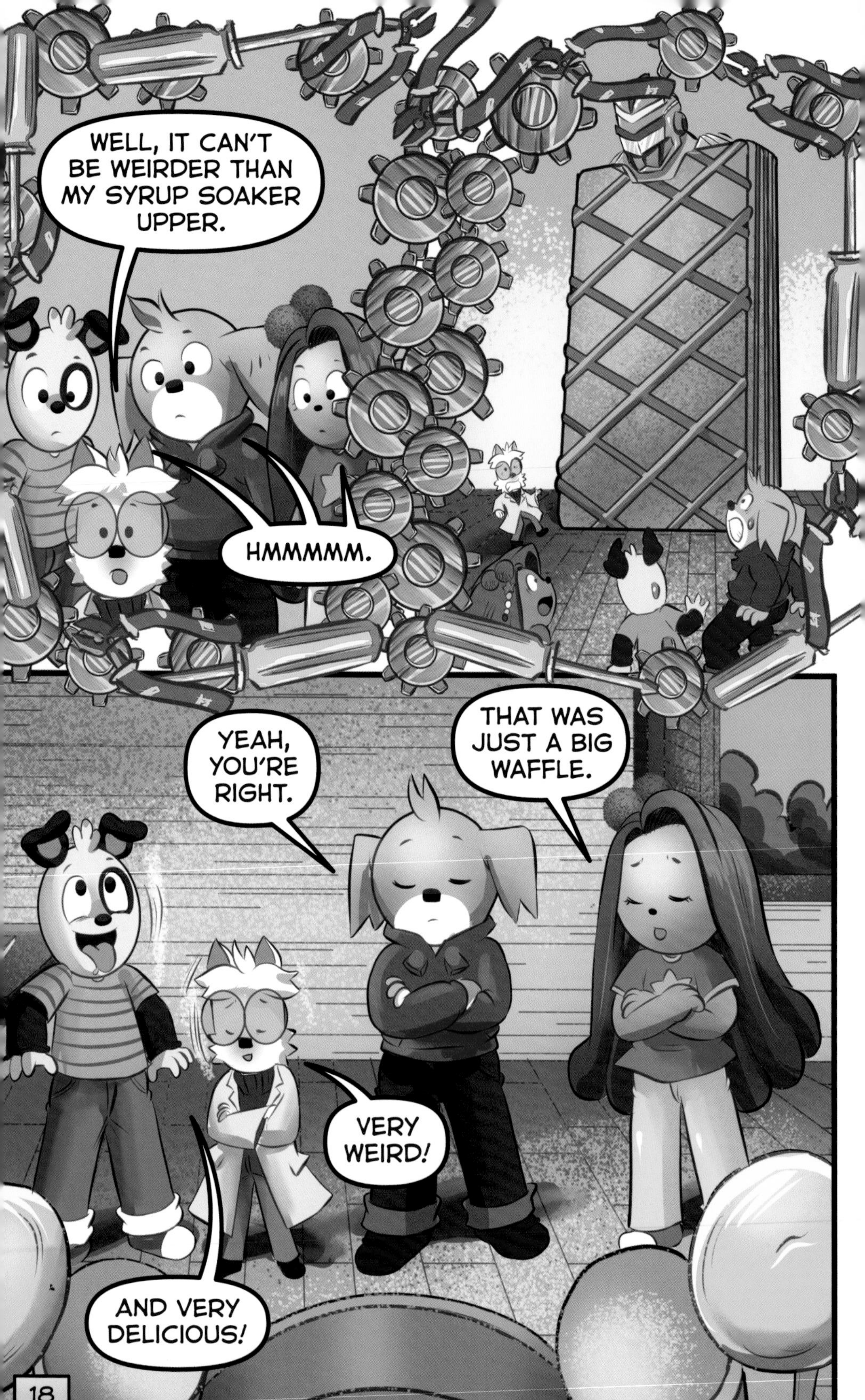
WELL, IT CAN'T BE WEIRDER THAN MY SYRUP SOAKER UPPER.
HMMMMM.
YEAH, YOU'RE RIGHT.
THAT WAS JUST A BIG WAFFLE.
VERY WEIRD!
AND VERY DELICIOUS!

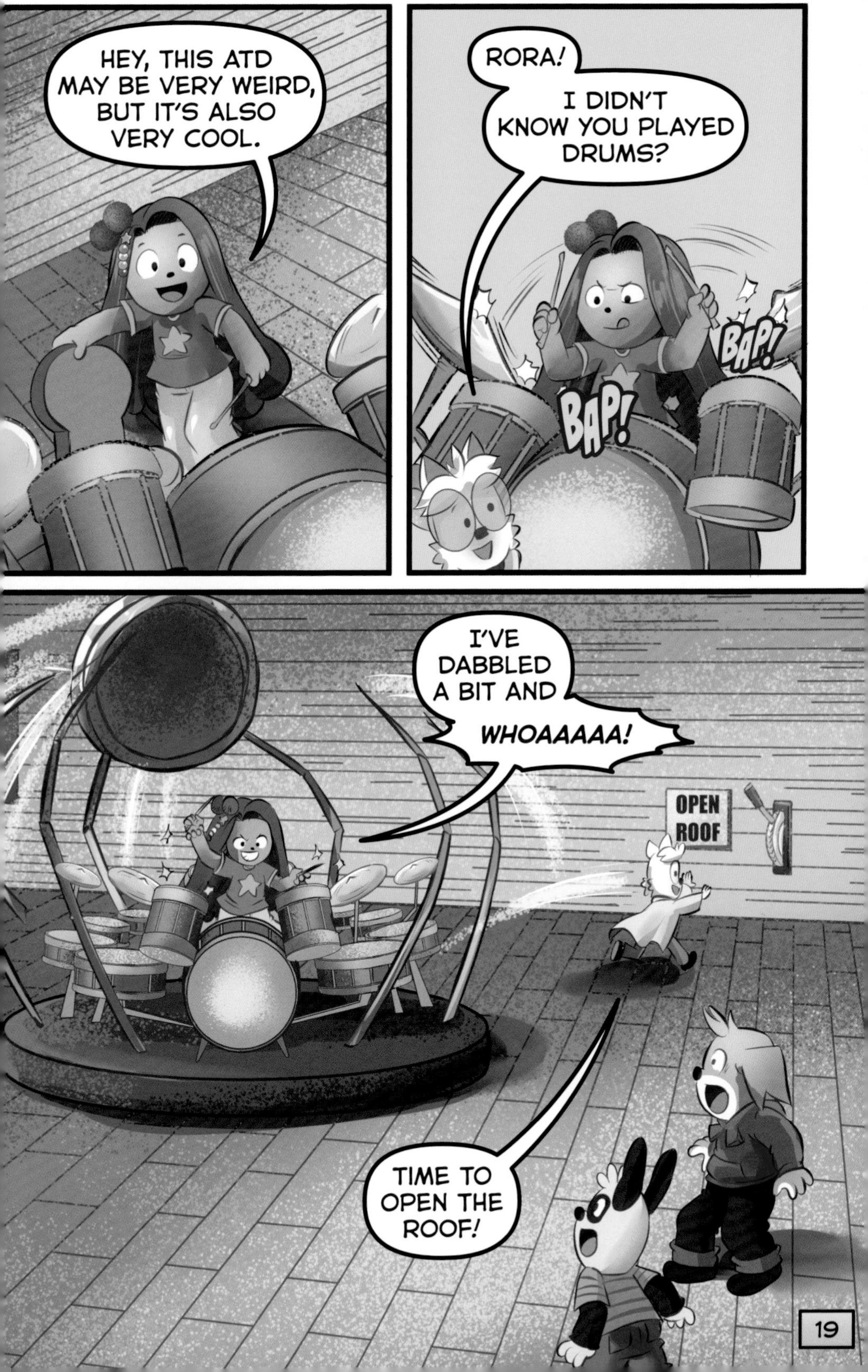
HEY, THIS ATD MAY BE VERY WEIRD, BUT IT'S ALSO VERY COOL.
RORA!
I DIDN'T KNOW YOU PLAYED DRUMS?
BAP!
BAP!
I'VE DABBLED A BIT AND
WHOAAAAA!
OPEN ROOF
TIME TO OPEN THE ROOF!

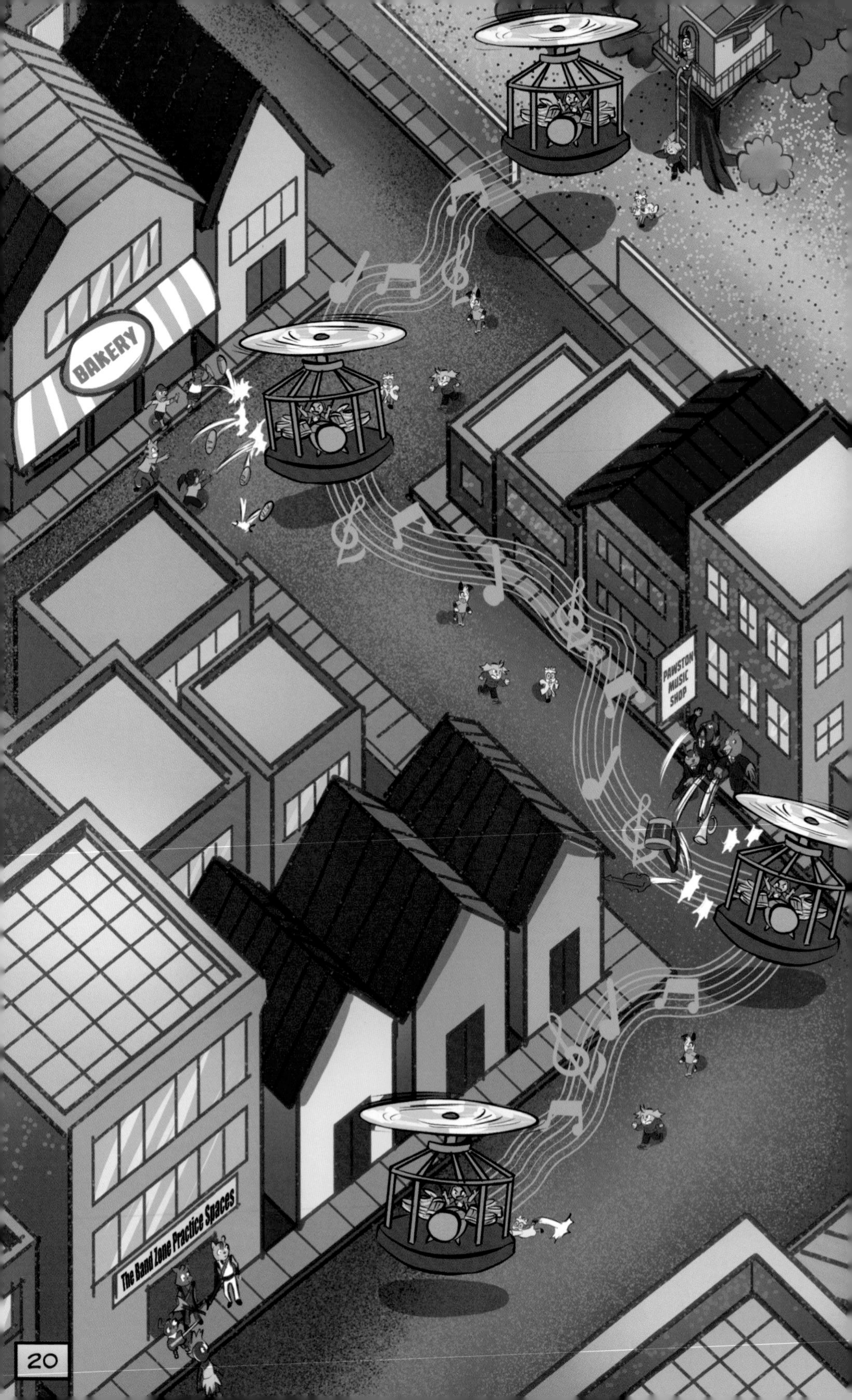
BAKERY
PAWSTON MUSIC SHOP
The Band Zone Practice Spaces

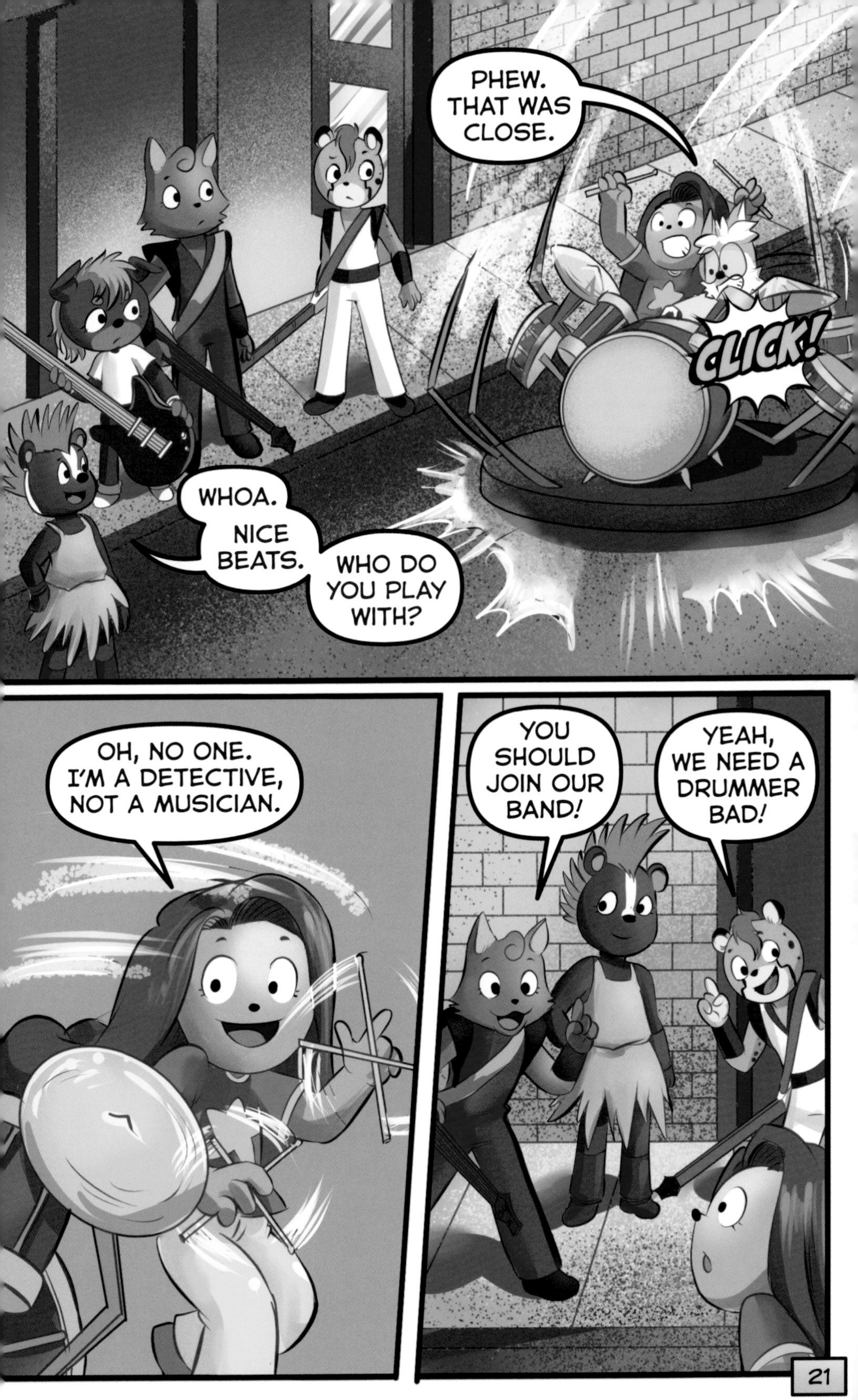
PHEW. THAT WAS CLOSE.
CLICK!
WHOA.
NICE BEATS.
WHO DO YOU PLAY WITH?
OH, NO ONE. I'M A DETECTIVE, NOT A MUSICIAN.
YOU SHOULD JOIN OUR BAND!
YEAH, WE NEED A DRUMMER BAD!

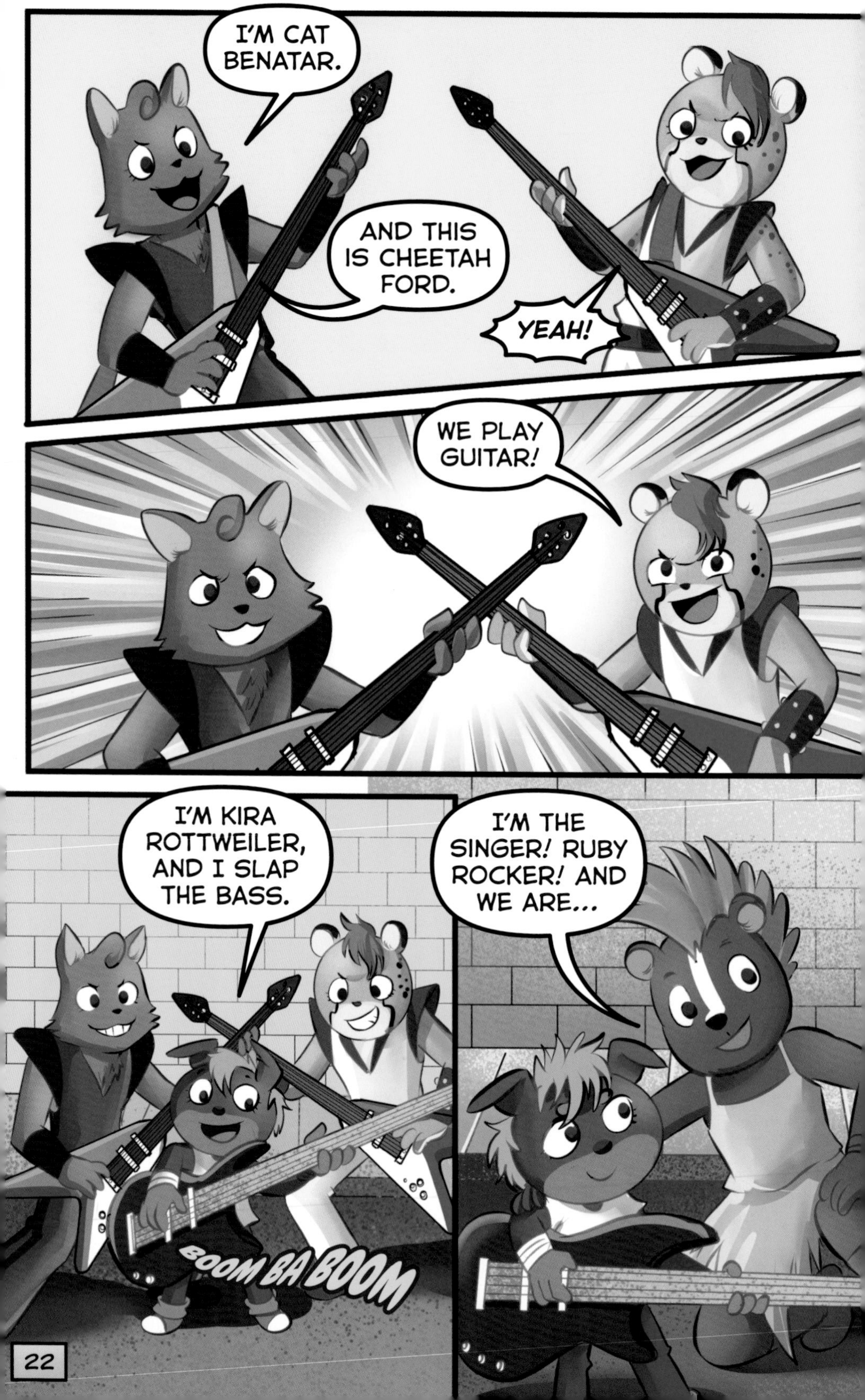
I'M CAT BENATAR.
AND THIS IS CHEETAH FORD.
YEAH!
WE PLAY GUITAR!
I'M KIRA ROTTWEILER, AND I SLAP THE BASS.
BOOM BA BOOM
I'M THE SINGER! RUBY ROCKER! AND WE ARE...

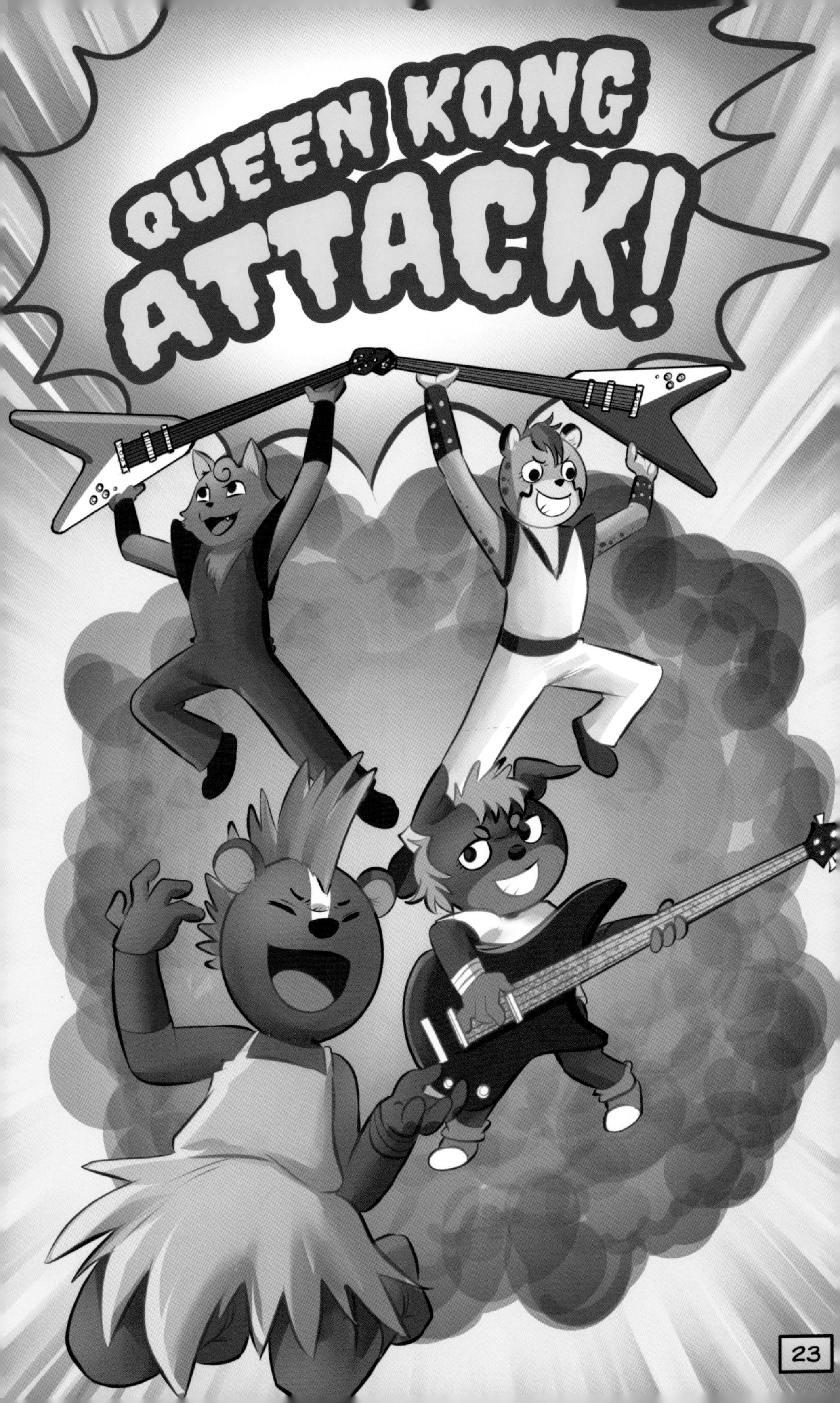
QUEEN KONG
ATTACK!

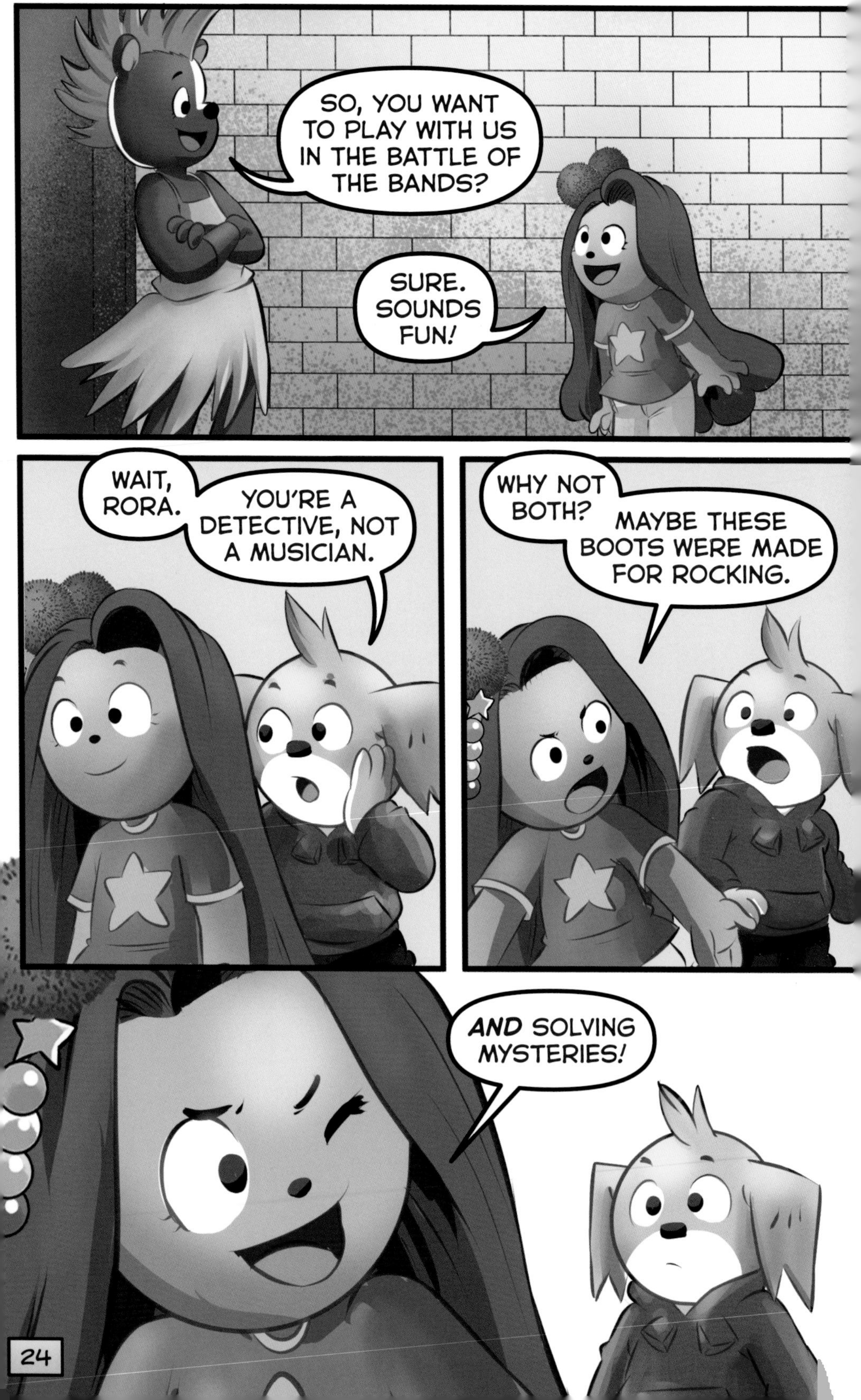
SO, YOU WANT TO PLAY WITH US IN THE BATTLE OF THE BANDS?
SURE. SOUNDS FUN!
WAIT, RORA.
YOU'RE A DETECTIVE, NOT A MUSICIAN.
WHY NOT BOTH?
MAYBE THESE BOOTS WERE MADE FOR ROCKING.
AND SOLVING MYSTERIES!

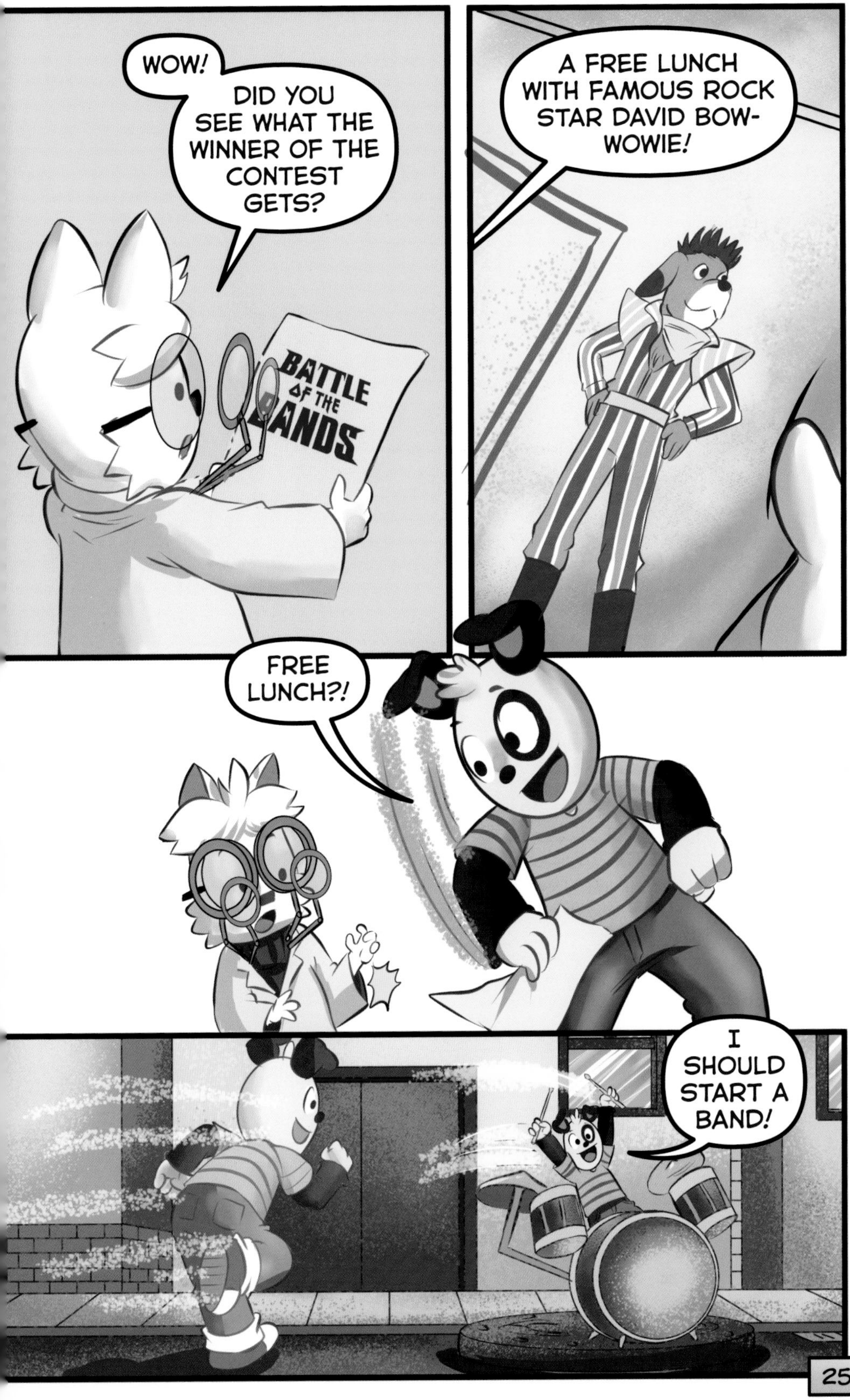
WOW!
DID YOU SEE WHAT THE WINNER OF THE CONTEST GETS?
BATTLE OF THE BANDS
A FREE LUNCH WITH FAMOUS ROCK STAR DAVID BOW-WOWIE!
FREE LUNCH?!
I SHOULD START A BAND!

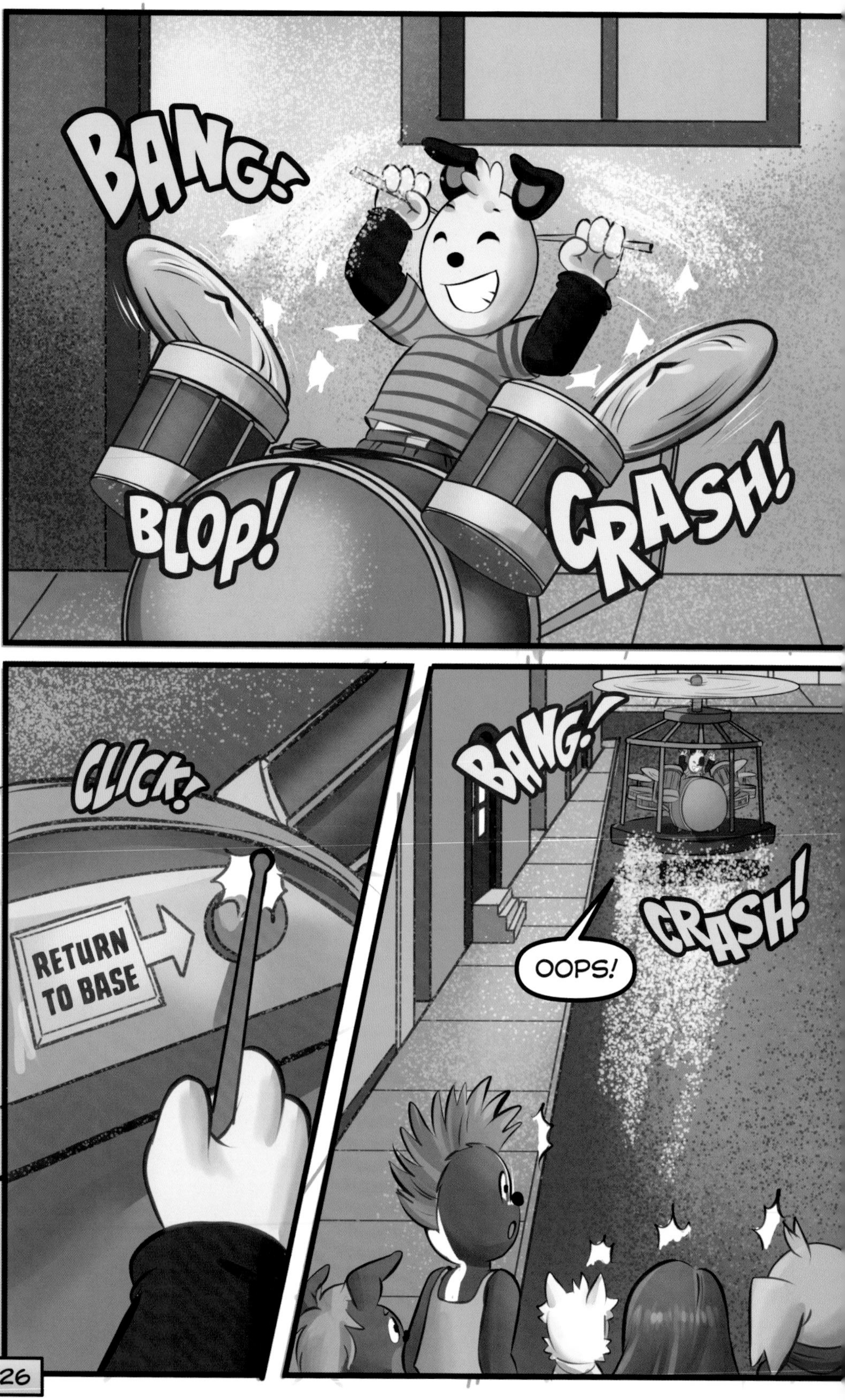
BANG!
BLOP!
CRASH!
CLICK!
RETURN TO BASE
BANG!
OOPS!
CRASH!

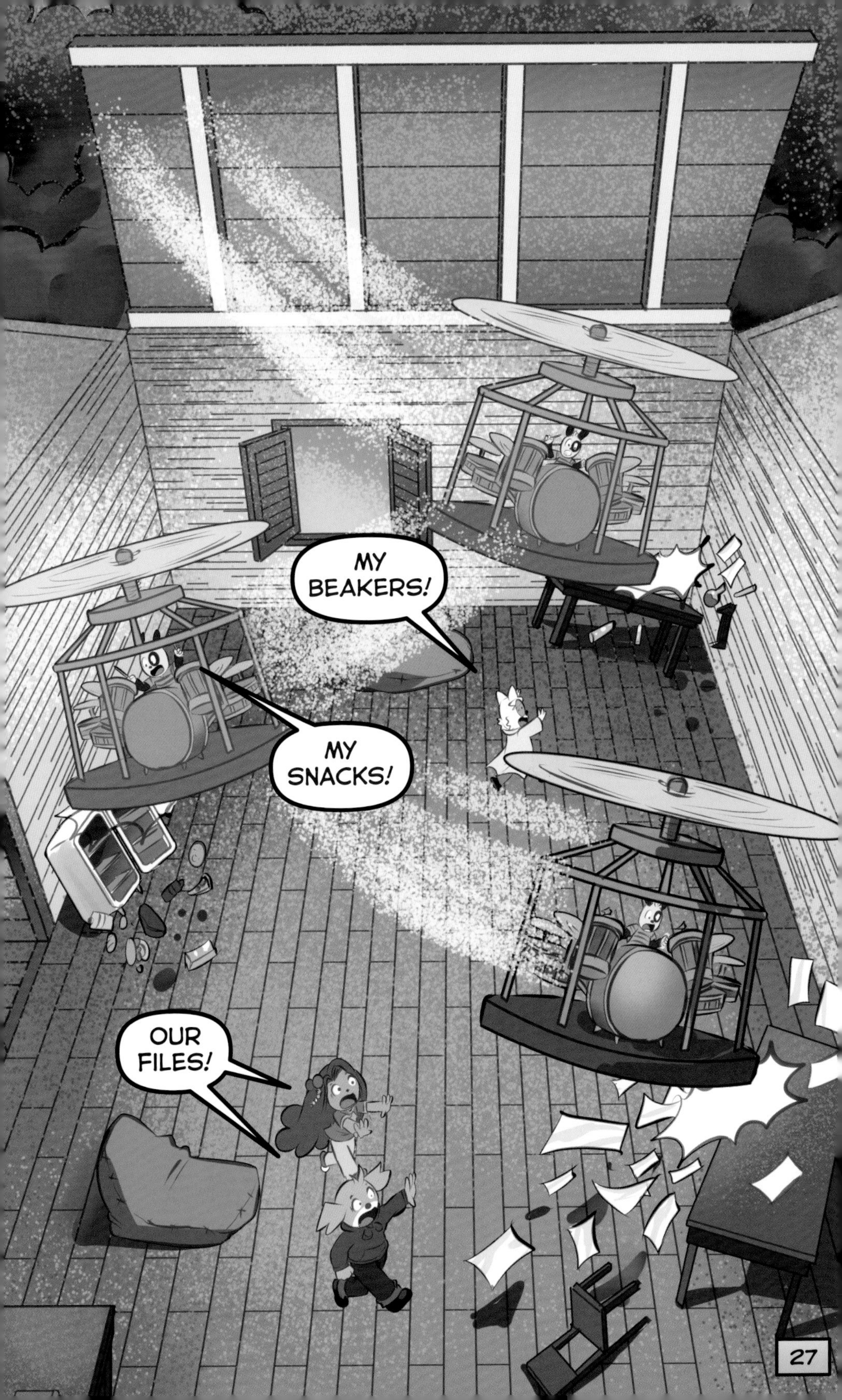
MY BEAKERS!
MY SNACKS!
OUR FILES!

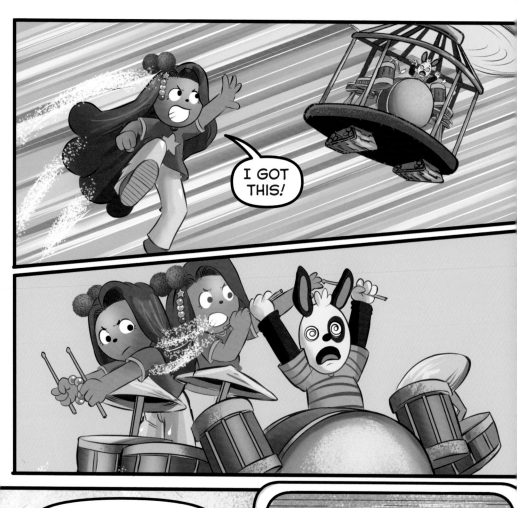

I GOT THIS!

BETTER LEAVE THE DRIVING TO A REAL DRUMMER...

...IF YOU WANT TO WIN THE BATTLE OF THE BANDS AND MEET DAVID BOW-WOWIE.

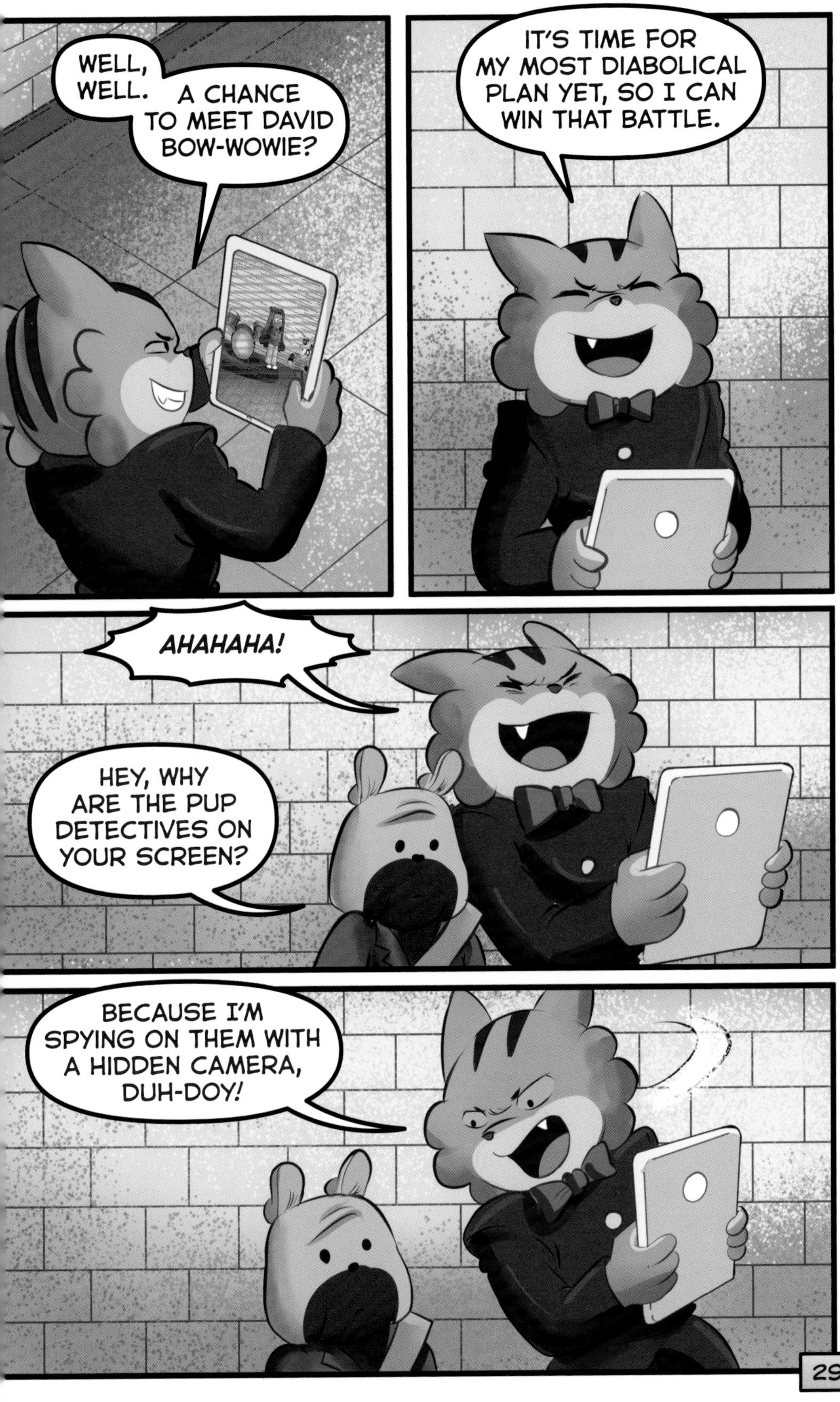
WELL, WELL.
A CHANCE TO MEET DAVID BOW-WOWIE?
IT'S TIME FOR MY MOST DIABOLICAL PLAN YET, SO I CAN WIN THAT BATTLE.
AHAHAHA!
HEY, WHY ARE THE PUP DETECTIVES ON YOUR SCREEN?
BECAUSE I'M SPYING ON THEM WITH A HIDDEN CAMERA, DUH-DOY!

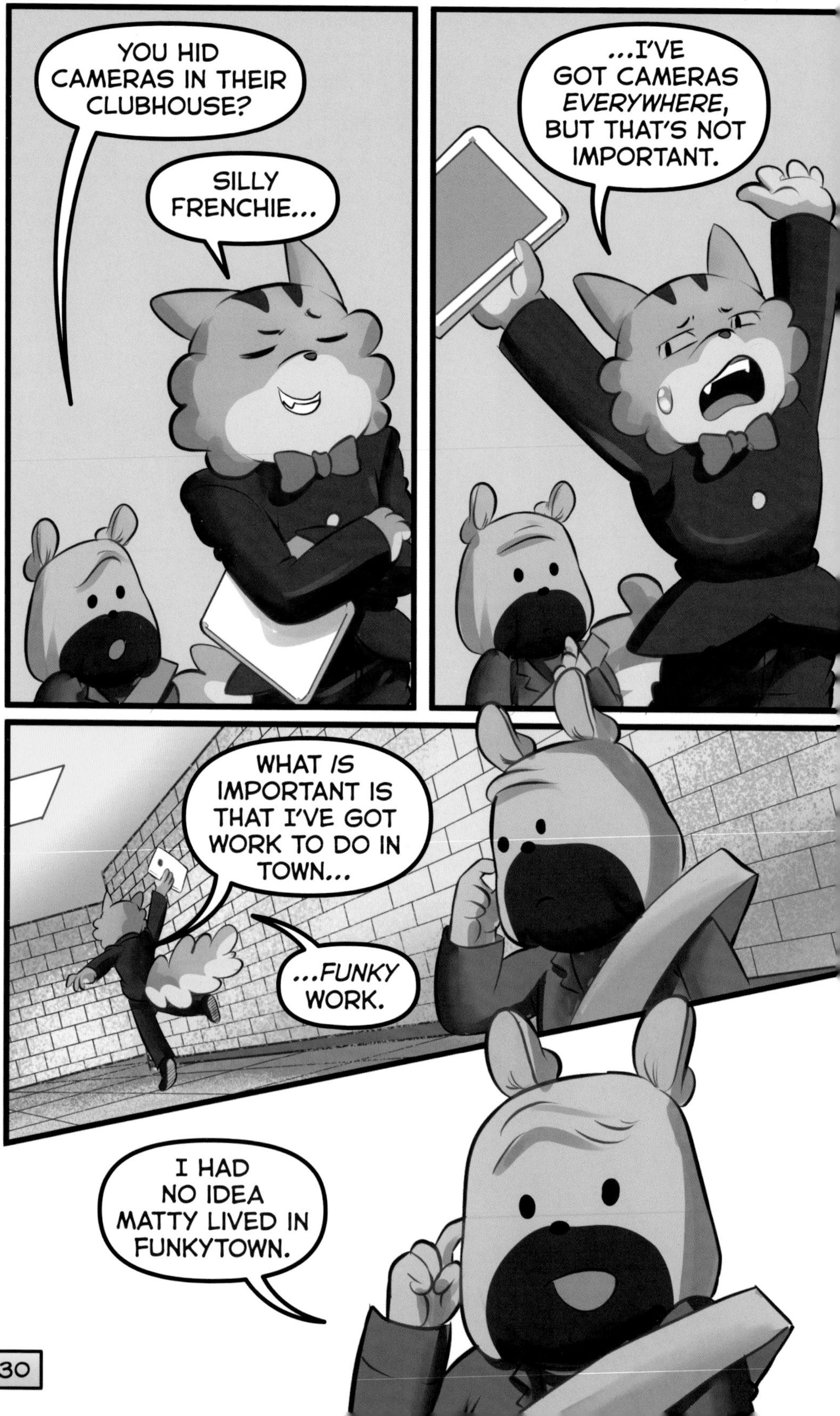
YOU HID CAMERAS IN THEIR CLUBHOUSE?
SILLY FRENCHIE...
...I'VE GOT CAMERAS *EVERYWHERE*, BUT THAT'S NOT IMPORTANT.
WHAT *IS* IMPORTANT IS THAT I'VE GOT WORK TO DO IN TOWN...
...*FUNKY* WORK.
I HAD NO IDEA MATTY LIVED IN FUNKYTOWN.

CHAPTER 3

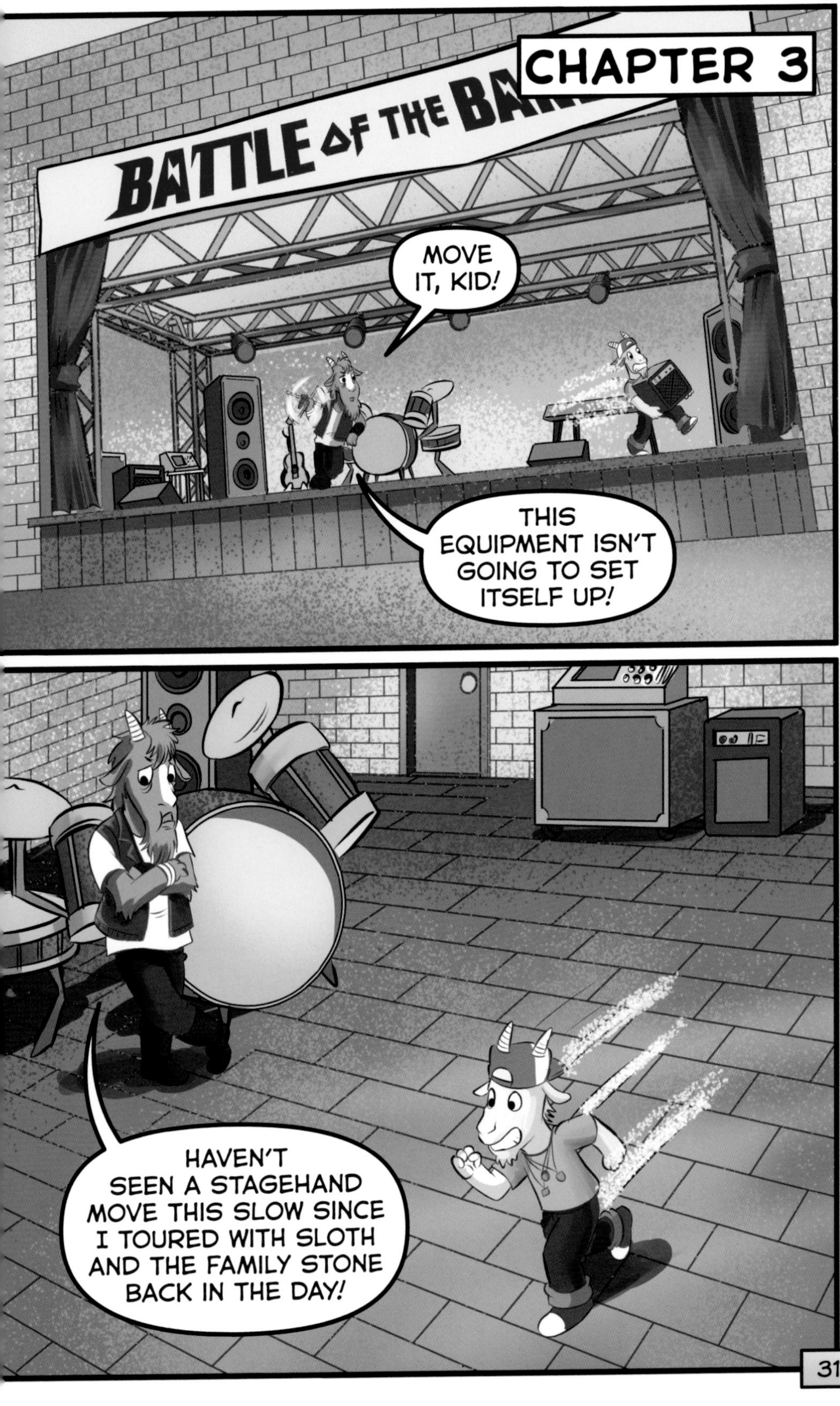

BATTLE OF THE BA
MOVE IT, KID!
THIS EQUIPMENT ISN'T GOING TO SET ITSELF UP!
HAVEN'T SEEN A STAGEHAND MOVE THIS SLOW SINCE I TOURED WITH SLOTH AND THE FAMILY STONE BACK IN THE DAY!

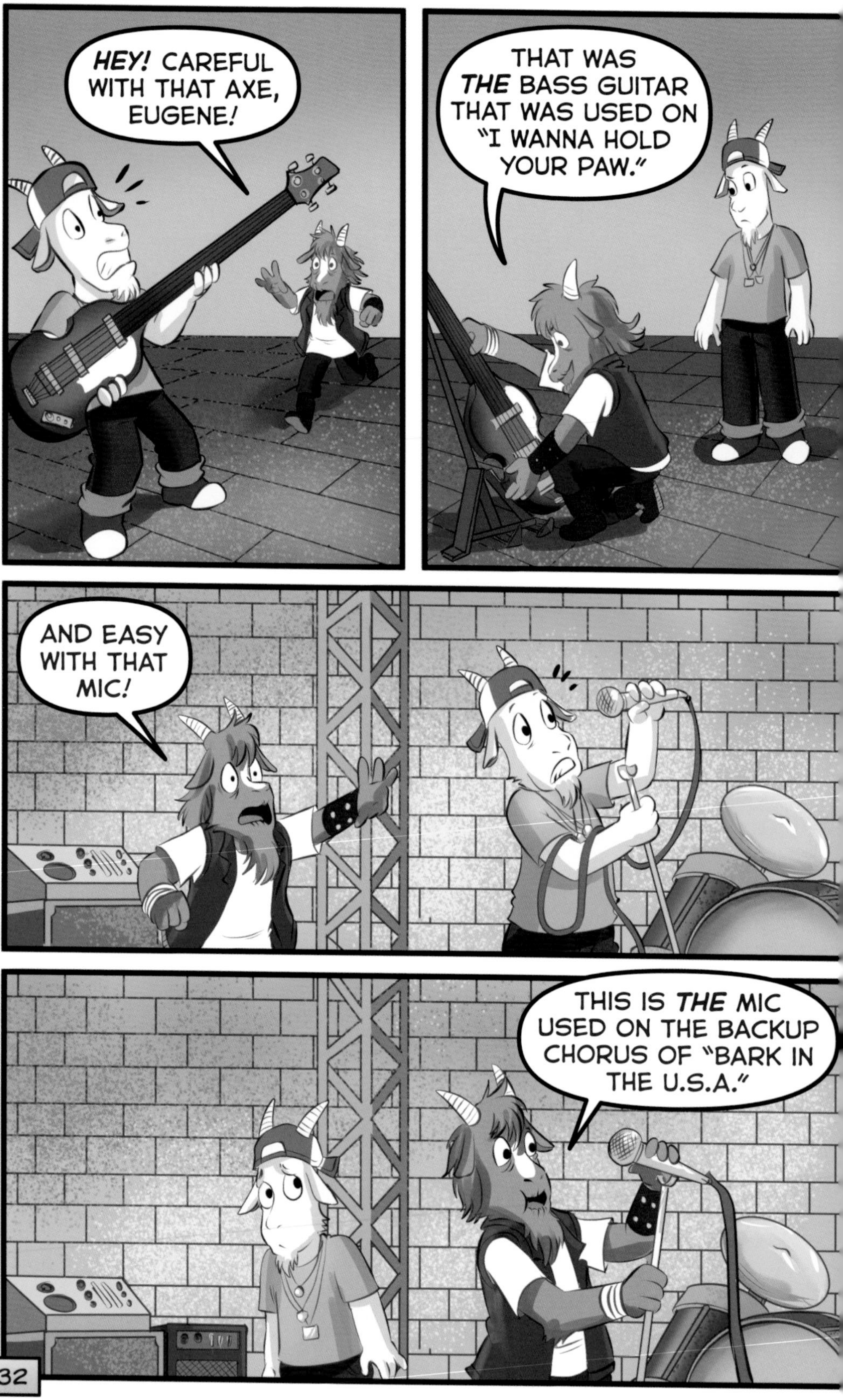
HEY! CAREFUL WITH THAT AXE, EUGENE!
THAT WAS THE BASS GUITAR THAT WAS USED ON "I WANNA HOLD YOUR PAW."
AND EASY WITH THAT MIC!
THIS IS THE MIC USED ON THE BACKUP CHORUS OF "BARK IN THE U.S.A."

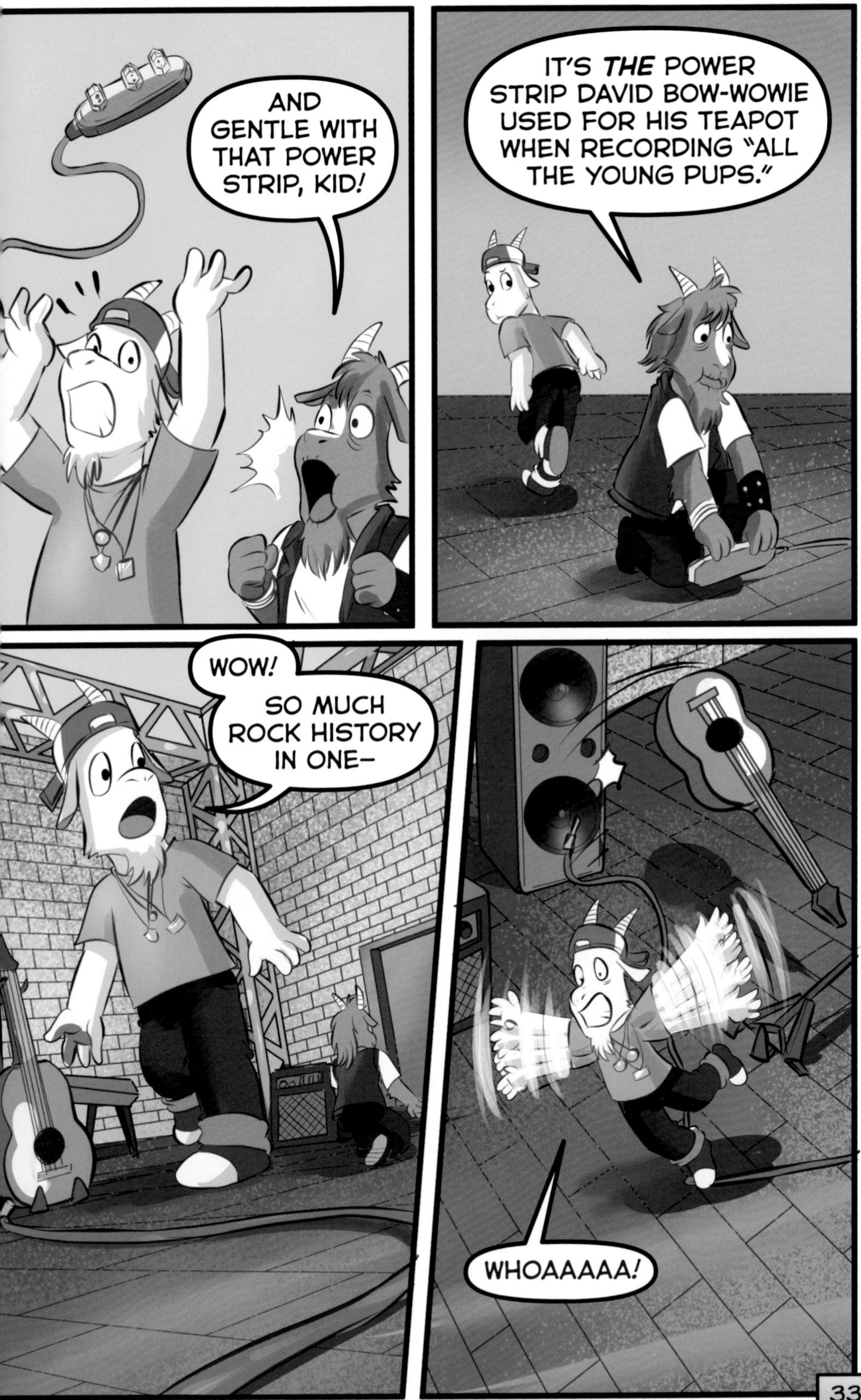
AND GENTLE WITH THAT POWER STRIP, KID!
IT'S *THE* POWER STRIP DAVID BOW-WOWIE USED FOR HIS TEAPOT WHEN RECORDING "ALL THE YOUNG PUPS."
WOW!
SO MUCH ROCK HISTORY IN ONE–
WHOAAAAA!

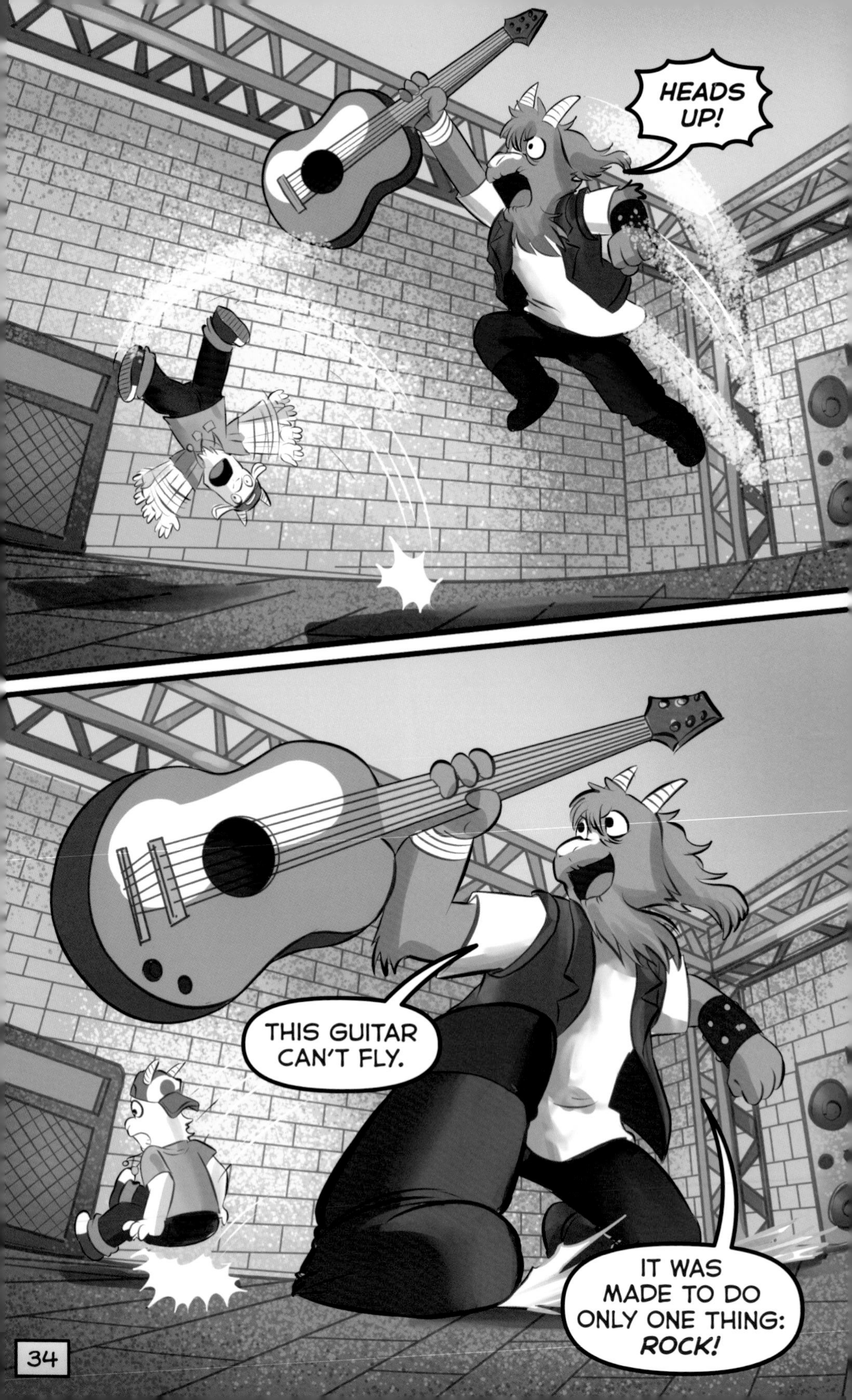
HEADS UP!
THIS GUITAR CAN'T FLY.
IT WAS MADE TO DO ONLY ONE THING: *ROCK!*

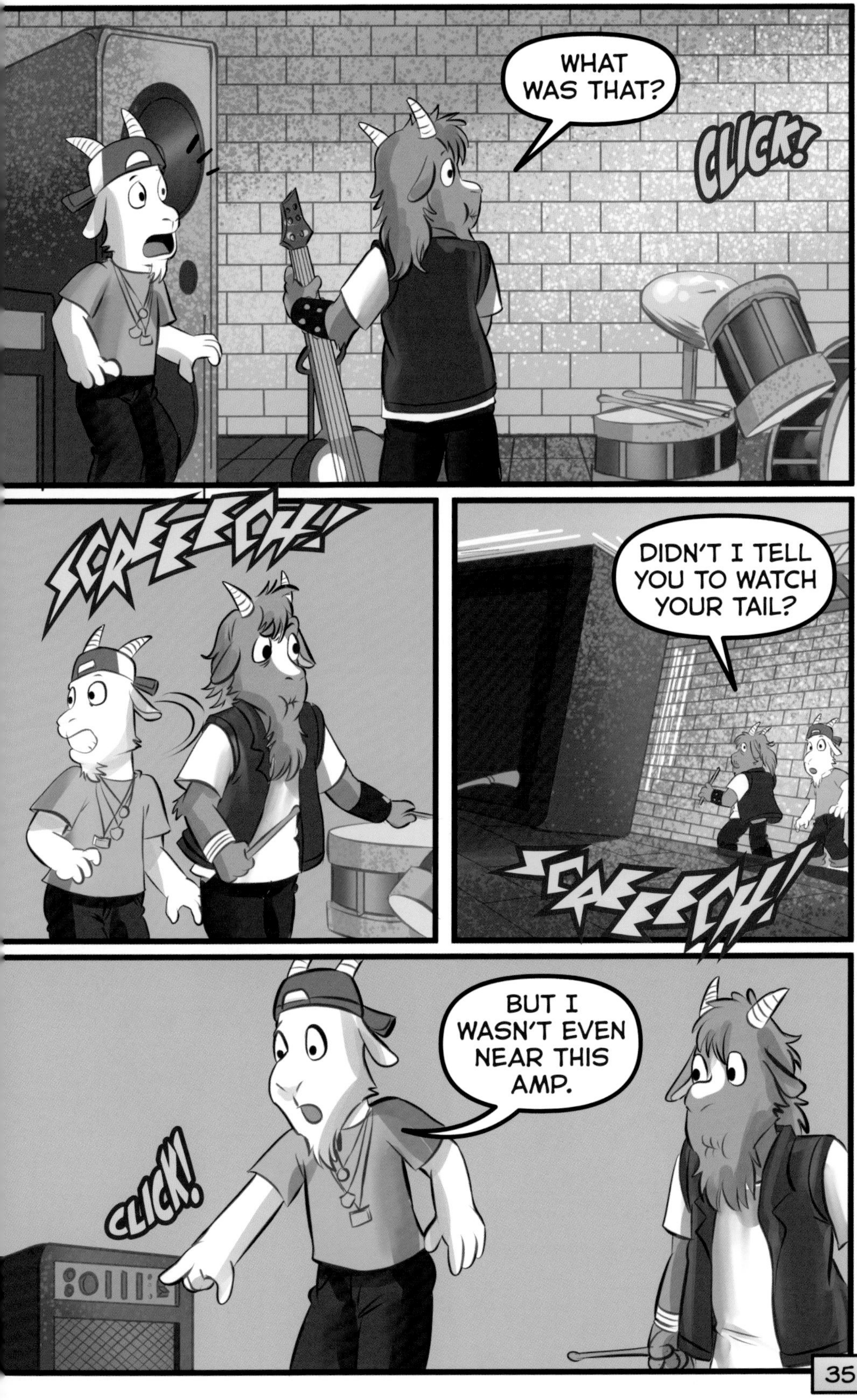
WHAT WAS THAT?
CLICK!
SCREEECH!
DIDN'T I TELL YOU TO WATCH YOUR TAIL?
SCREEECH!
BUT I WASN'T EVEN NEAR THIS AMP.
CLICK!

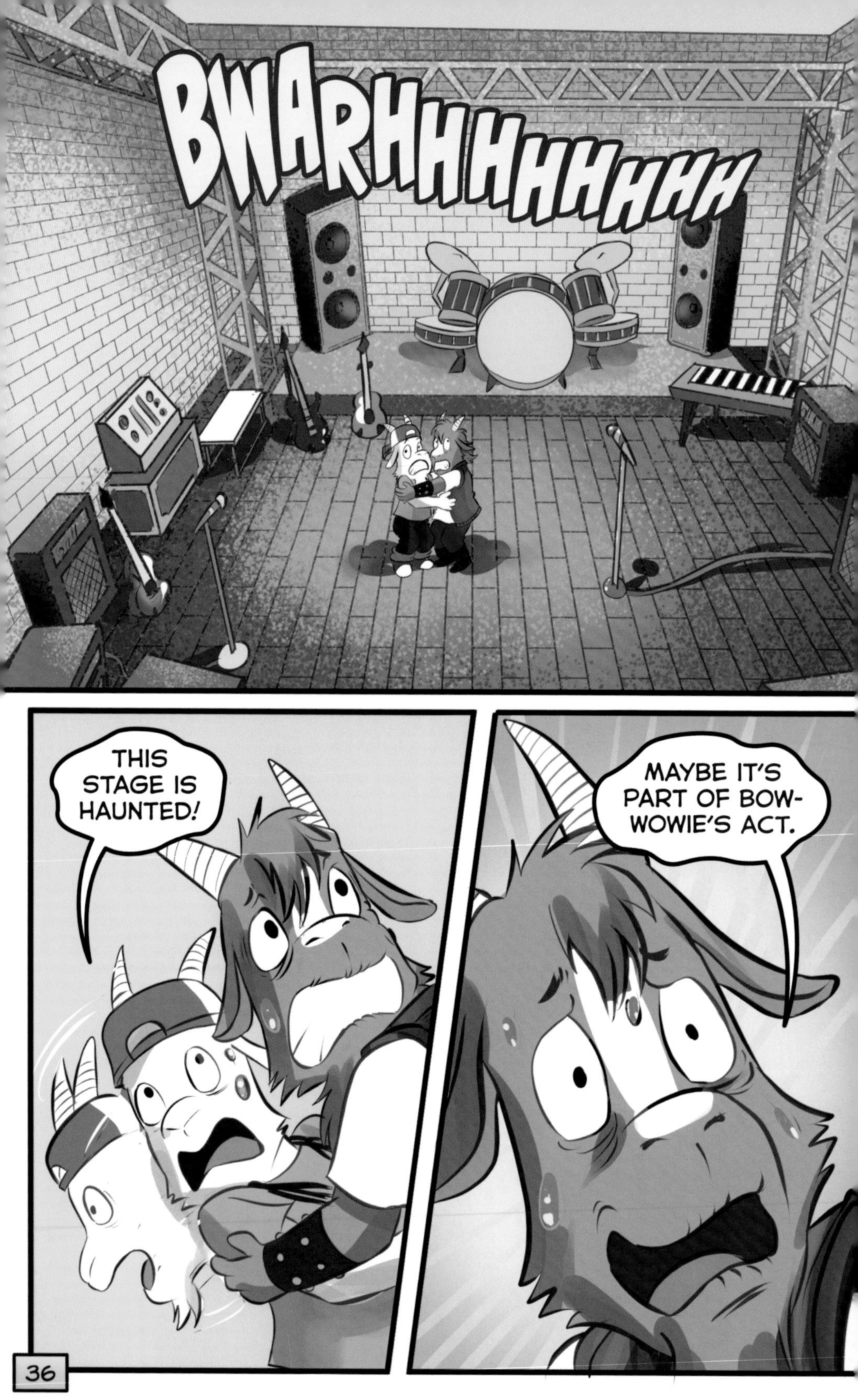
BWARHHHHHHHH
THIS STAGE IS HAUNTED!
MAYBE IT'S PART OF BOW-WOWIE'S ACT.

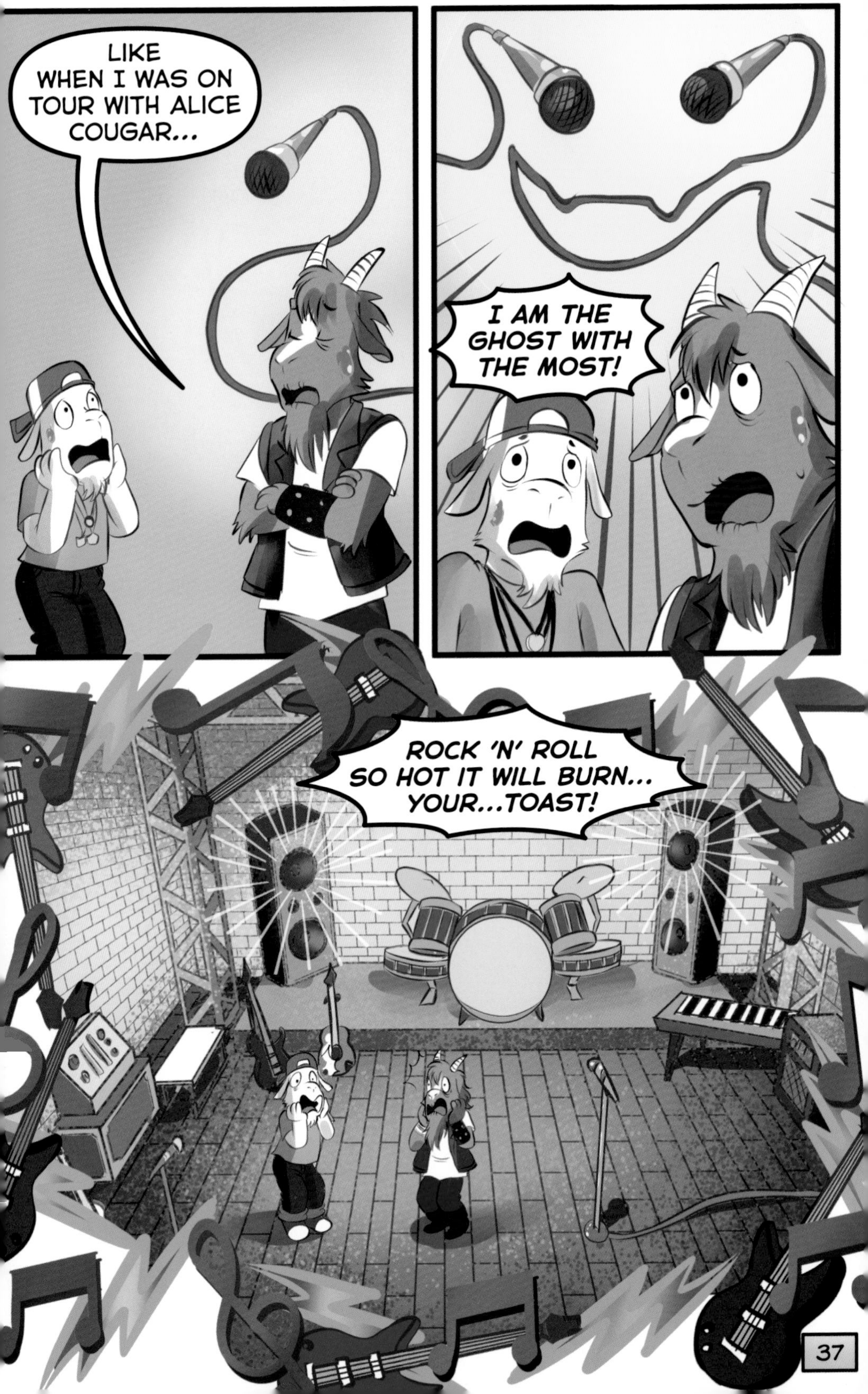
LIKE WHEN I WAS ON TOUR WITH ALICE COUGAR...
I AM THE GHOST WITH THE MOST!
ROCK 'N' ROLL SO HOT IT WILL BURN... YOUR...TOAST!

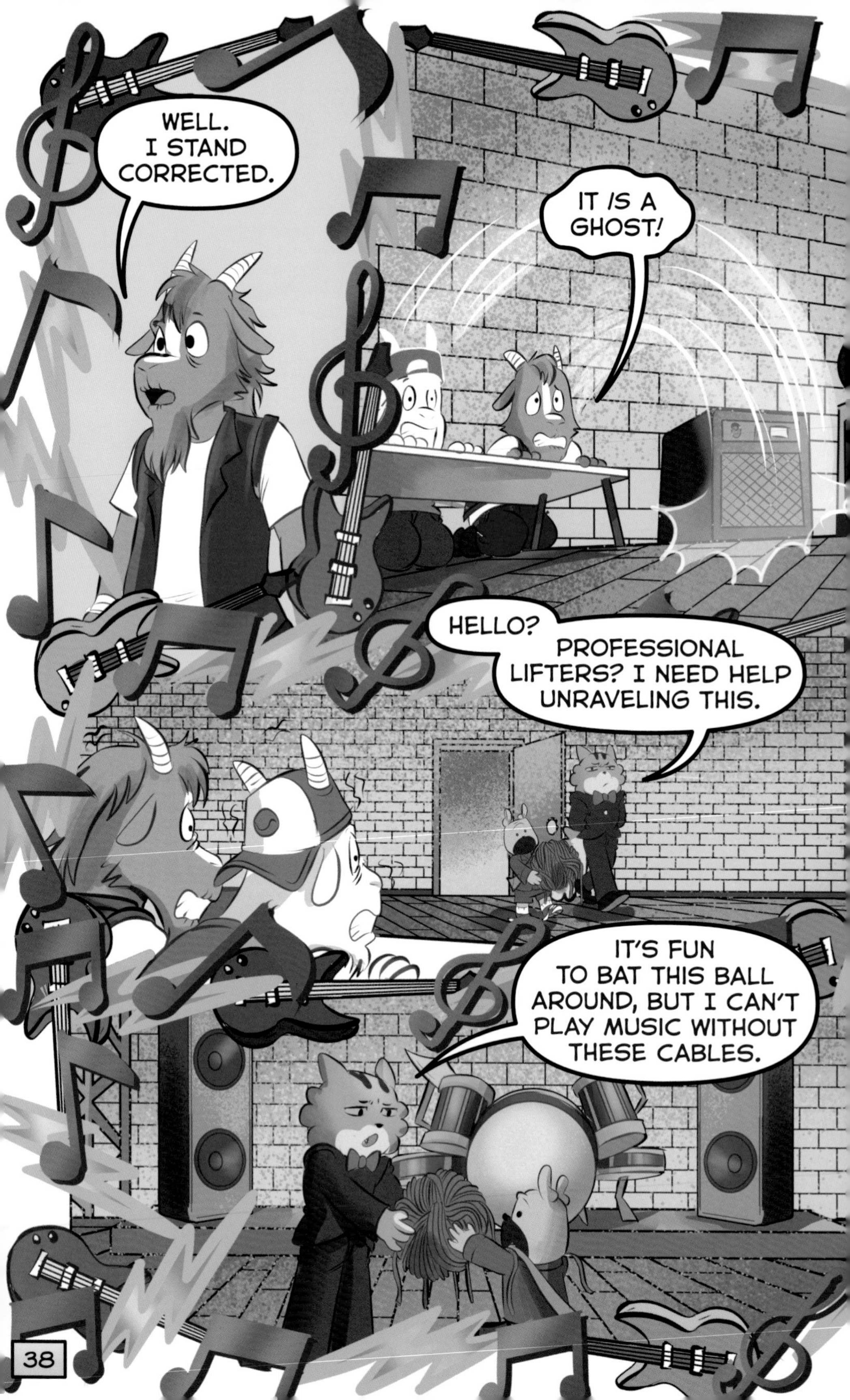
WELL. I STAND CORRECTED.
IT IS A GHOST!
HELLO? PROFESSIONAL LIFTERS? I NEED HELP UNRAVELING THIS.
IT'S FUN TO BAT THIS BALL AROUND, BUT I CAN'T PLAY MUSIC WITHOUT THESE CABLES.

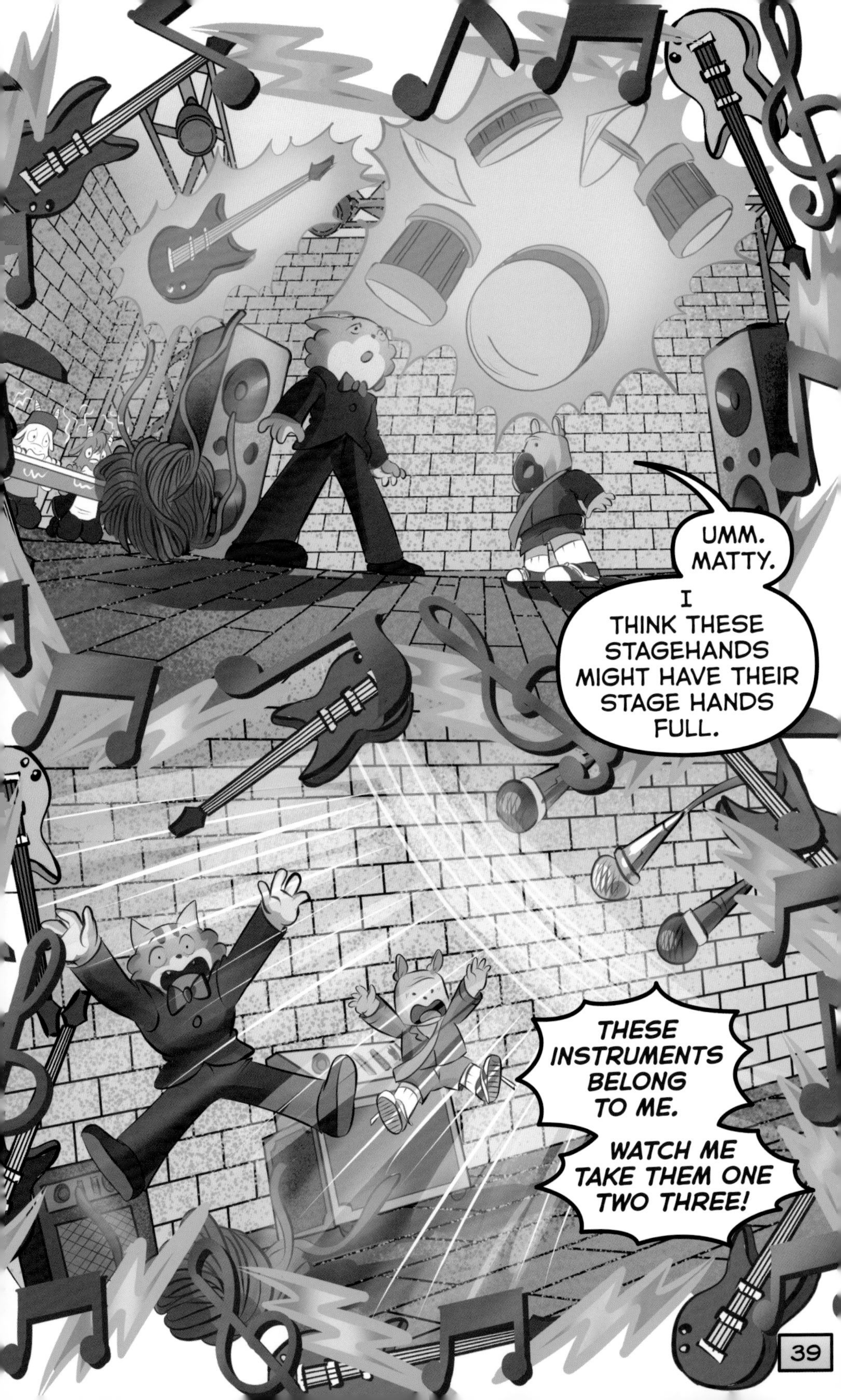
UMM. MATTY.
I THINK THESE STAGEHANDS MIGHT HAVE THEIR STAGE HANDS FULL.
THESE INSTRUMENTS BELONG TO ME.
WATCH ME TAKE THEM ONE TWO THREE!

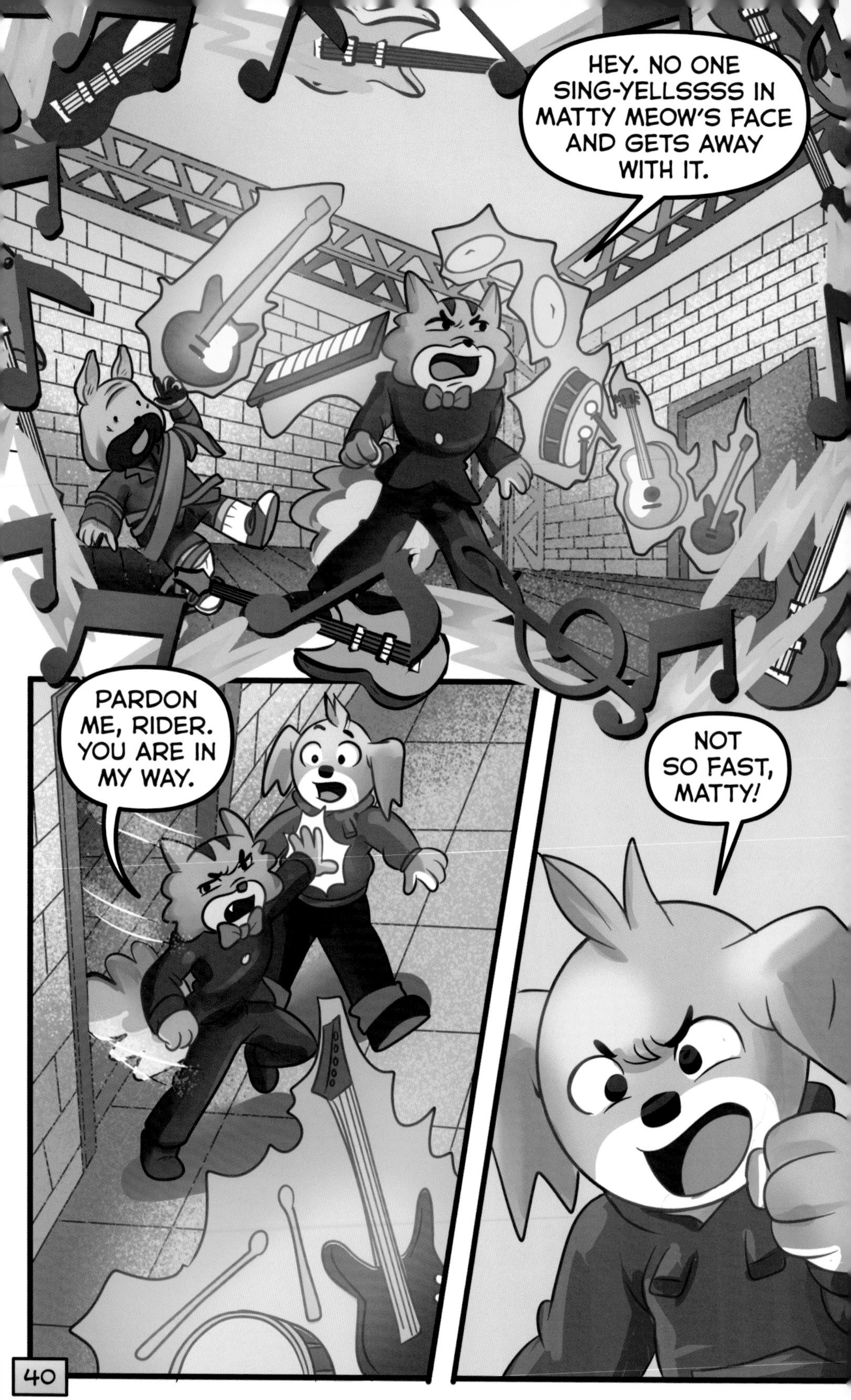
HEY. NO ONE SING-YELLSSSS IN MATTY MEOW'S FACE AND GETS AWAY WITH IT.
PARDON ME, RIDER. YOU ARE IN MY WAY.
NOT SO FAST, MATTY!

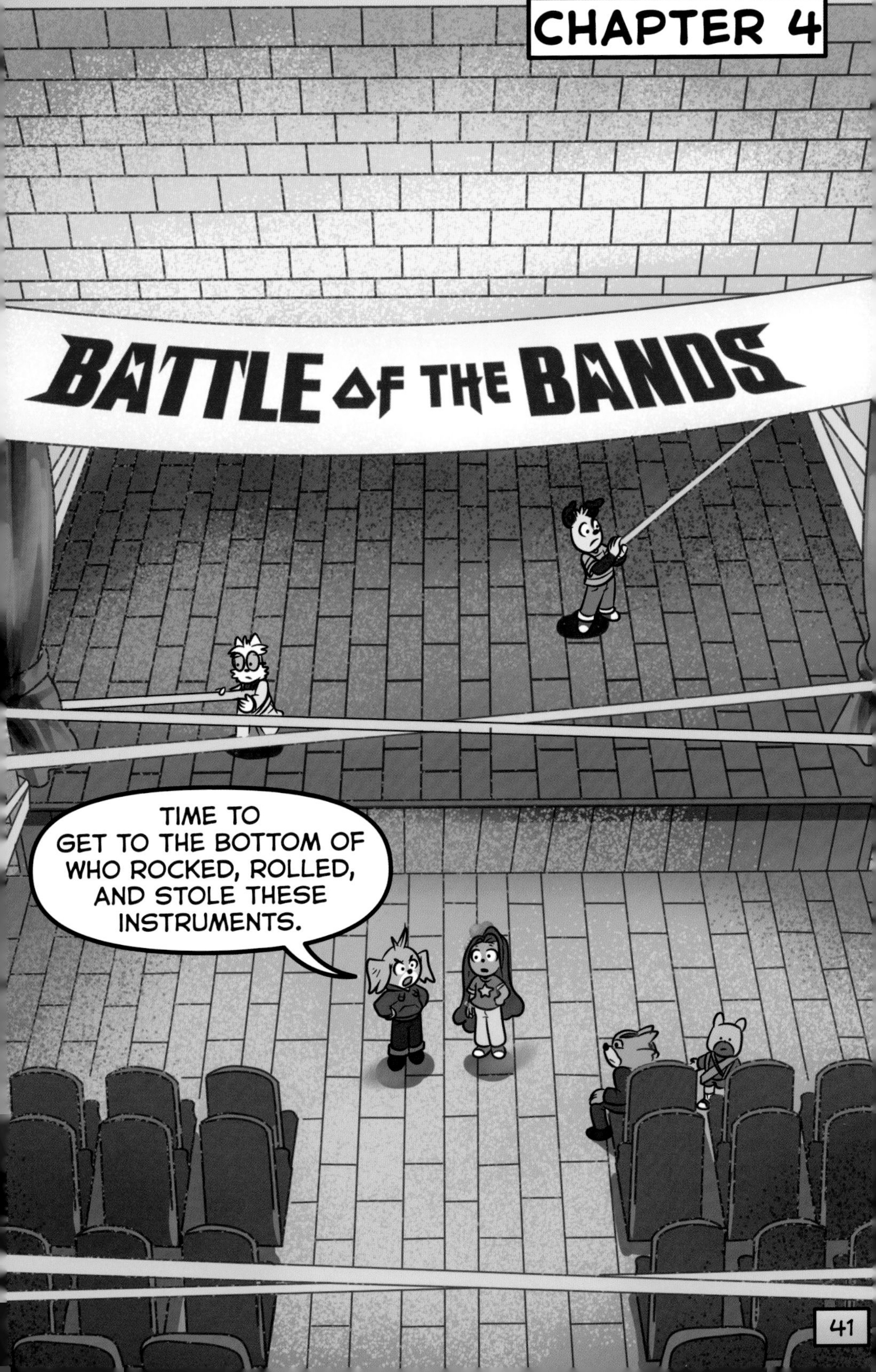
CHAPTER 4
BATTLE OF THE BANDS
TIME TO GET TO THE BOTTOM OF WHO ROCKED, ROLLED, AND STOLE THESE INSTRUMENTS.

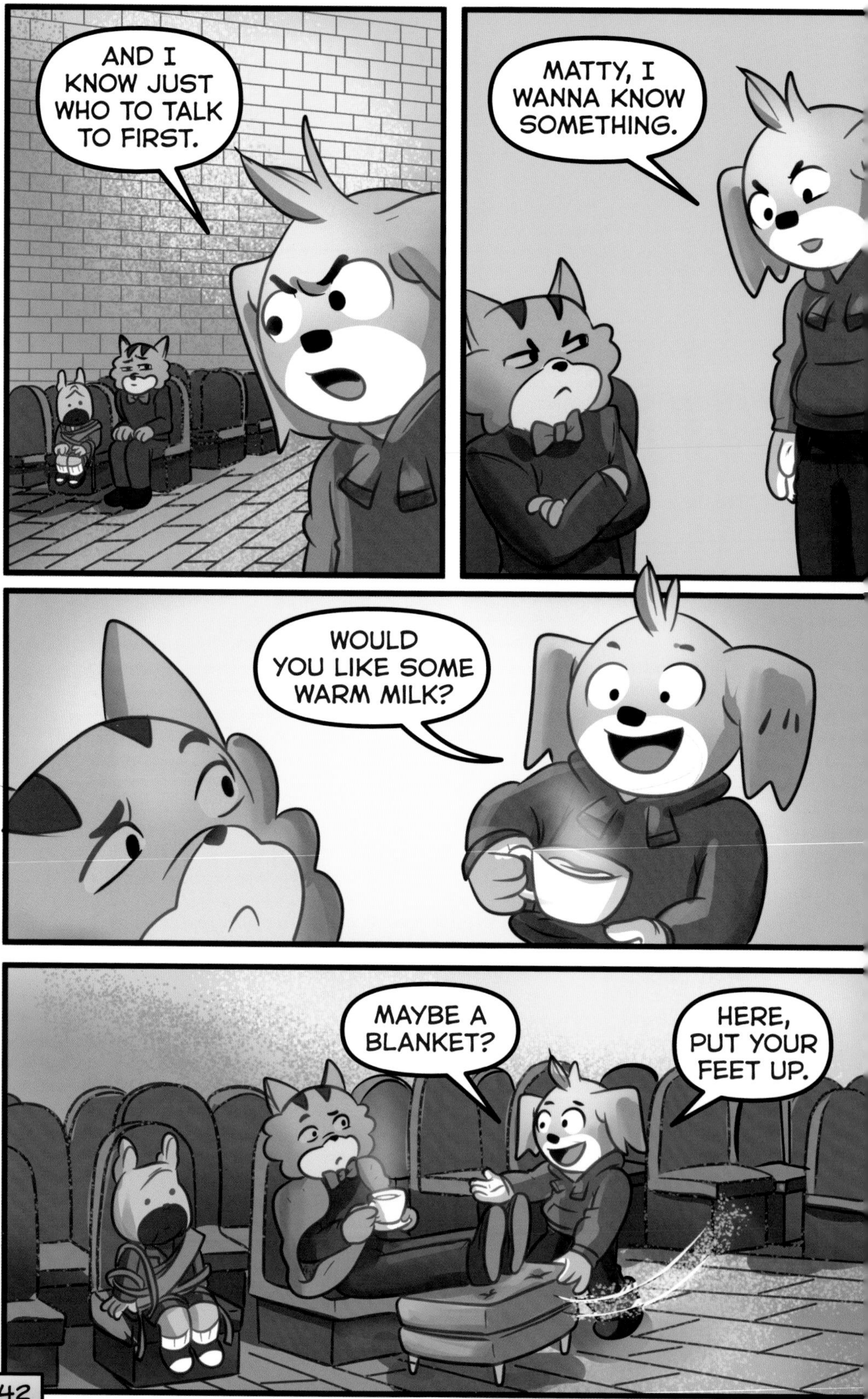
AND I KNOW JUST WHO TO TALK TO FIRST.
MATTY, I WANNA KNOW SOMETHING.
WOULD YOU LIKE SOME WARM MILK?
MAYBE A BLANKET?
HERE, PUT YOUR FEET UP.

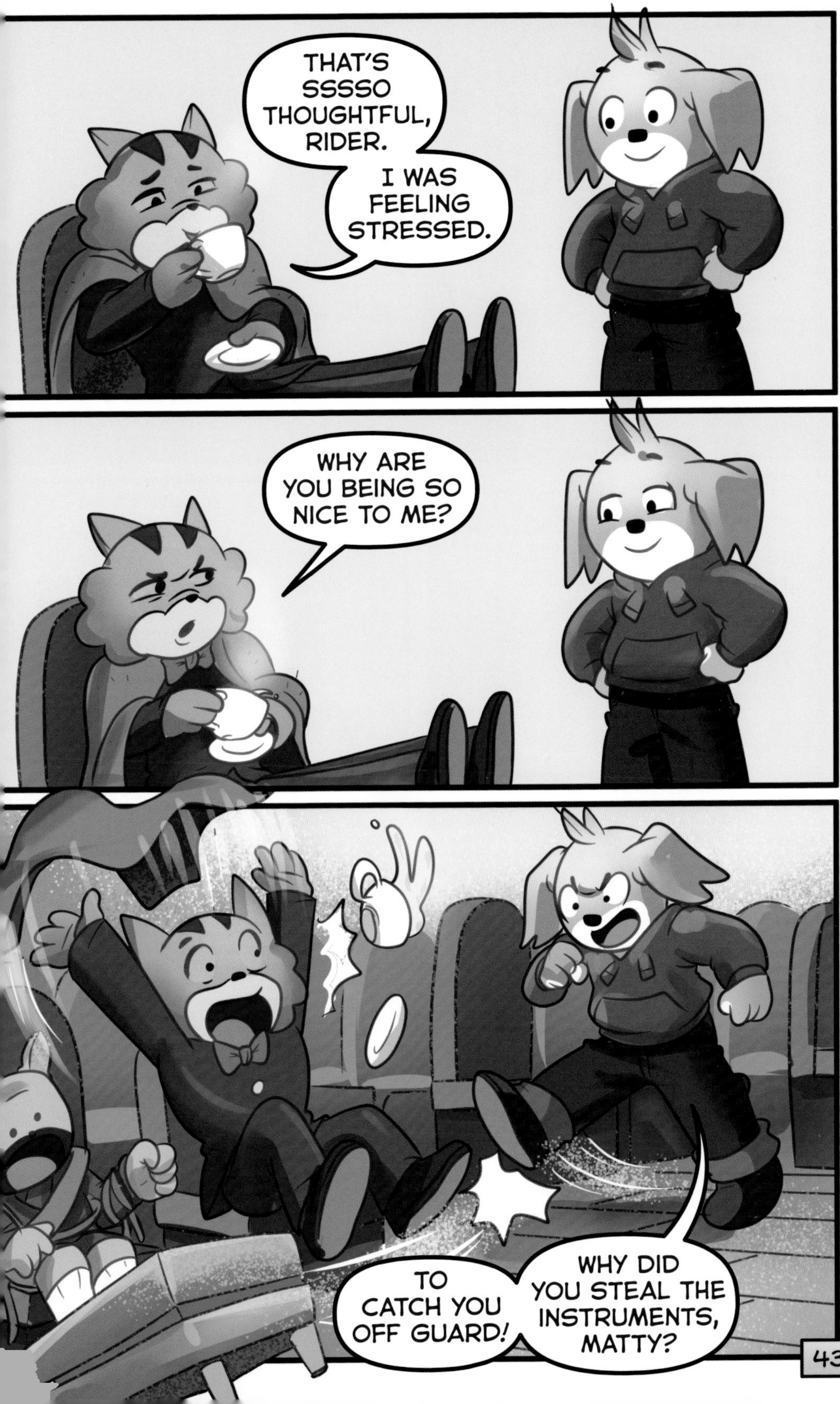
THAT'S SSSSO THOUGHTFUL, RIDER.
I WAS FEELING STRESSED.
WHY ARE YOU BEING SO NICE TO ME?
TO CATCH YOU OFF GUARD!
WHY DID YOU STEAL THE INSTRUMENTS, MATTY?

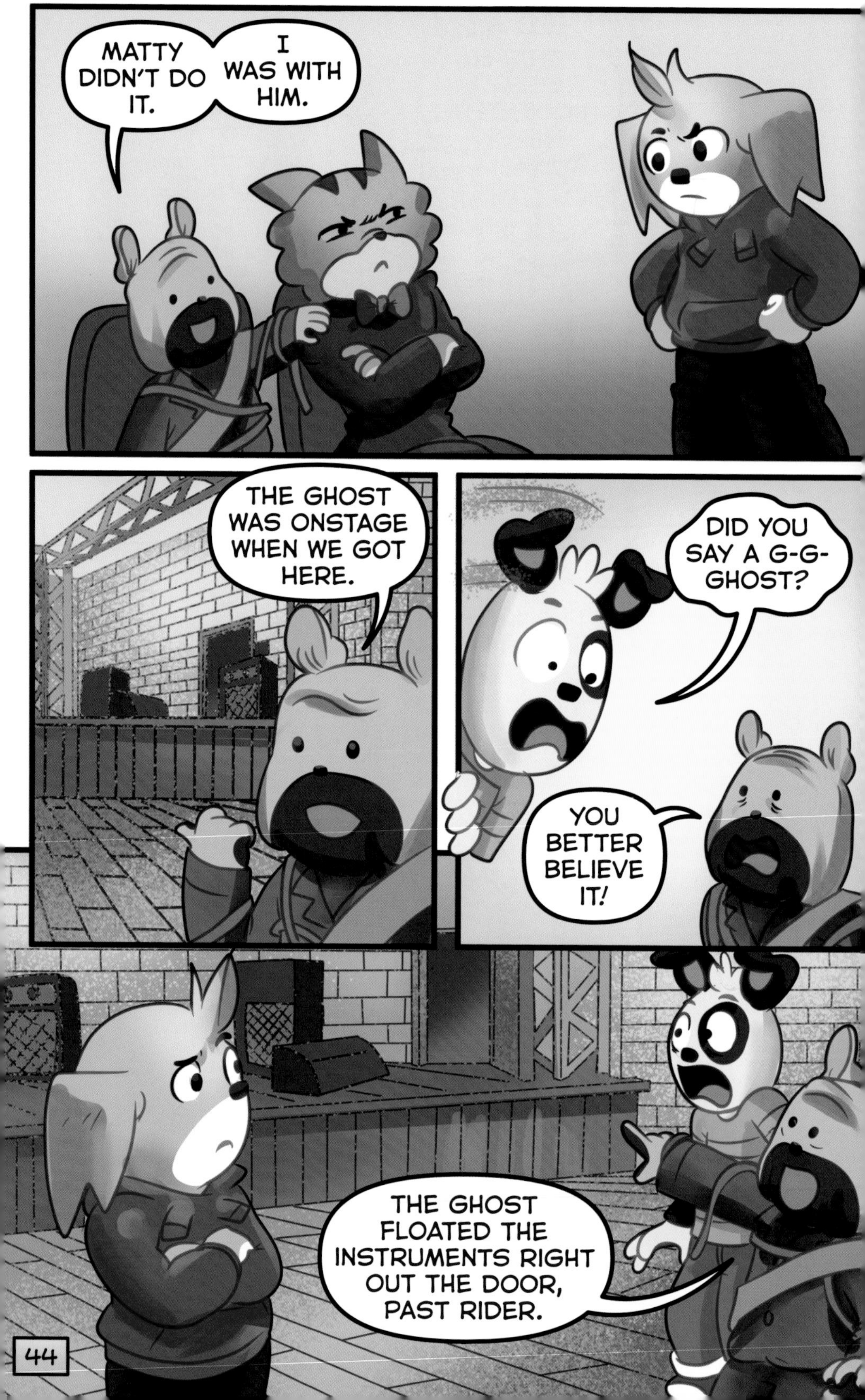
MATTY DIDN'T DO IT.
I WAS WITH HIM.
THE GHOST WAS ONSTAGE WHEN WE GOT HERE.
DID YOU SAY A G-G-GHOST?
YOU BETTER BELIEVE IT!
THE GHOST FLOATED THE INSTRUMENTS RIGHT OUT THE DOOR, PAST RIDER.

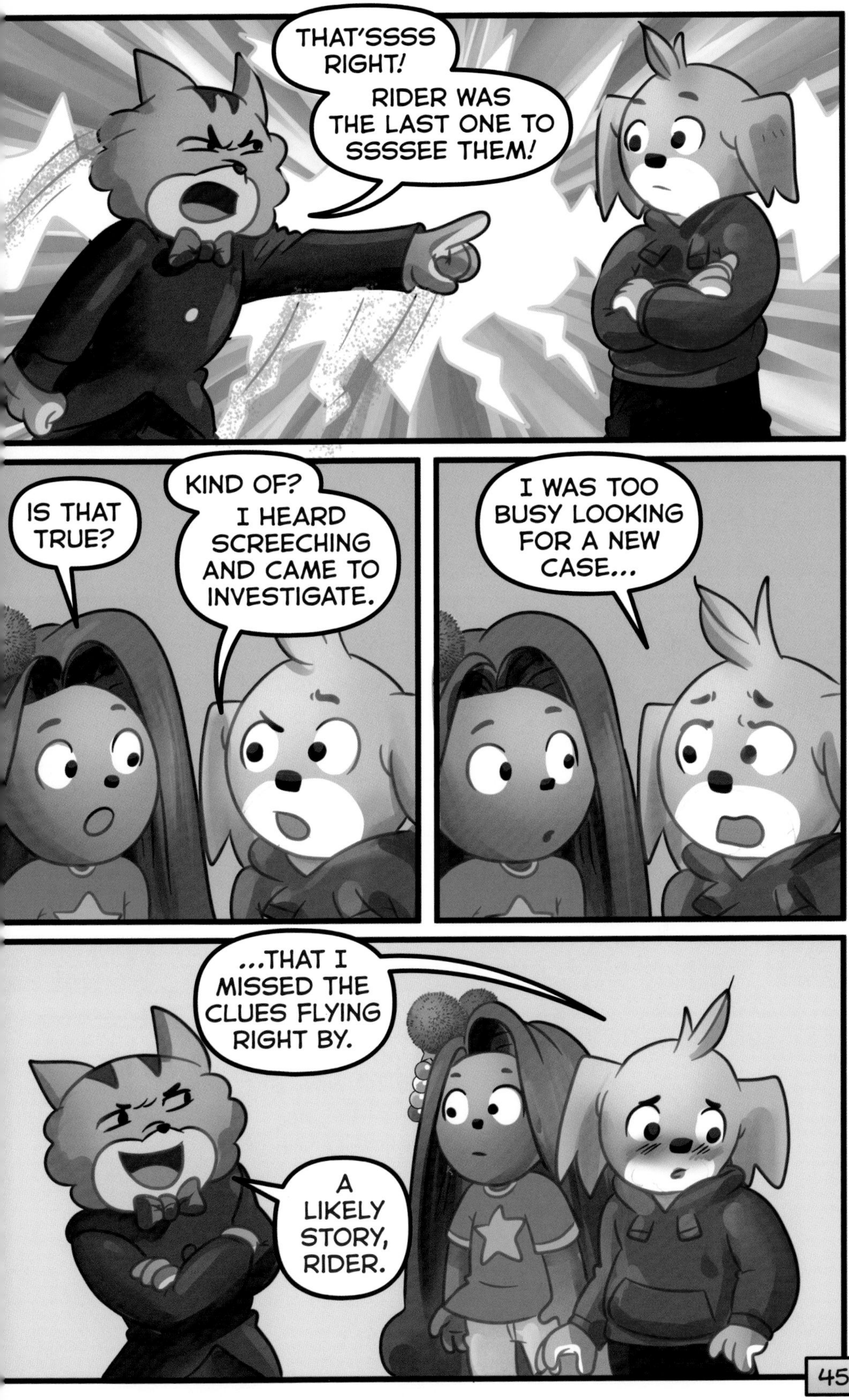
THAT'SSSS RIGHT!
RIDER WAS THE LAST ONE TO SSSSEE THEM!
IS THAT TRUE?
KIND OF?
I HEARD SCREECHING AND CAME TO INVESTIGATE.
I WAS TOO BUSY LOOKING FOR A NEW CASE...
...THAT I MISSED THE CLUES FLYING RIGHT BY.
A LIKELY STORY, RIDER.

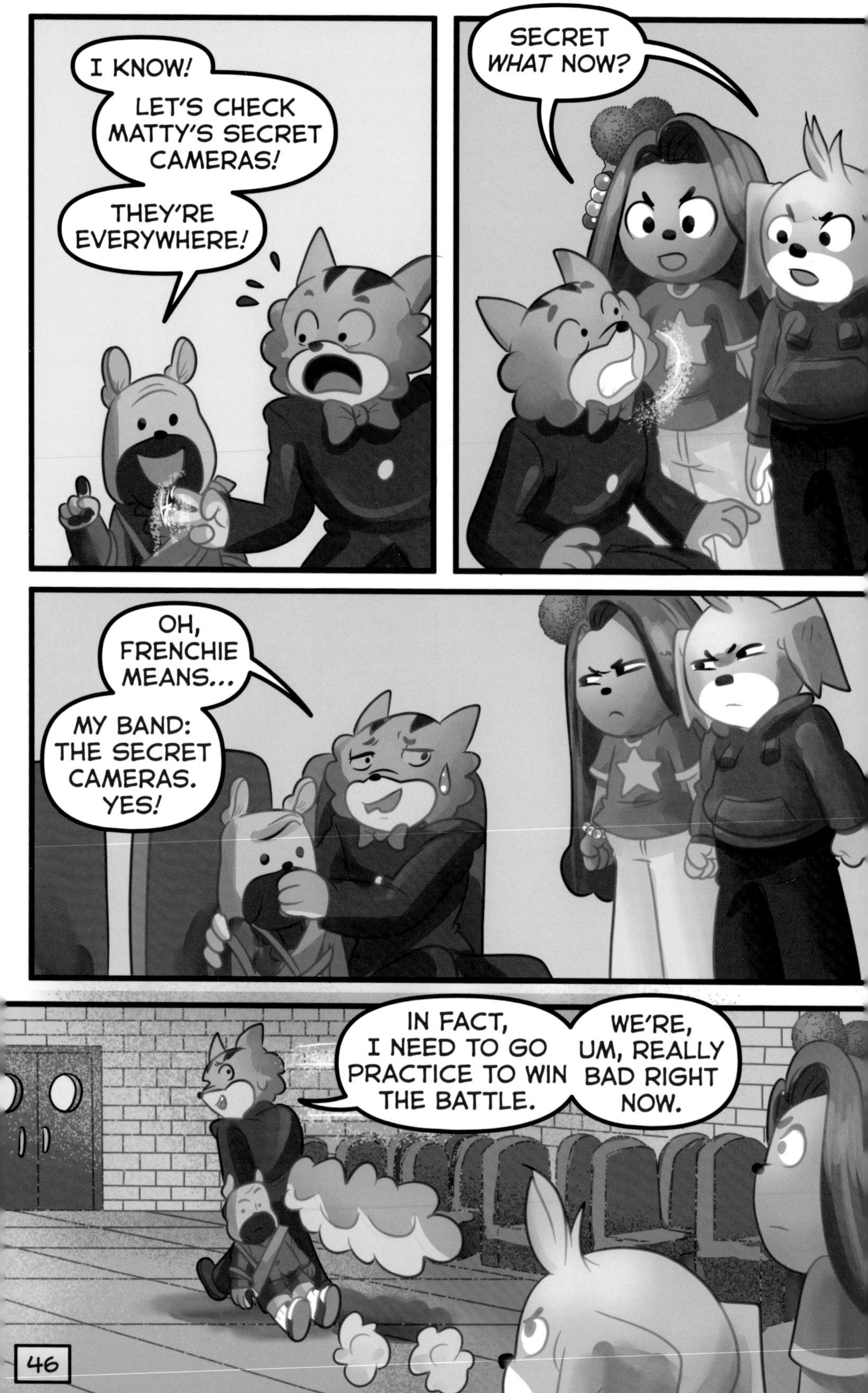
I KNOW!
LET'S CHECK MATTY'S SECRET CAMERAS!
THEY'RE EVERYWHERE!
SECRET *WHAT* NOW?
OH, FRENCHIE MEANS...
MY BAND: THE SECRET CAMERAS. YES!
IN FACT, I NEED TO GO PRACTICE TO WIN THE BATTLE.
WE'RE, UM, REALLY BAD RIGHT NOW.

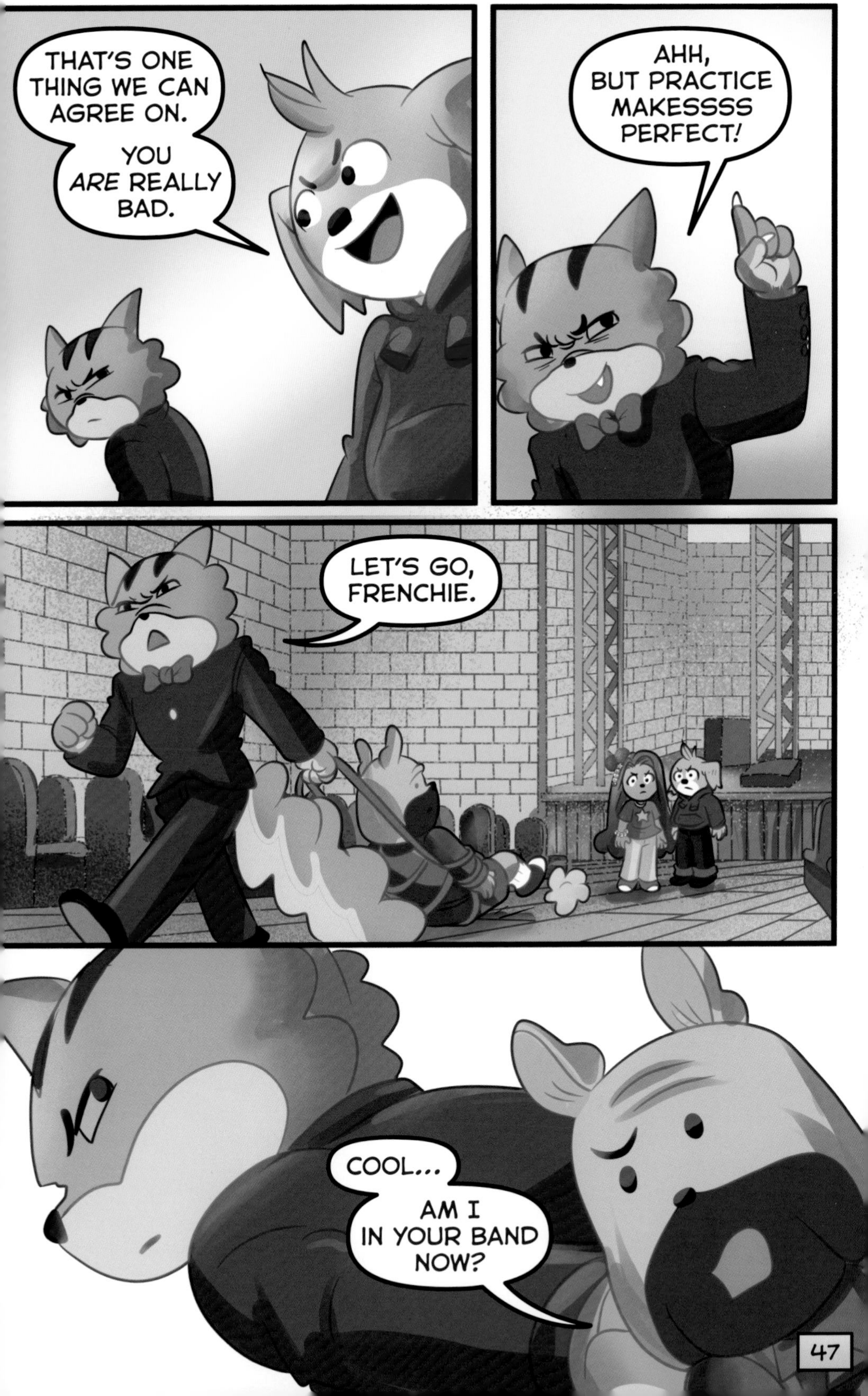
THAT'S ONE THING WE CAN AGREE ON.
YOU ARE REALLY BAD.
AHH, BUT PRACTICE MAKESSSS PERFECT!
LET'S GO, FRENCHIE.
COOL...
AM I IN YOUR BAND NOW?

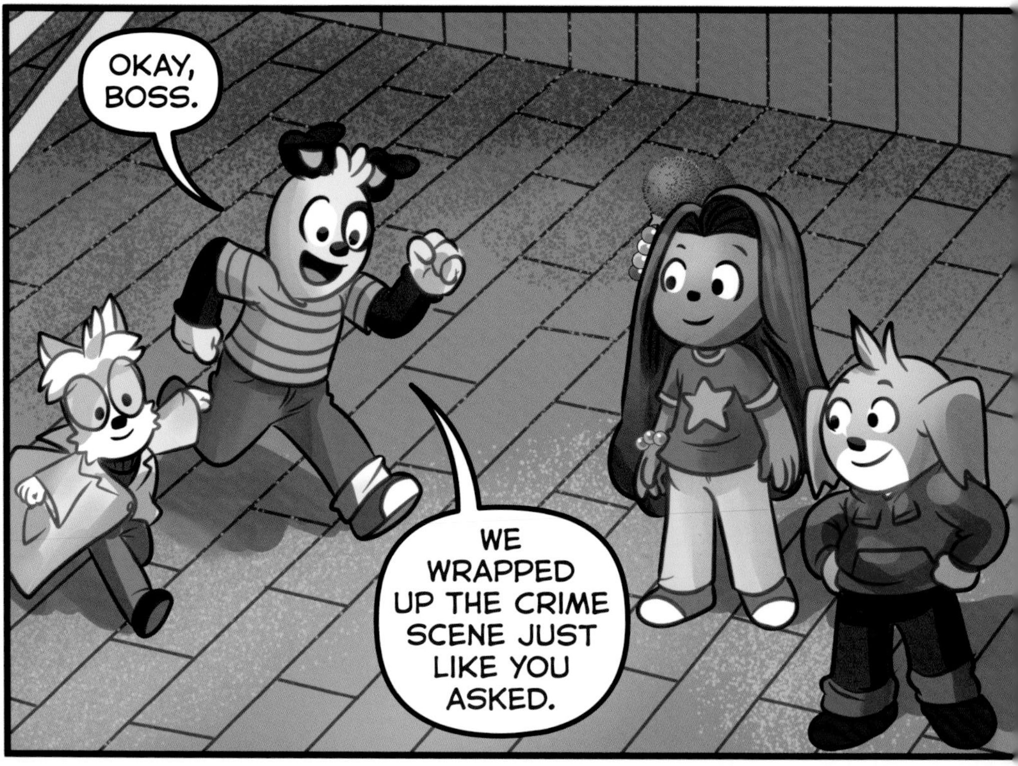
OKAY, BOSS.
WE WRAPPED UP THE CRIME SCENE JUST LIKE YOU ASKED.

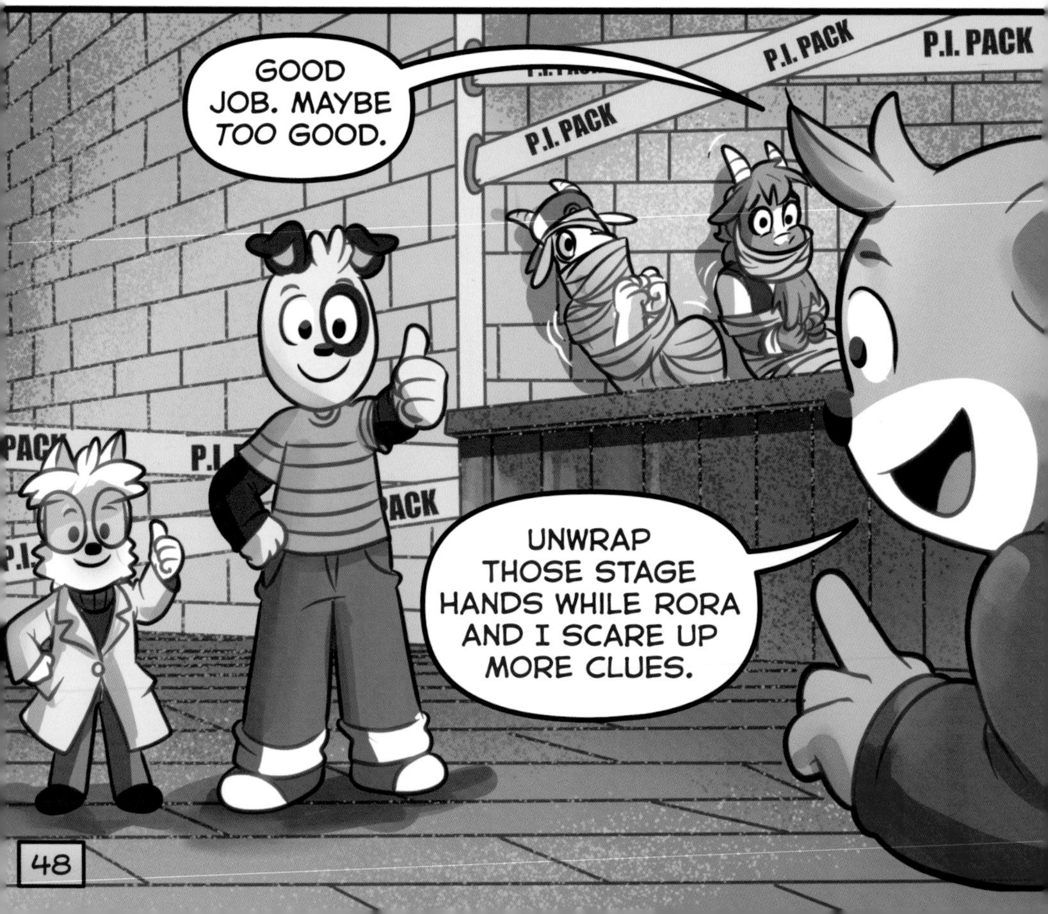
GOOD JOB. MAYBE TOO GOOD.
P.I. PACK
P.I. PACK
P.I. PACK
UNWRAP THOSE STAGE HANDS WHILE RORA AND I SCARE UP MORE CLUES.

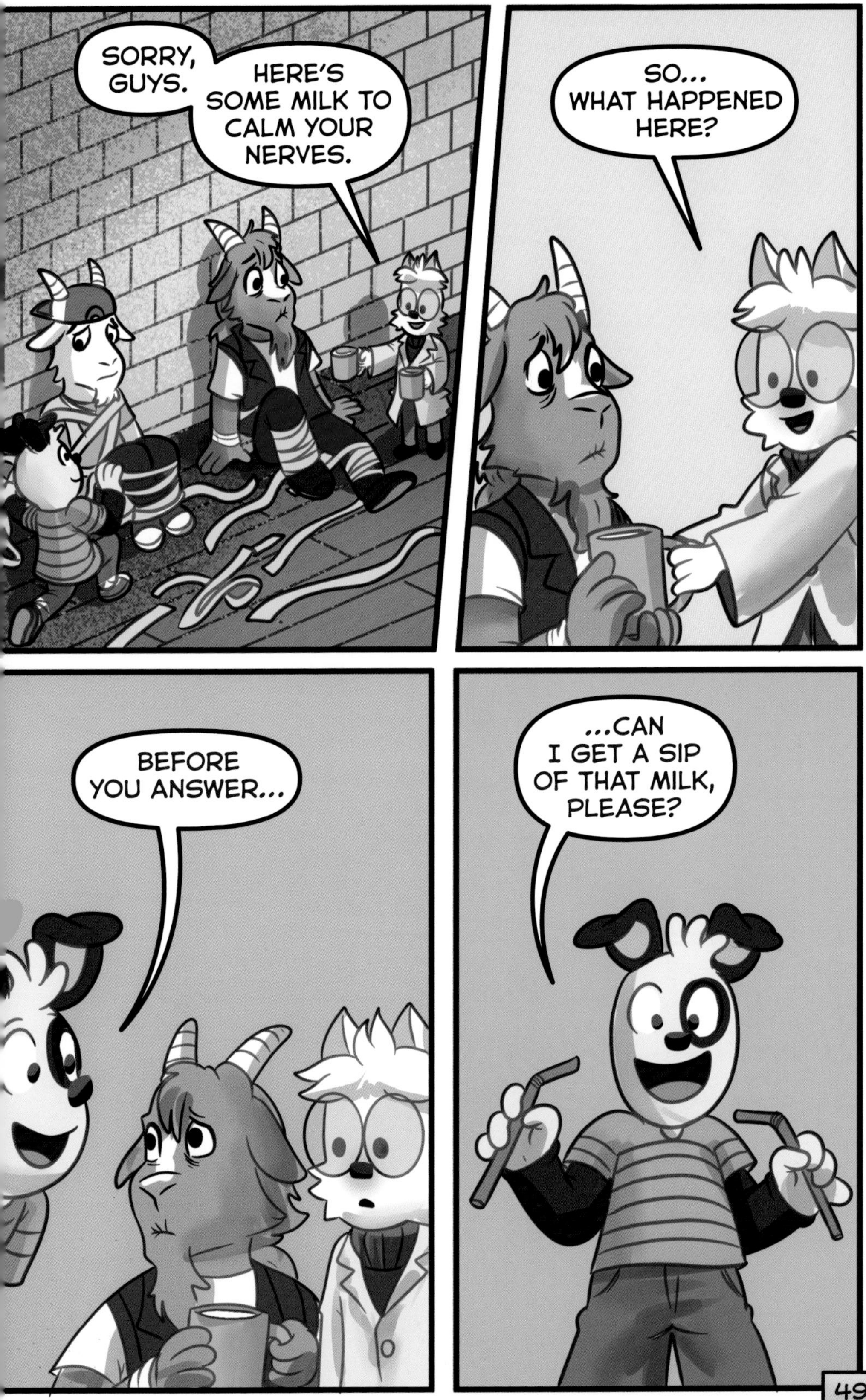
SORRY, GUYS.
HERE'S SOME MILK TO CALM YOUR NERVES.
SO... WHAT HAPPENED HERE?
BEFORE YOU ANSWER...
...CAN I GET A SIP OF THAT MILK, PLEASE?

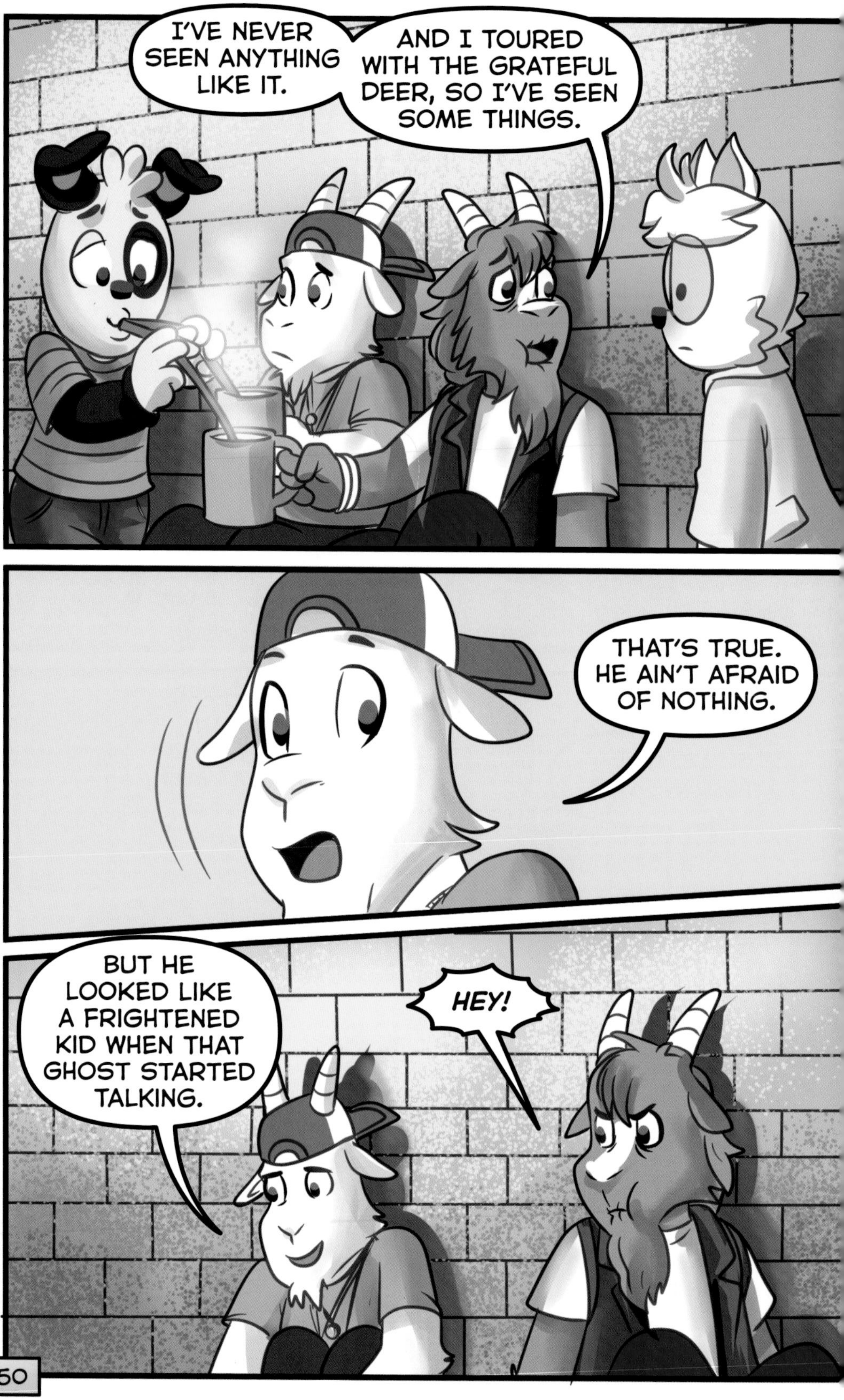
I'VE NEVER SEEN ANYTHING LIKE IT.
AND I TOURED WITH THE GRATEFUL DEER, SO I'VE SEEN SOME THINGS.
THAT'S TRUE. HE AIN'T AFRAID OF NOTHING.
BUT HE LOOKED LIKE A FRIGHTENED KID WHEN THAT GHOST STARTED TALKING.
HEY!

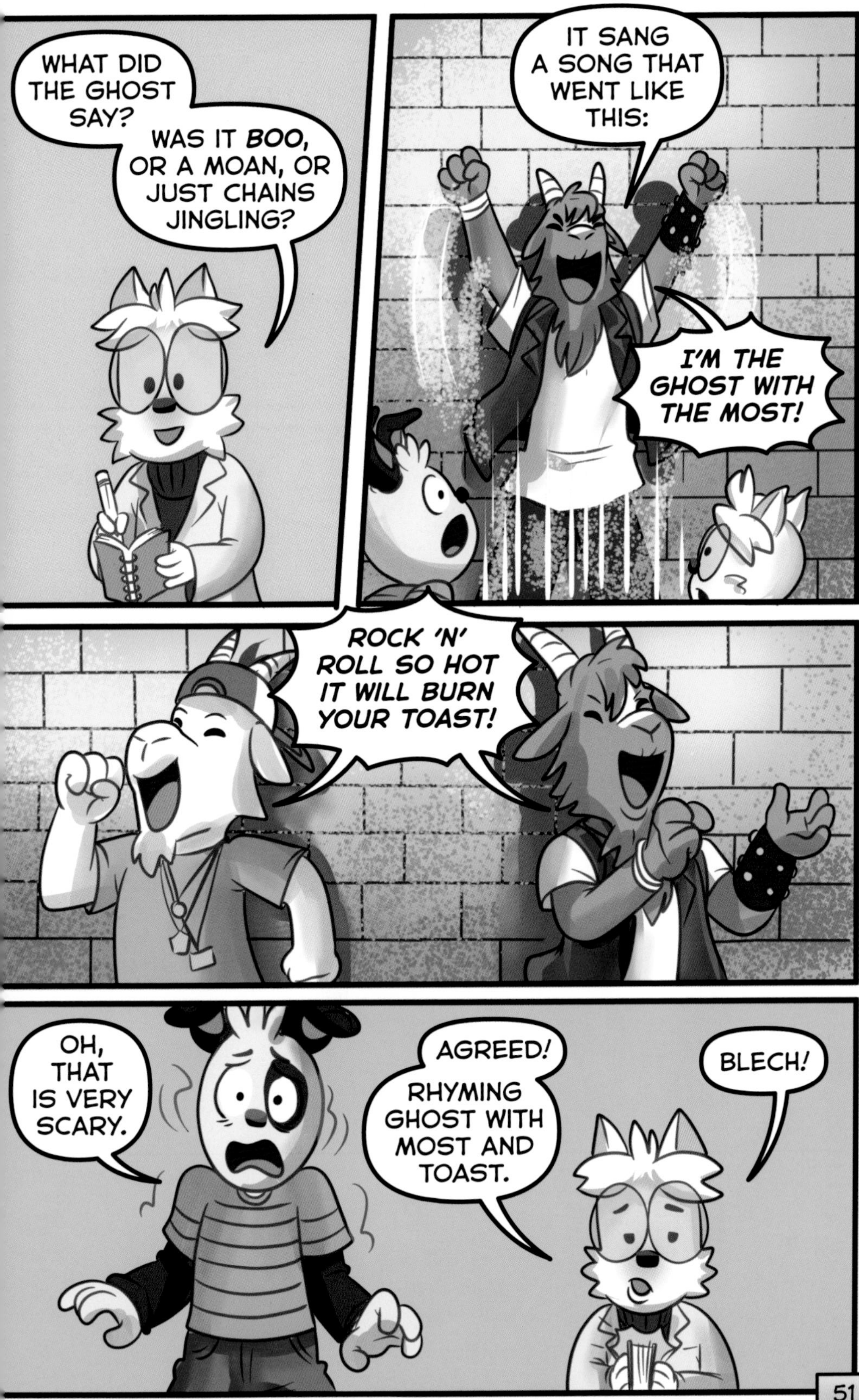
WHAT DID THE GHOST SAY?
WAS IT *BOO*, OR A MOAN, OR JUST CHAINS JINGLING?
IT SANG A SONG THAT WENT LIKE THIS:
I'M THE GHOST WITH THE MOST!
ROCK 'N' ROLL SO HOT IT WILL BURN YOUR TOAST!
OH, THAT IS VERY SCARY.
AGREED!
RHYMING GHOST WITH MOST AND TOAST.
BLECH!

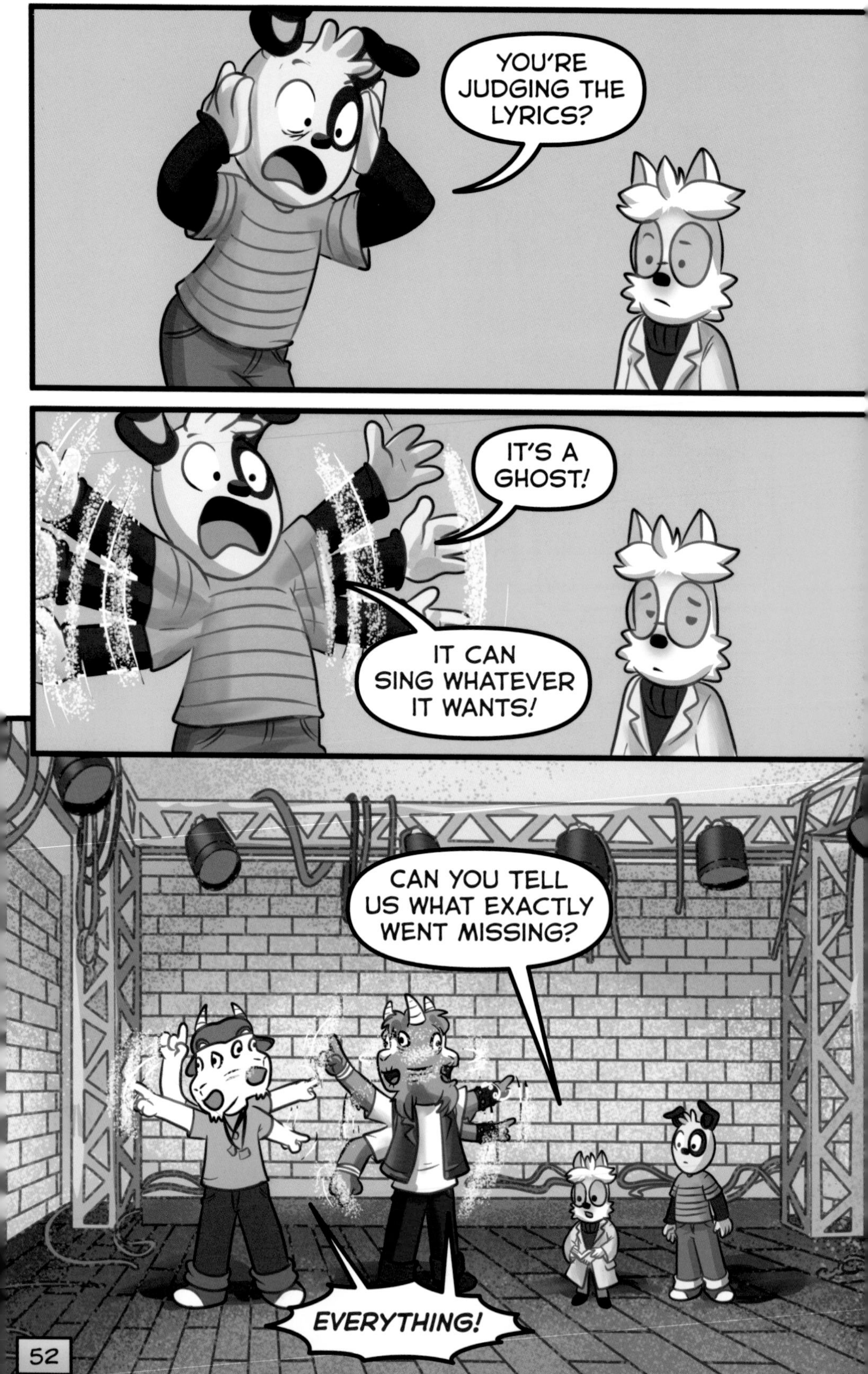
YOU'RE JUDGING THE LYRICS?
IT'S A GHOST!
IT CAN SING WHATEVER IT WANTS!
CAN YOU TELL US WHAT EXACTLY WENT MISSING?
EVERYTHING!

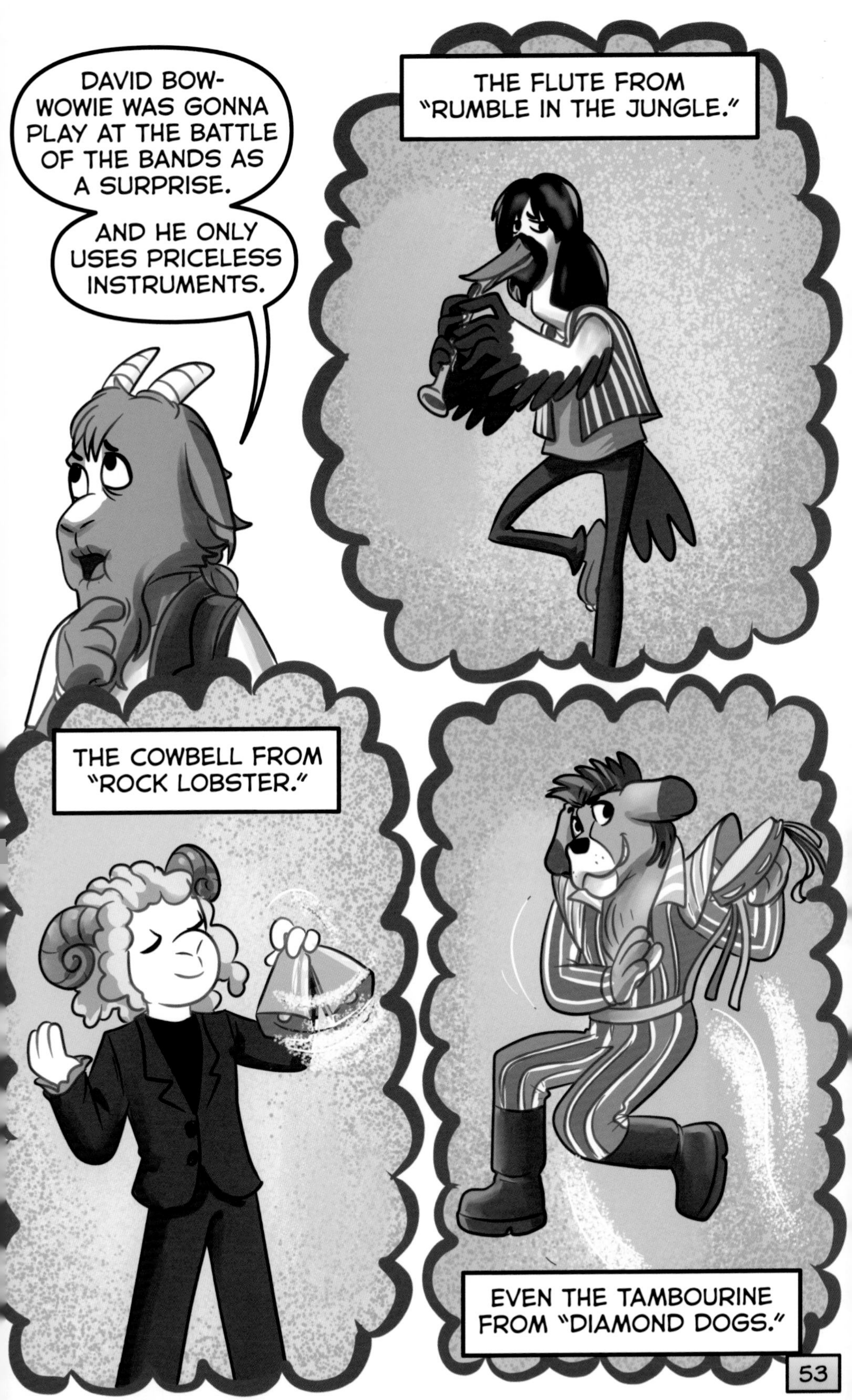

DAVID BOW-WOWIE WAS GONNA PLAY AT THE BATTLE OF THE BANDS AS A SURPRISE.
AND HE ONLY USES PRICELESS INSTRUMENTS.
THE FLUTE FROM "RUMBLE IN THE JUNGLE."
THE COWBELL FROM "ROCK LOBSTER."
EVEN THE TAMBOURINE FROM "DIAMOND DOGS."

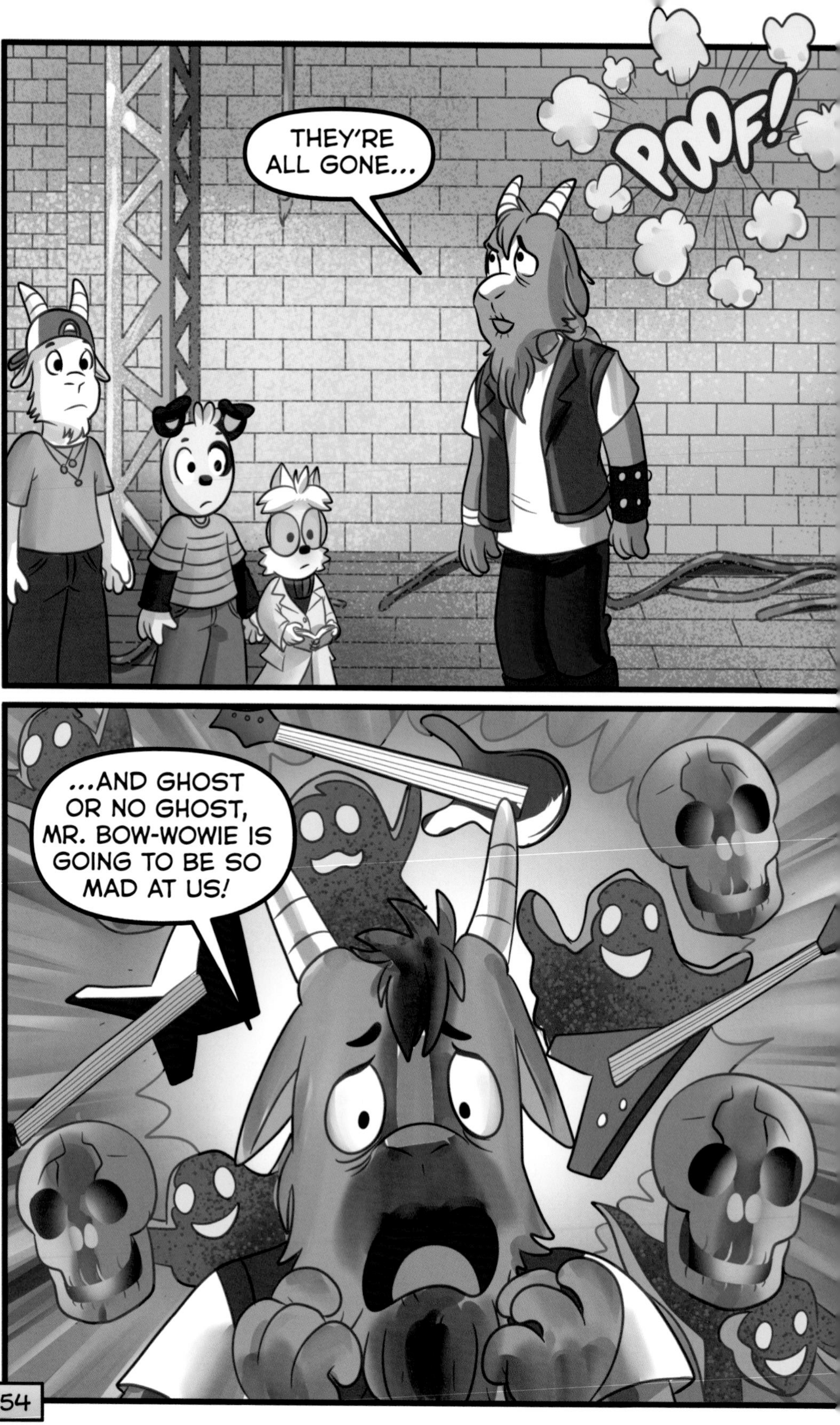
POOF!
THEY'RE ALL GONE...
...AND GHOST OR NO GHOST, MR. BOW-WOWIE IS GOING TO BE SO MAD AT US!

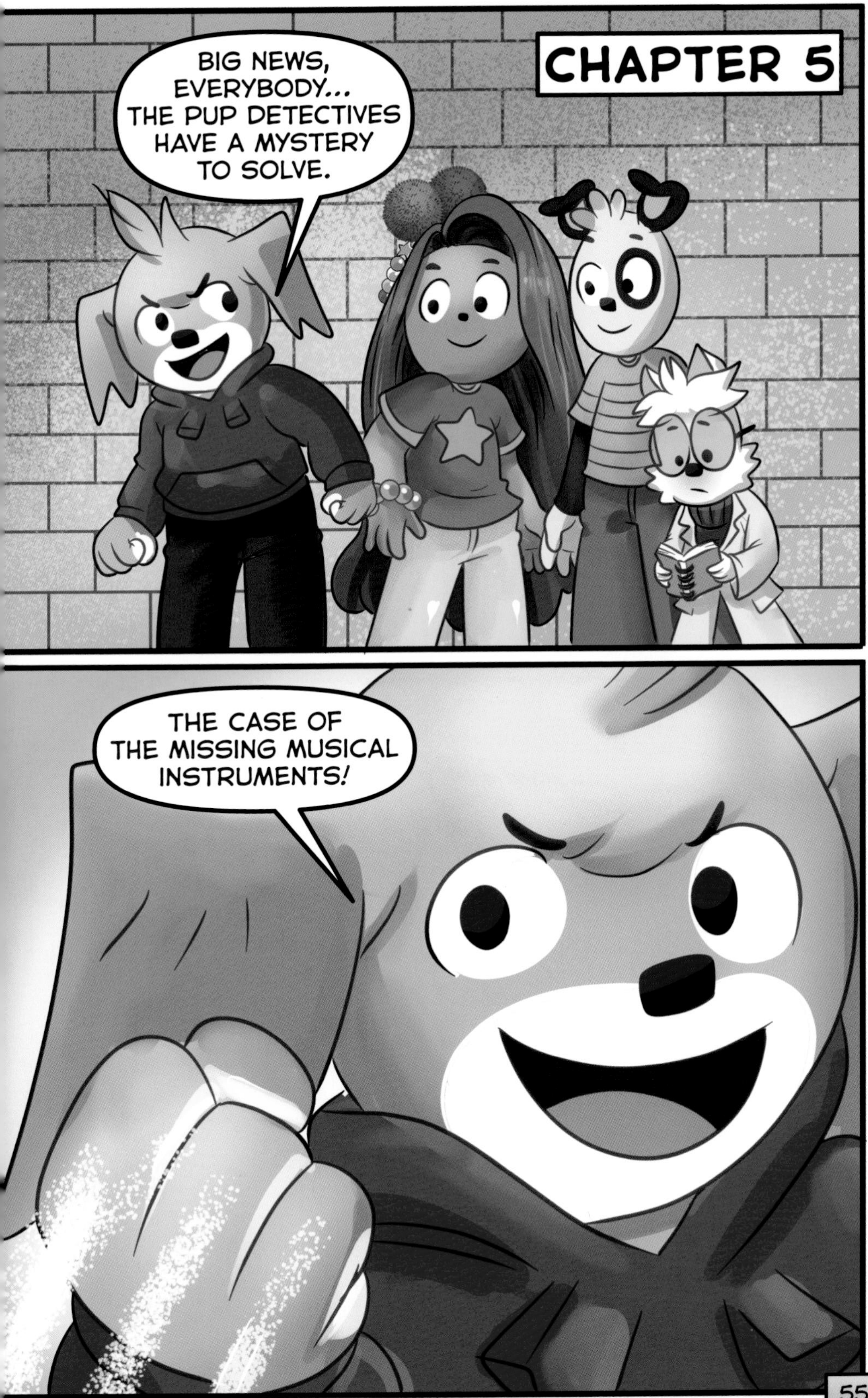
CHAPTER 5
BIG NEWS, EVERYBODY... THE PUP DETECTIVES HAVE A MYSTERY TO SOLVE.
THE CASE OF THE MISSING MUSICAL INSTRUMENTS!

57

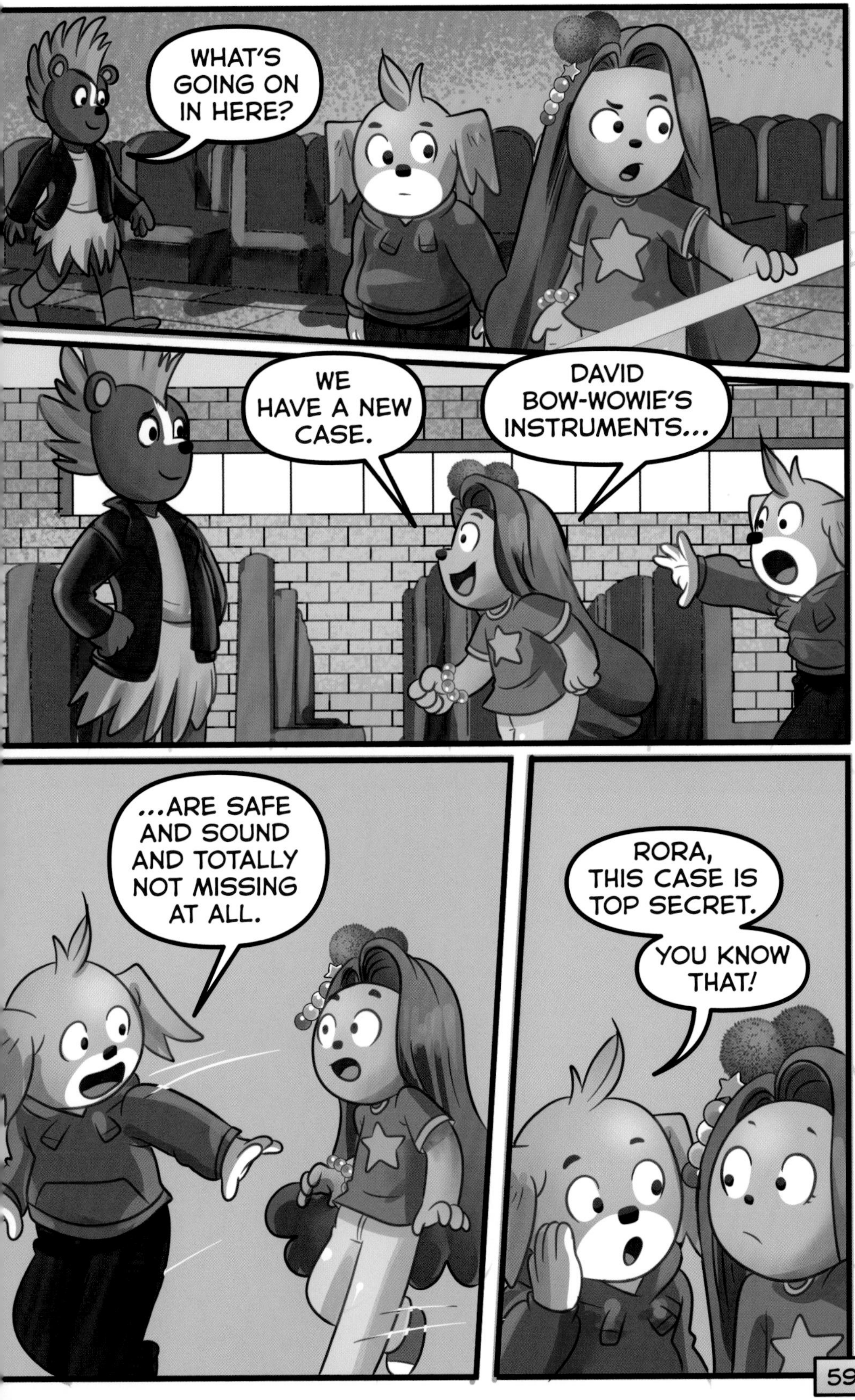
WHAT'S GOING ON IN HERE?
WE HAVE A NEW CASE.
DAVID BOW-WOWIE'S INSTRUMENTS...
...ARE SAFE AND SOUND AND TOTALLY NOT MISSING AT ALL.
RORA, THIS CASE IS TOP SECRET.
YOU KNOW THAT!

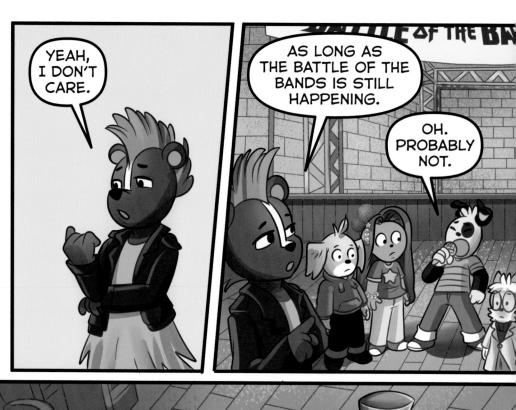

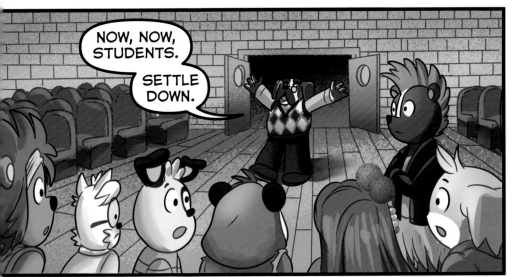

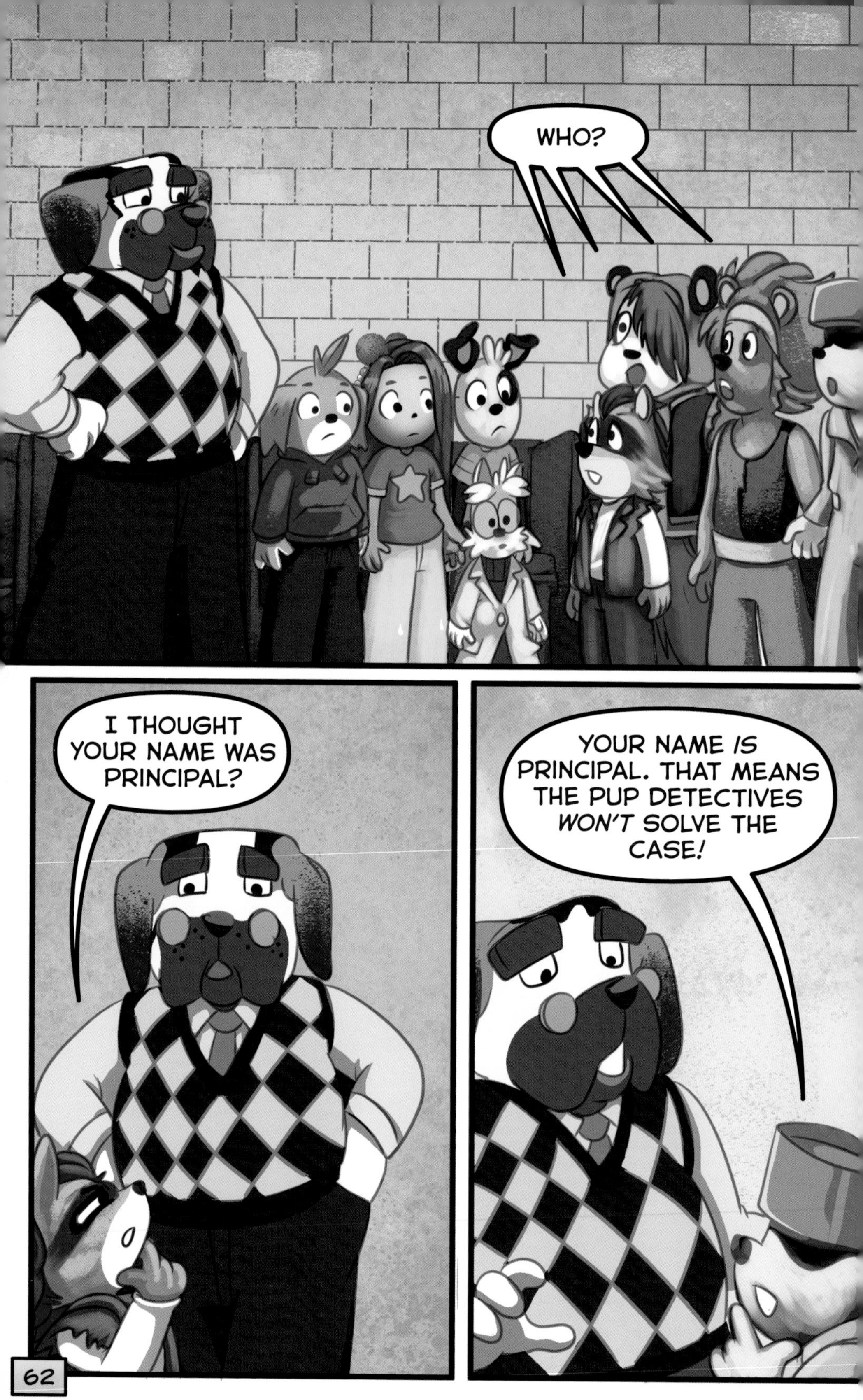
WHO?
I THOUGHT YOUR NAME WAS PRINCIPAL?
YOUR NAME *IS* PRINCIPAL. THAT MEANS THE PUP DETECTIVES *WON'T* SOLVE THE CASE!

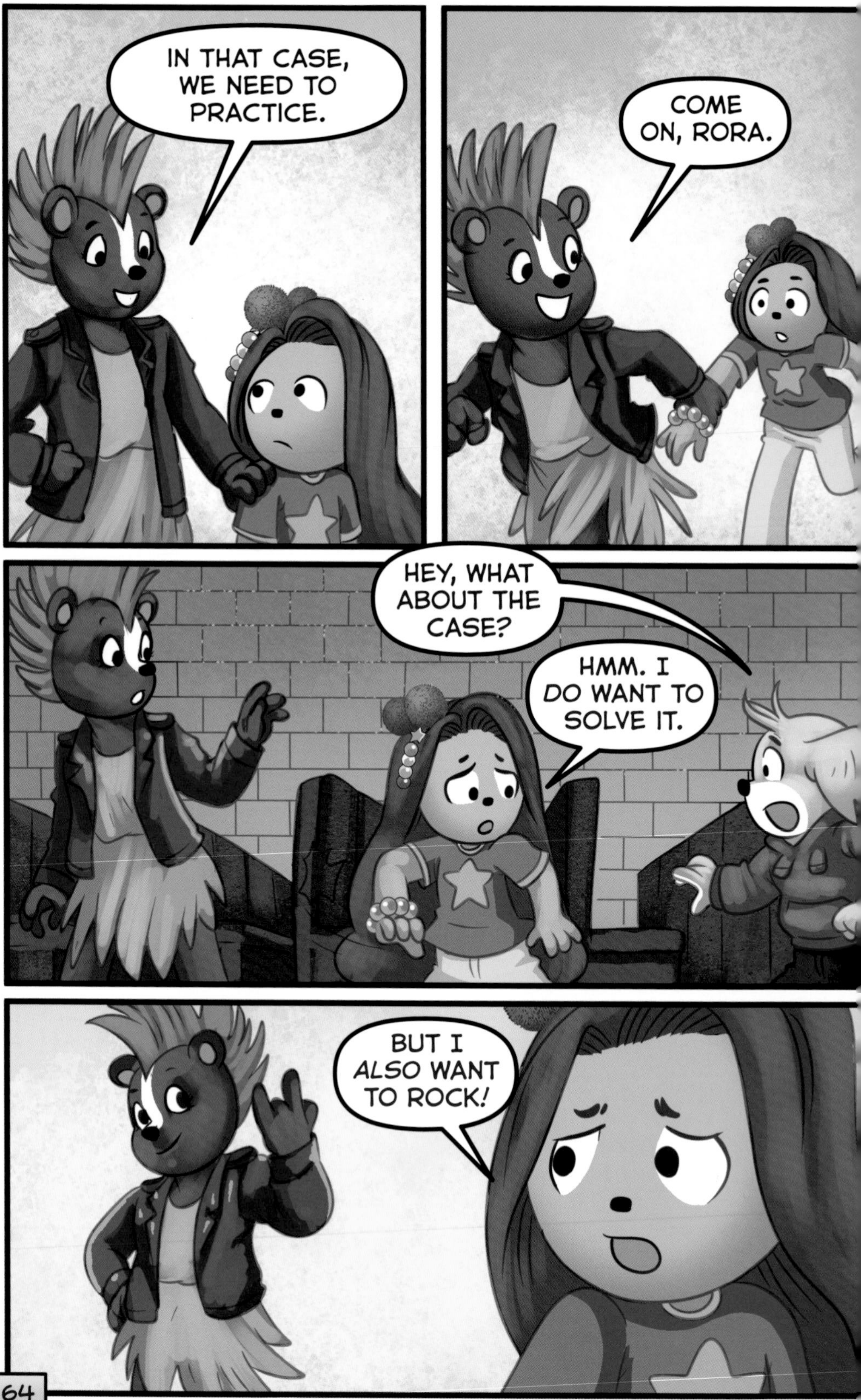
IN THAT CASE, WE NEED TO PRACTICE.
COME ON, RORA.
HEY, WHAT ABOUT THE CASE?
HMM. I *DO* WANT TO SOLVE IT.
BUT I *ALSO* WANT TO ROCK!

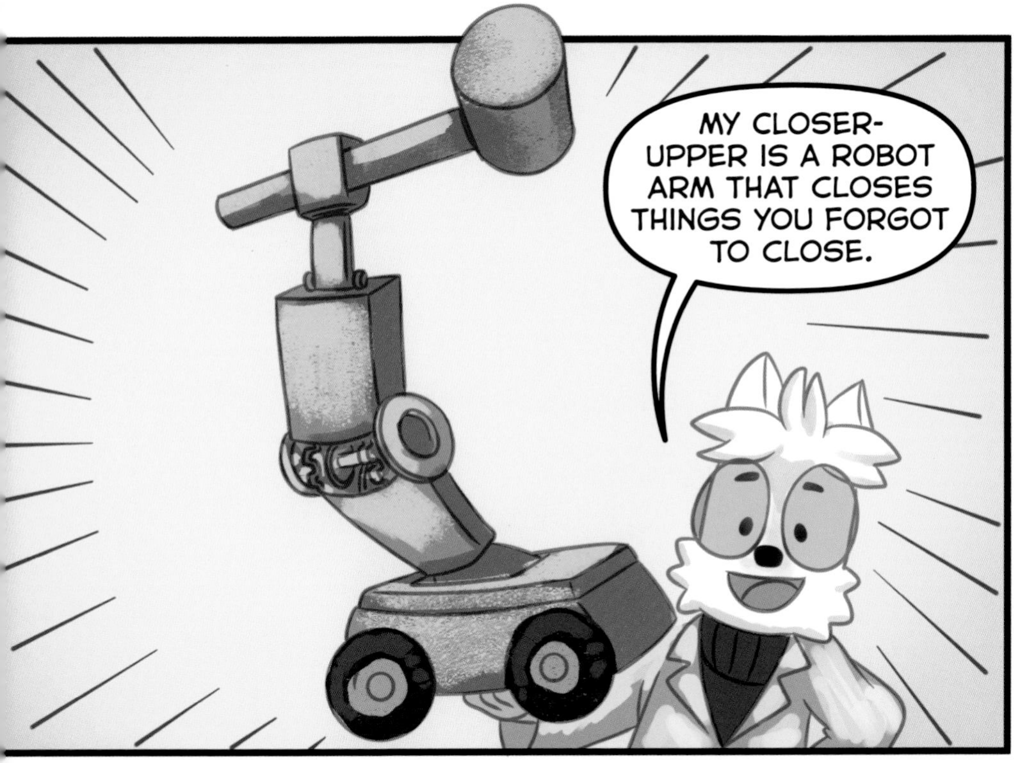
MY CLOSER-UPPER IS A ROBOT ARM THAT CLOSES THINGS YOU FORGOT TO CLOSE.

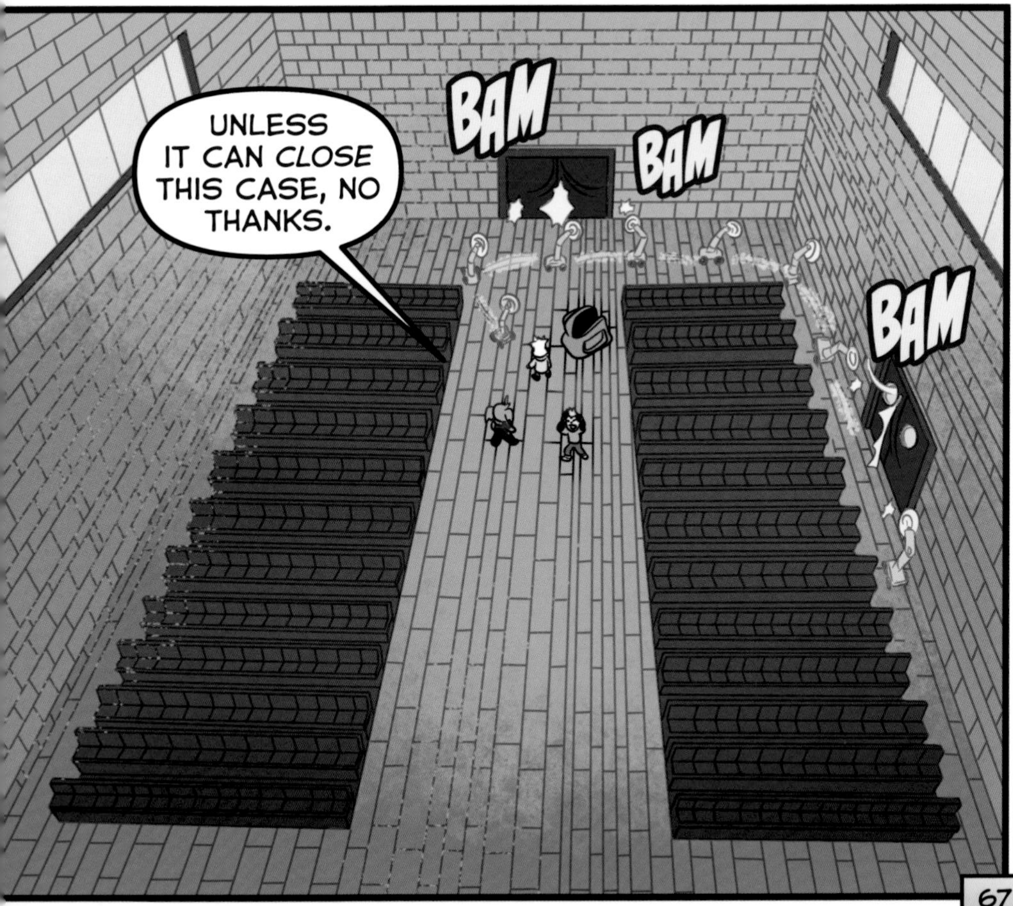
BAM
BAM
UNLESS IT CAN *CLOSE* THIS CASE, NO THANKS.
BAM

YOU GOT ANY NON-ROBOT ARM INVENTIONS, WESTIE?

JUST ONE.

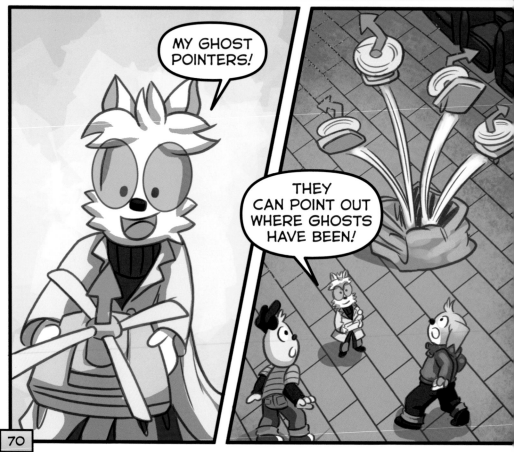

MY GHOST POINTERS!

THEY CAN POINT OUT WHERE GHOSTS HAVE BEEN!

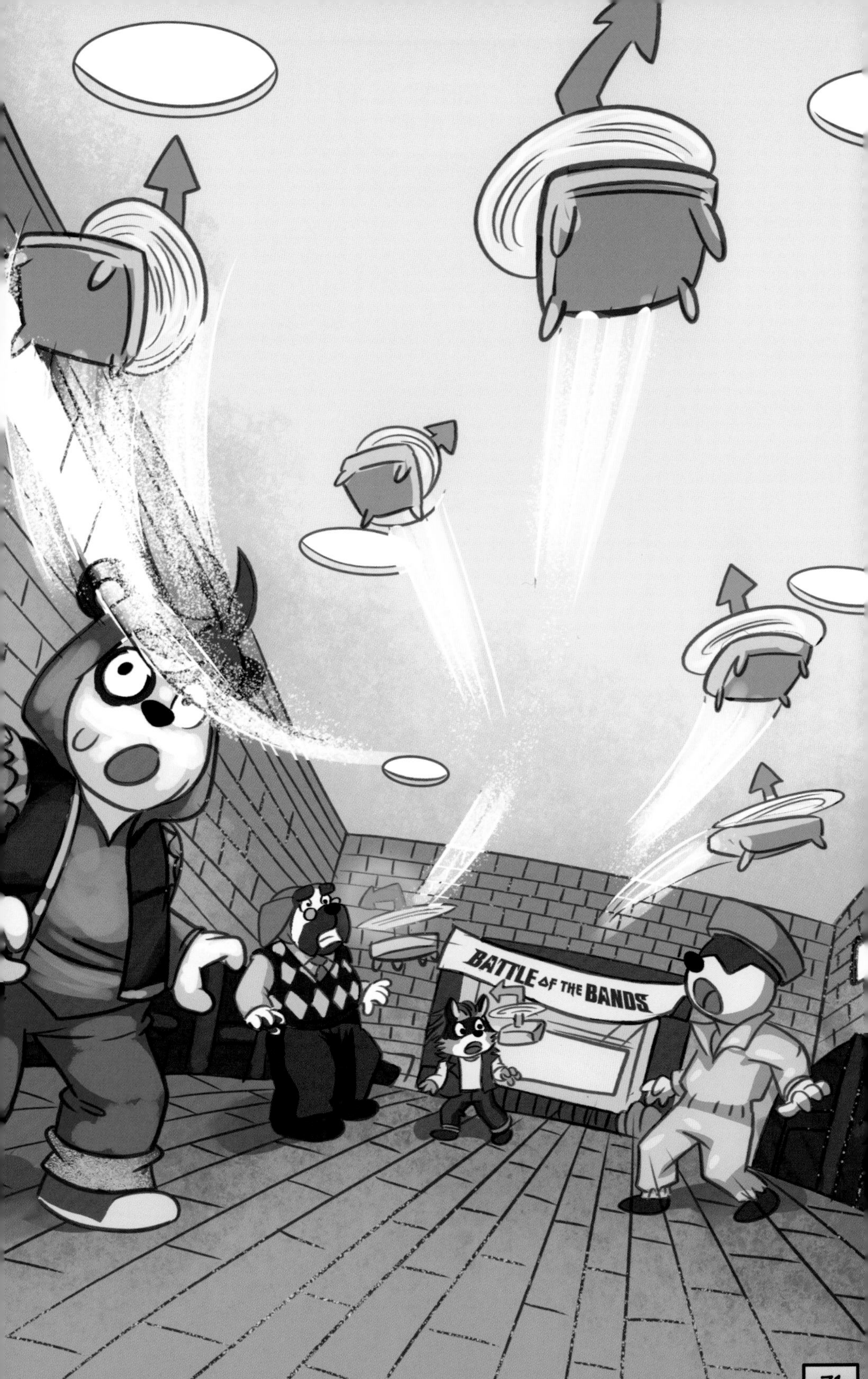
BATTLE OF THE BANDS

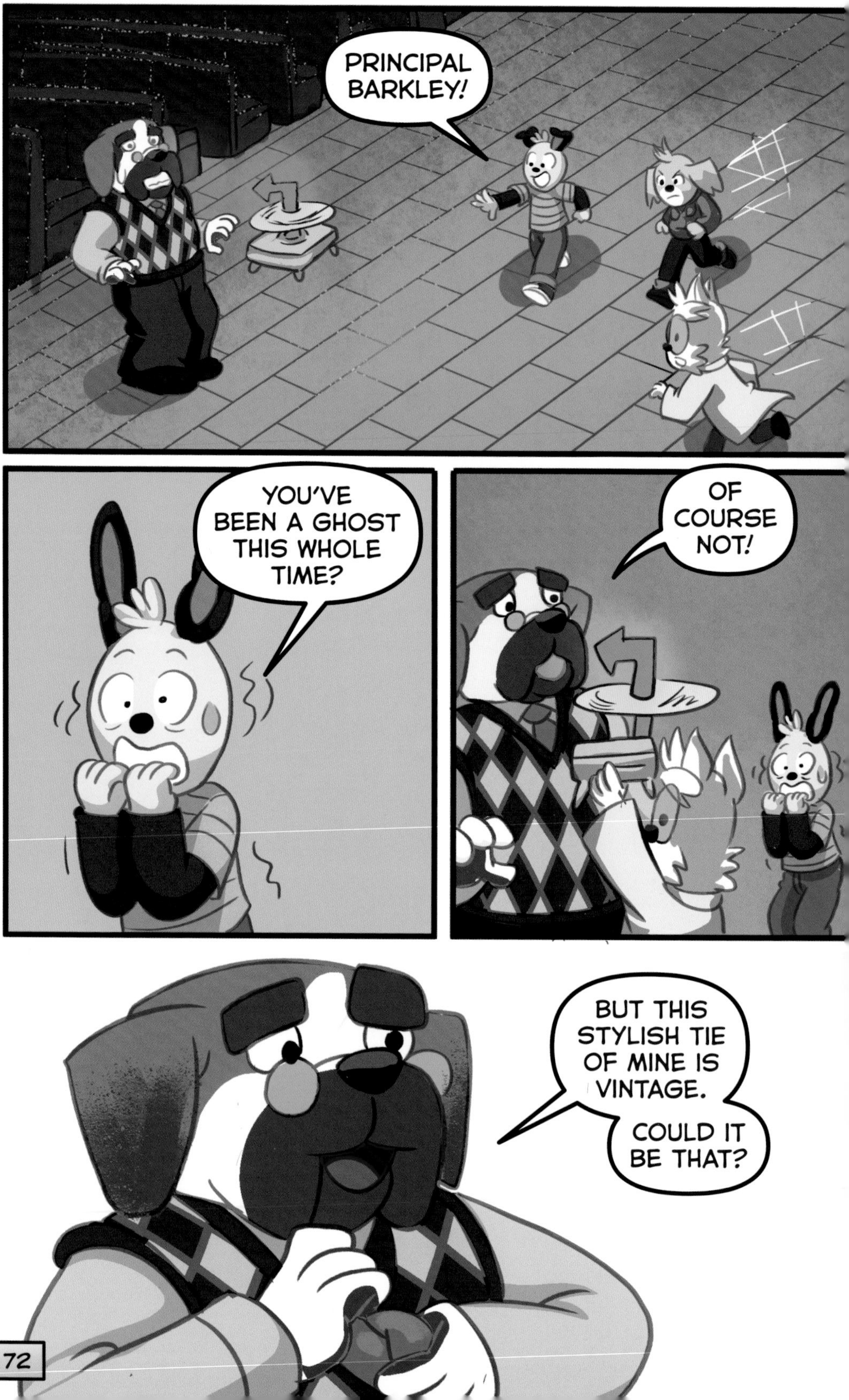
PRINCIPAL BARKLEY!
YOU'VE BEEN A GHOST THIS WHOLE TIME?
OF COURSE NOT!
BUT THIS STYLISH TIE OF MINE IS VINTAGE.
COULD IT BE THAT?

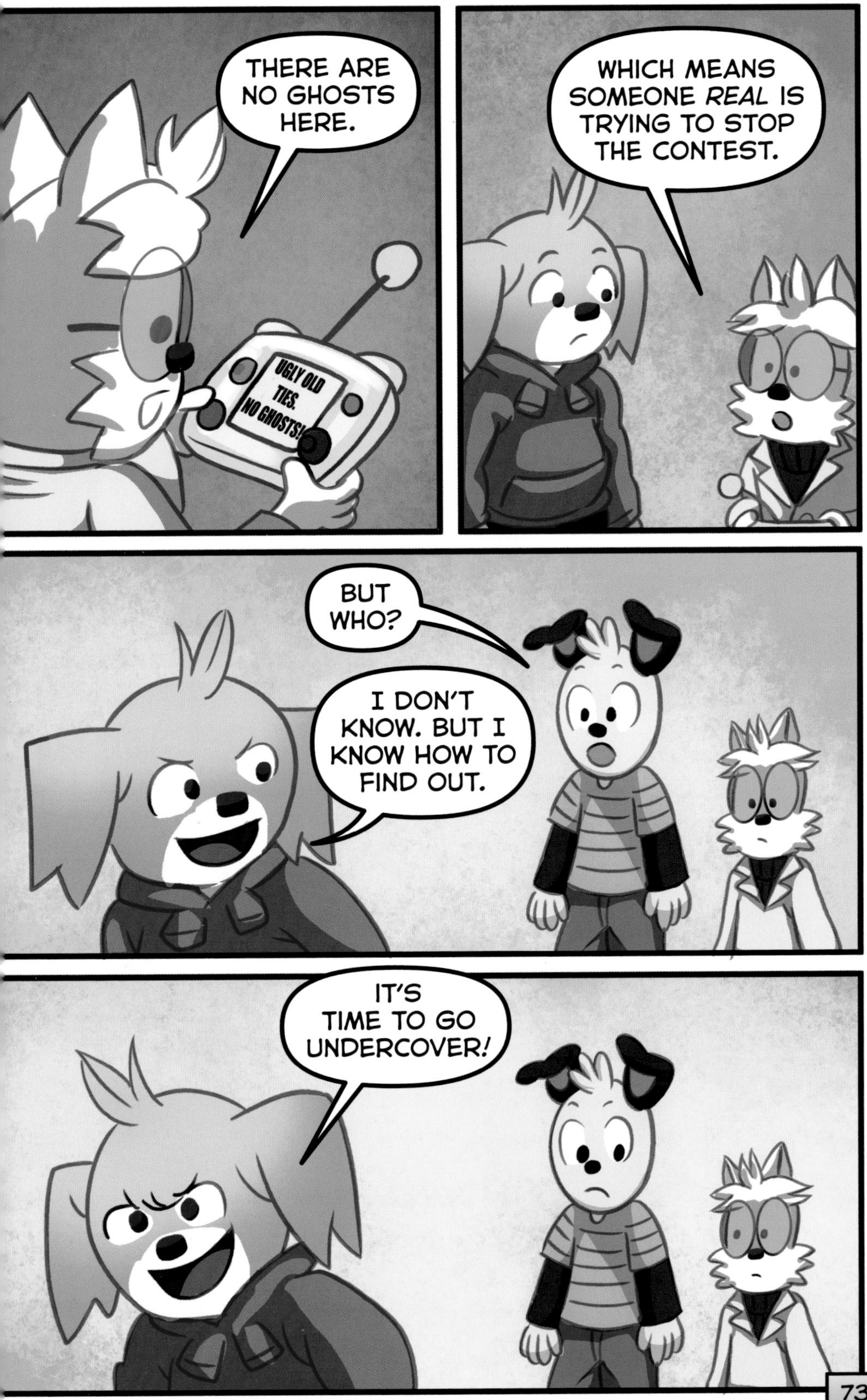
THERE ARE NO GHOSTS HERE.
UGLY OLD TIES. NO GHOSTS!
WHICH MEANS SOMEONE *REAL* IS TRYING TO STOP THE CONTEST.
BUT WHO?
I DON'T KNOW. BUT I KNOW HOW TO FIND OUT.
IT'S TIME TO GO UNDERCOVER!

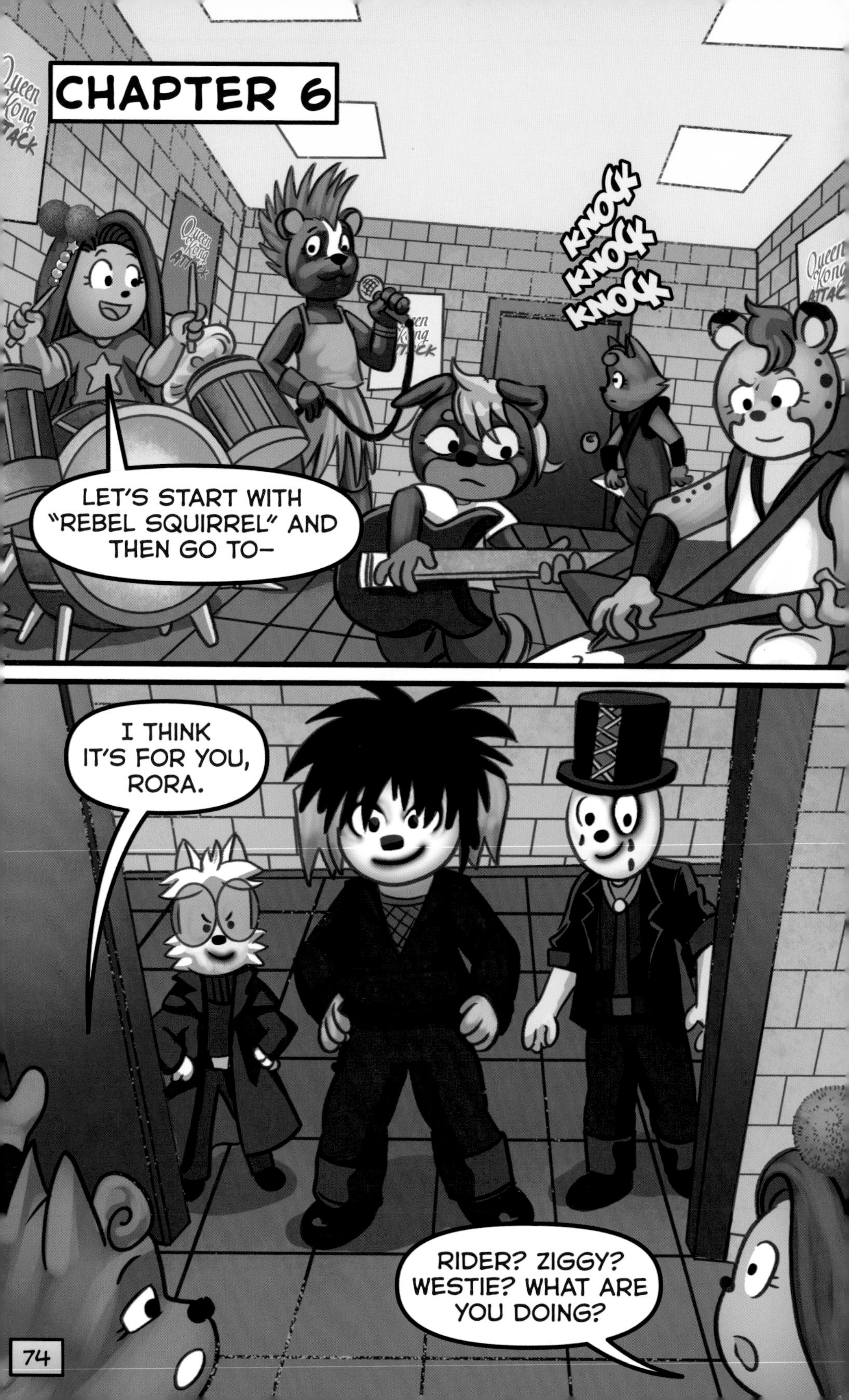
CHAPTER 6
Queen Kong Attack
KNOCK KNOCK KNOCK
LET'S START WITH "REBEL SQUIRREL" AND THEN GO TO—
I THINK IT'S FOR YOU, RORA.
RIDER? ZIGGY? WESTIE? WHAT ARE YOU DOING?

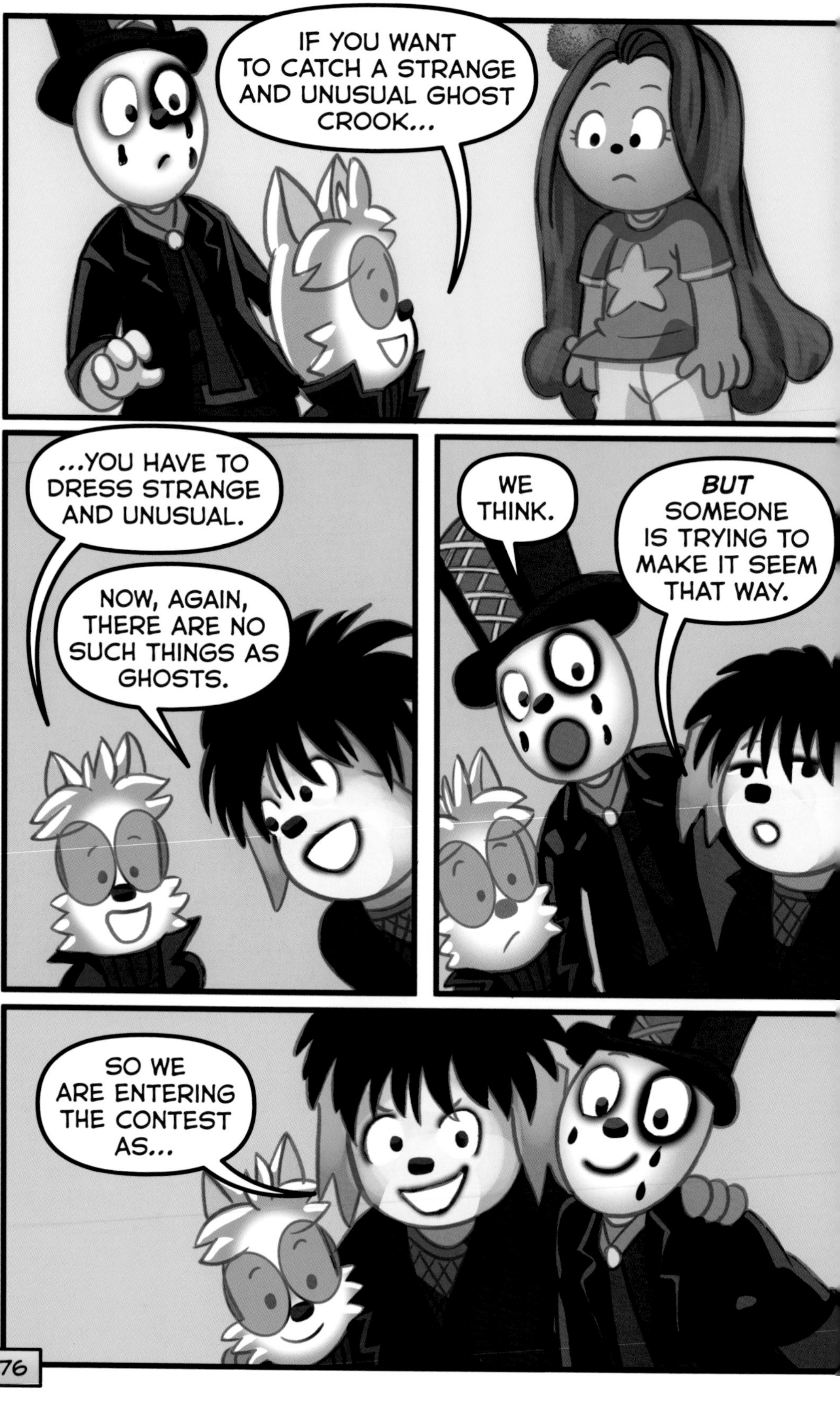
IF YOU WANT TO CATCH A STRANGE AND UNUSUAL GHOST CROOK...
...YOU HAVE TO DRESS STRANGE AND UNUSUAL.
NOW, AGAIN, THERE ARE NO SUCH THINGS AS GHOSTS.
WE THINK.
BUT SOMEONE IS TRYING TO MAKE IT SEEM THAT WAY.
SO WE ARE ENTERING THE CONTEST AS...

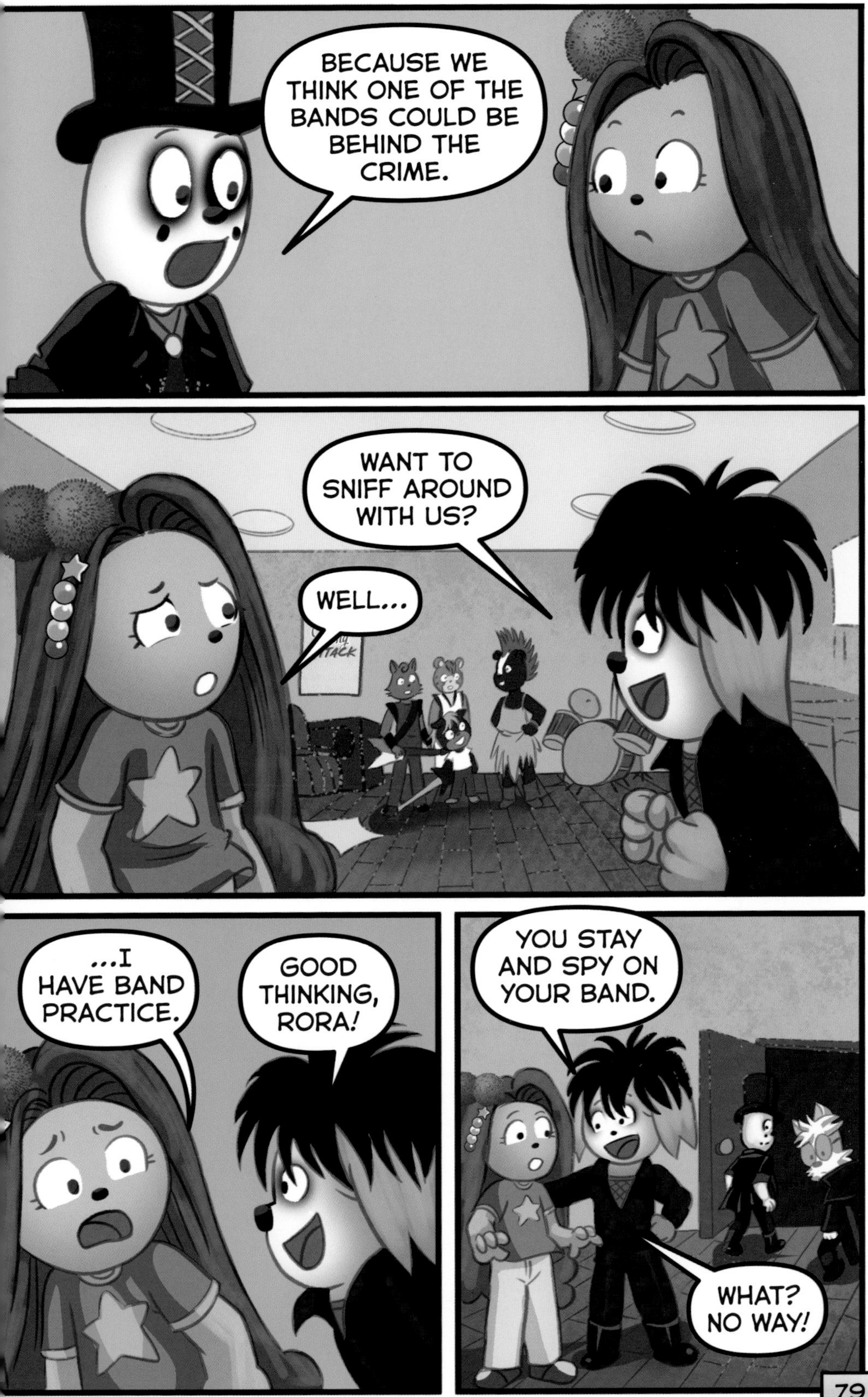
BECAUSE WE THINK ONE OF THE BANDS COULD BE BEHIND THE CRIME.
WANT TO SNIFF AROUND WITH US?
WELL...
...I HAVE BAND PRACTICE.
GOOD THINKING, RORA!
YOU STAY AND SPY ON YOUR BAND.
WHAT? NO WAY!

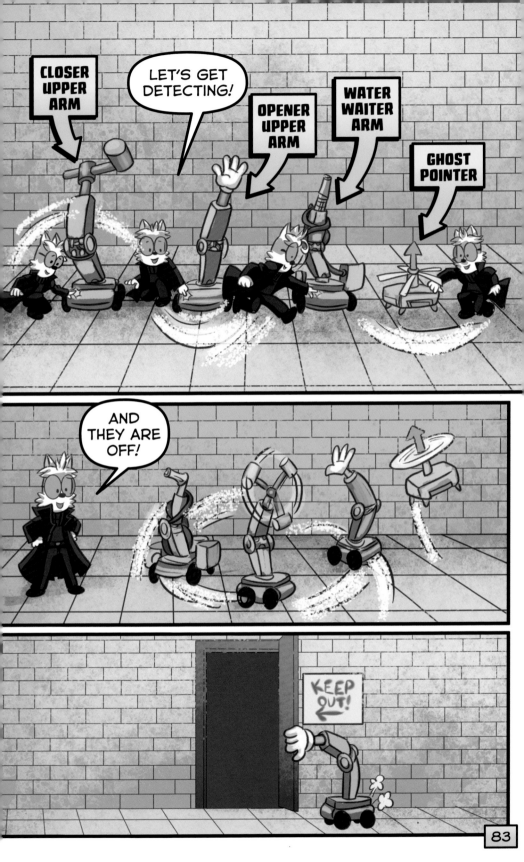

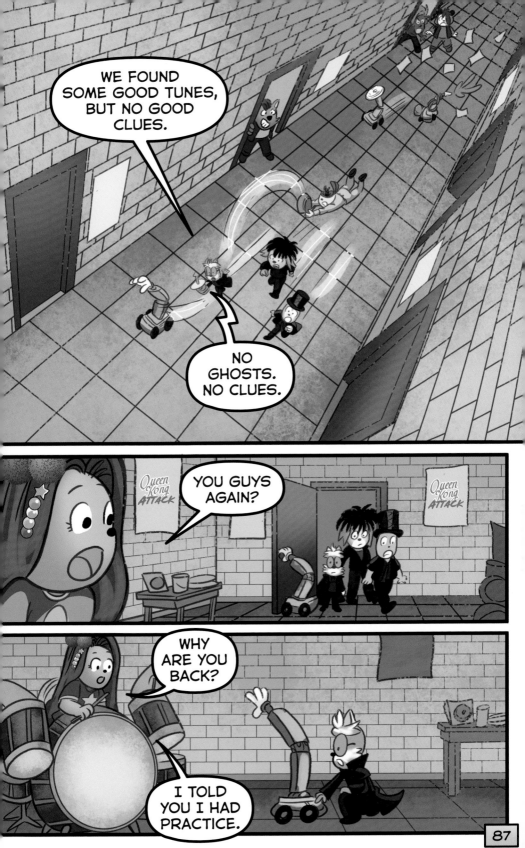

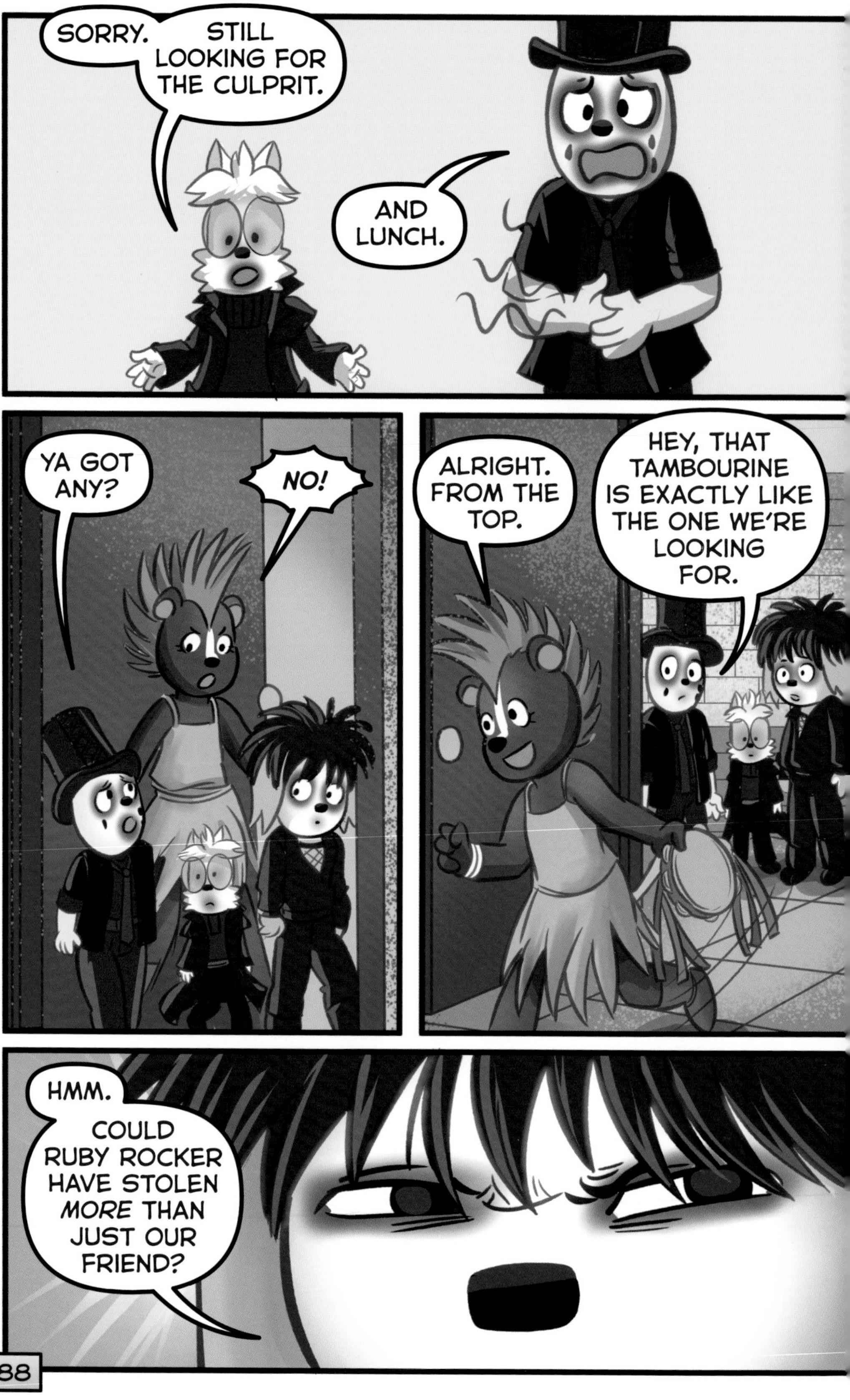
SORRY.
STILL LOOKING FOR THE CULPRIT.
AND LUNCH.
YA GOT ANY?
NO!
ALRIGHT. FROM THE TOP.
HEY, THAT TAMBOURINE IS EXACTLY LIKE THE ONE WE'RE LOOKING FOR.
HMM.
COULD RUBY ROCKER HAVE STOLEN *MORE* THAN JUST OUR FRIEND?

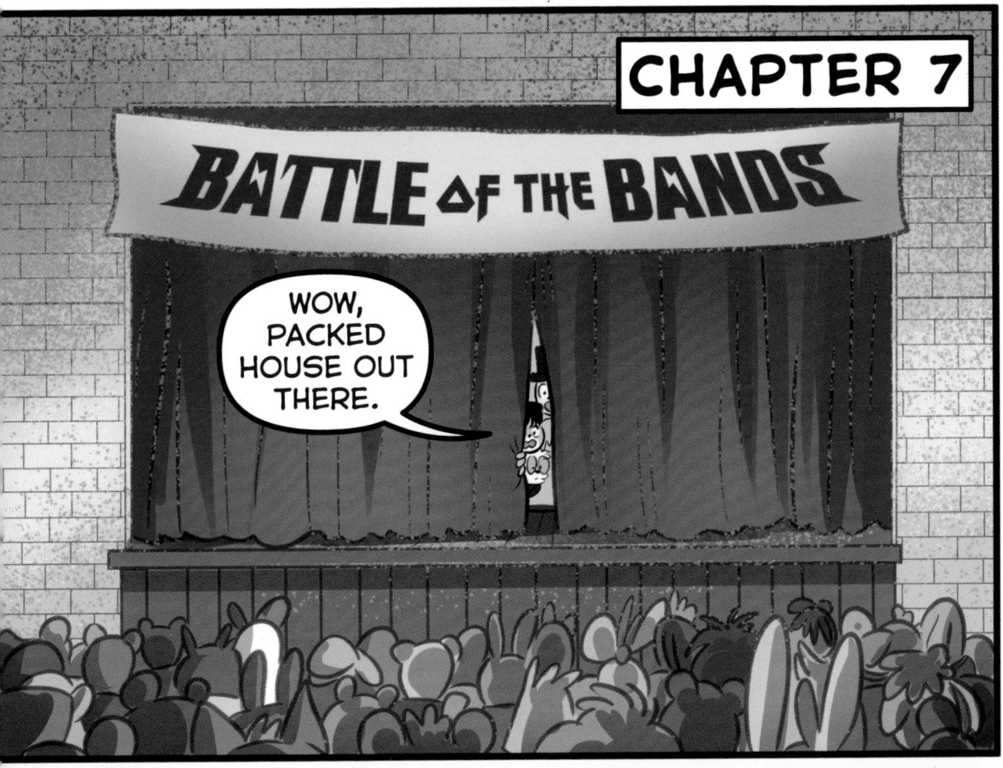
CHAPTER 7
BATTLE OF THE BANDS
WOW, PACKED HOUSE OUT THERE.

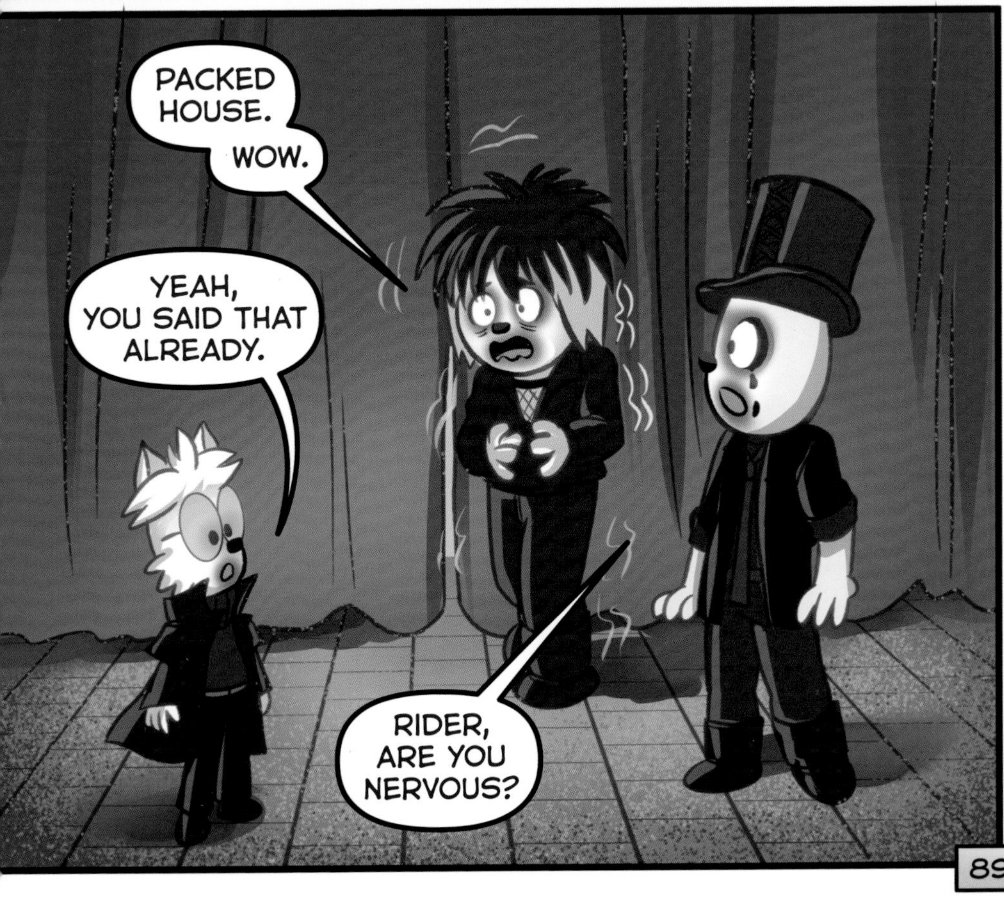
PACKED HOUSE.
WOW.
YEAH, YOU SAID THAT ALREADY.
RIDER, ARE YOU NERVOUS?

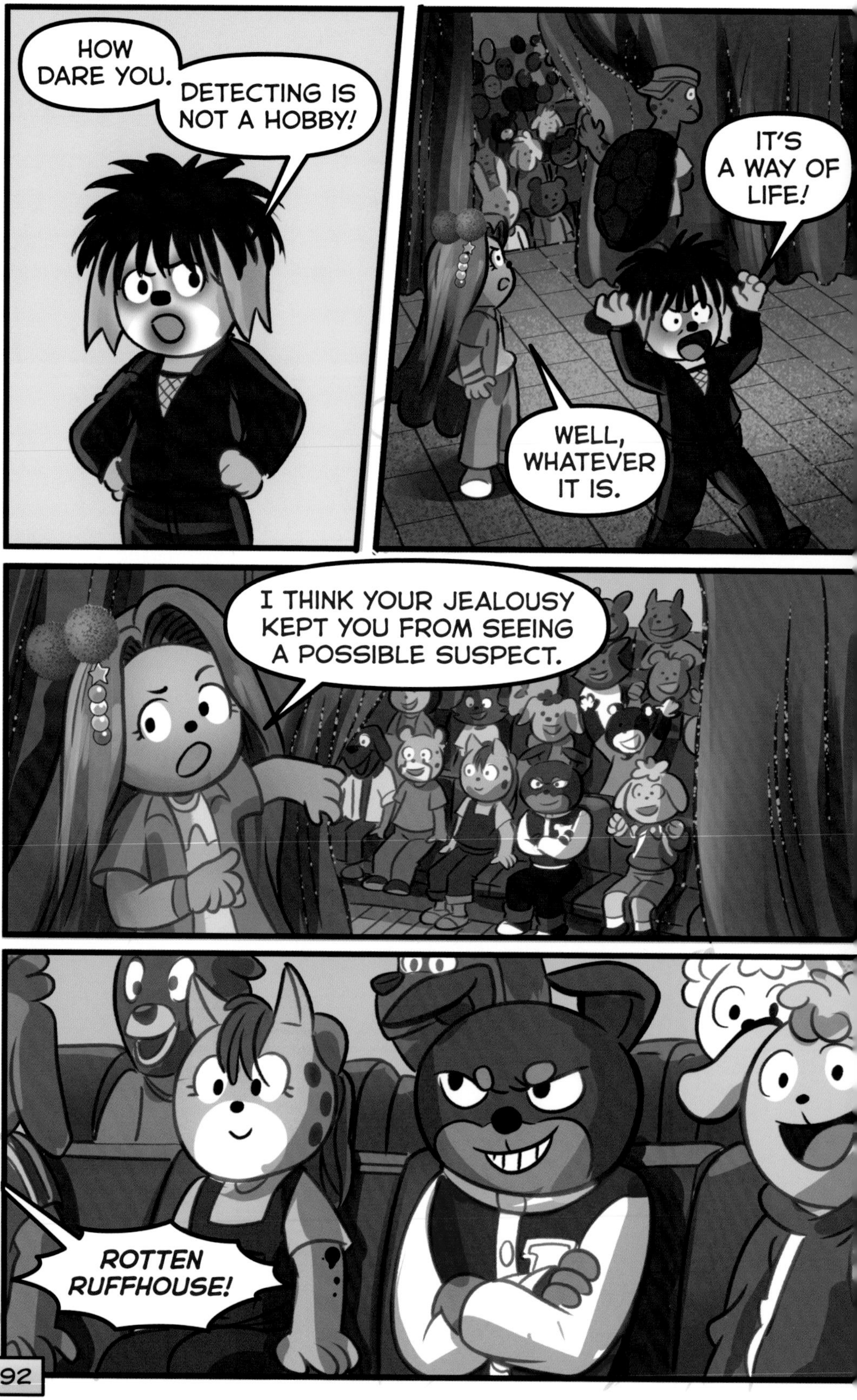
HOW DARE YOU.
DETECTING IS NOT A HOBBY!
IT'S A WAY OF LIFE!
WELL, WHATEVER IT IS.
I THINK YOUR JEALOUSY KEPT YOU FROM SEEING A POSSIBLE SUSPECT.
ROTTEN RUFFHOUSE!

WHAT IS ROTTEN DOING HERE?

HE HATES HEALTHY COMPETITION.

EXACTLY WHAT I WAS THINKING!

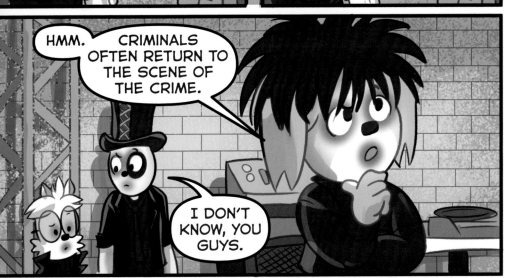

HMM. CRIMINALS OFTEN RETURN TO THE SCENE OF THE CRIME.

I DON'T KNOW, YOU GUYS.

COULD YOUR FEELINGS BE GETTING IN THE WAY OF SOLID DETECTIVE WORK?

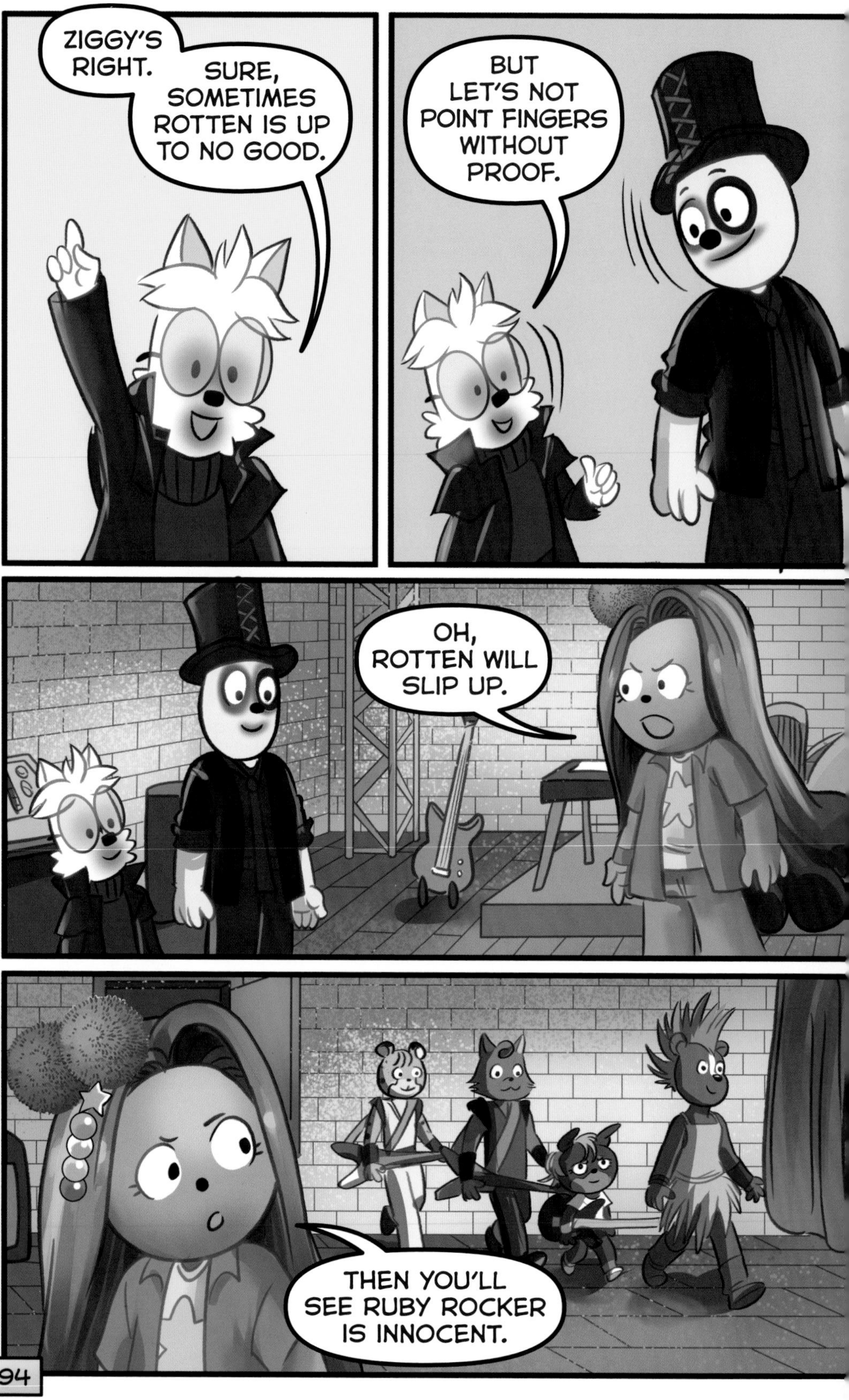
ZIGGY'S RIGHT.
SURE, SOMETIMES ROTTEN IS UP TO NO GOOD.
BUT LET'S NOT POINT FINGERS WITHOUT PROOF.
OH, ROTTEN WILL SLIP UP.
THEN YOU'LL SEE RUBY ROCKER IS INNOCENT.

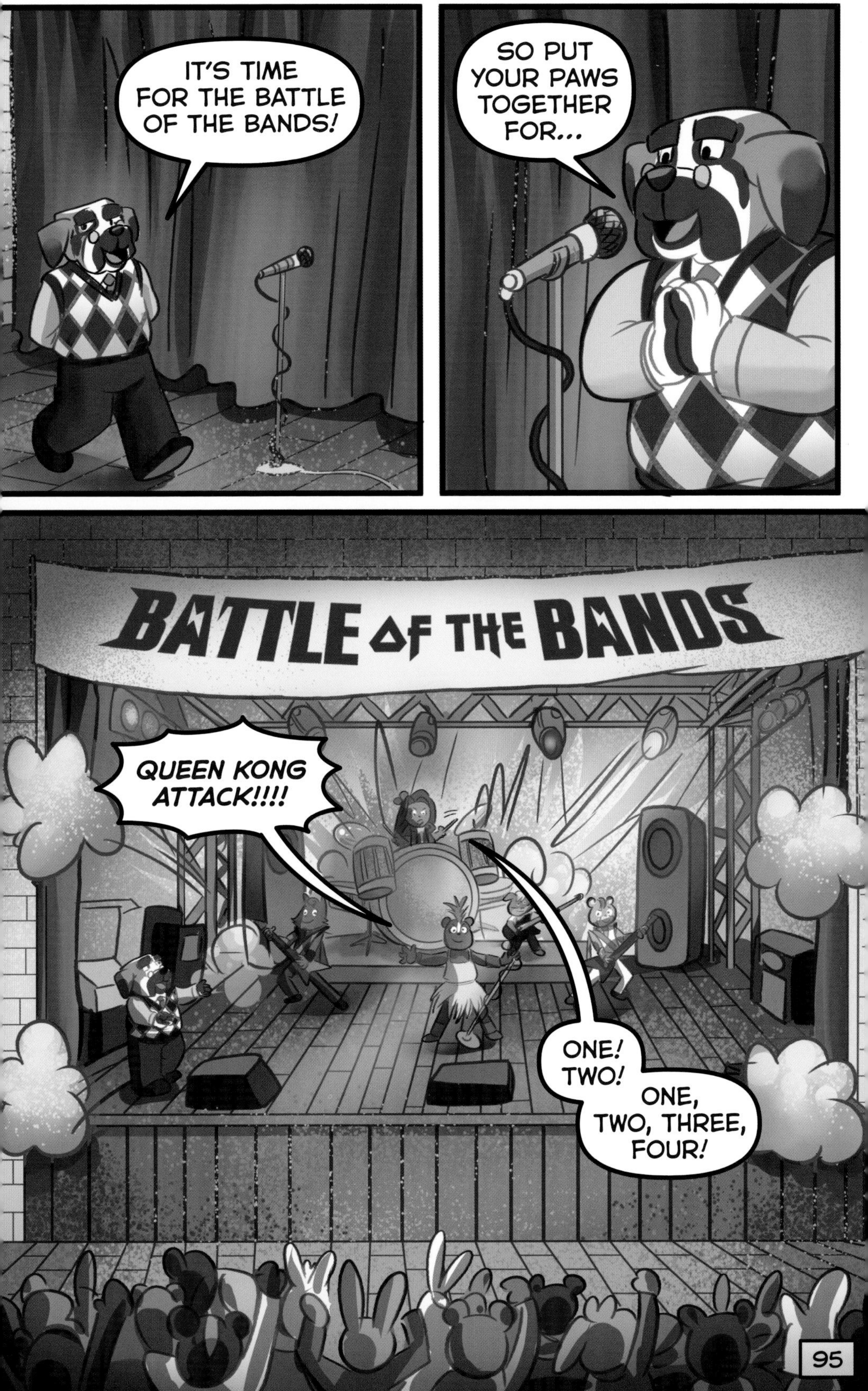
IT'S TIME FOR THE BATTLE OF THE BANDS!
SO PUT YOUR PAWS TOGETHER FOR...
BATTLE OF THE BANDS
QUEEN KONG ATTACK!!!!
ONE! TWO!
ONE, TWO, THREE, FOUR!

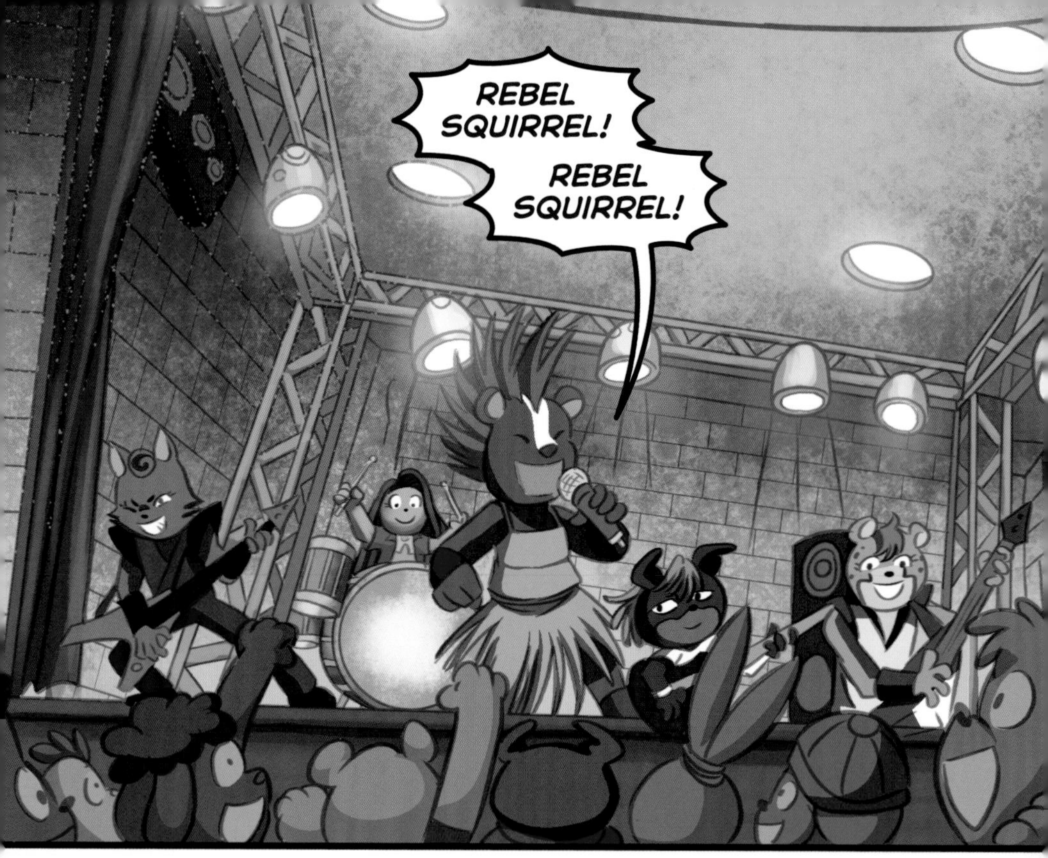
REBEL SQUIRREL!
REBEL SQUIRREL!

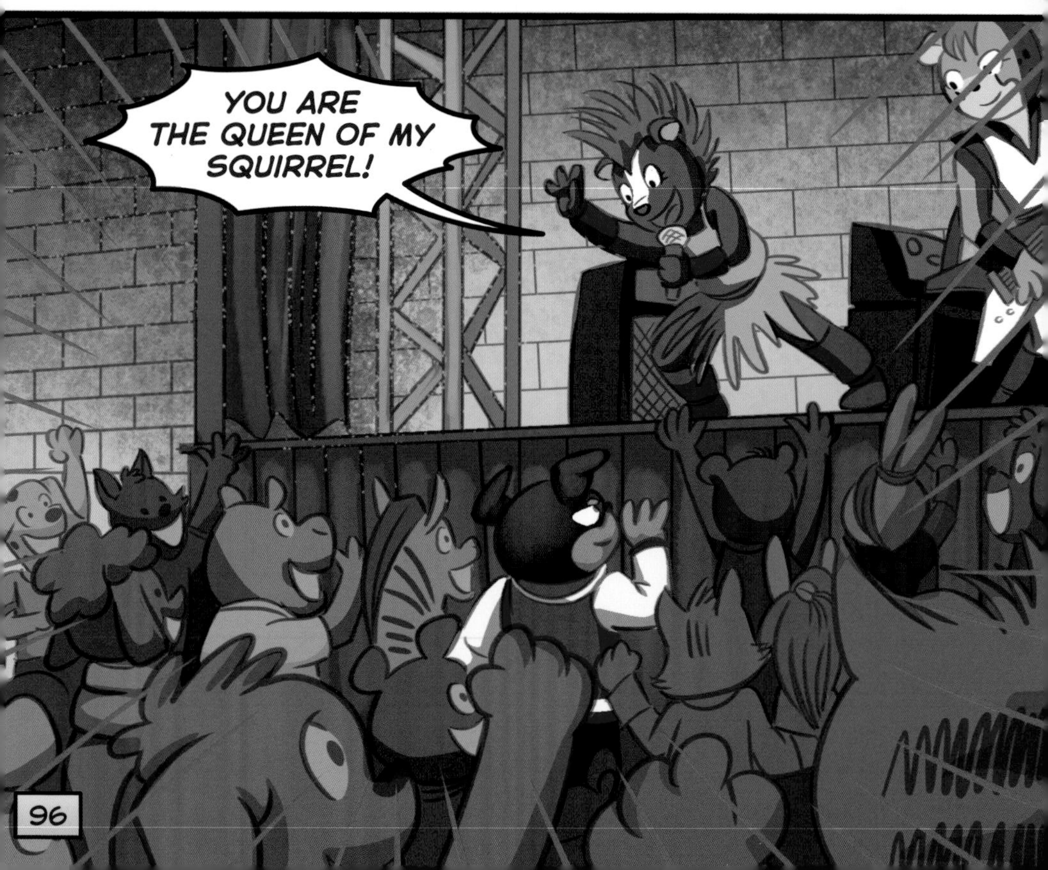
YOU ARE THE QUEEN OF MY SQUIRREL!

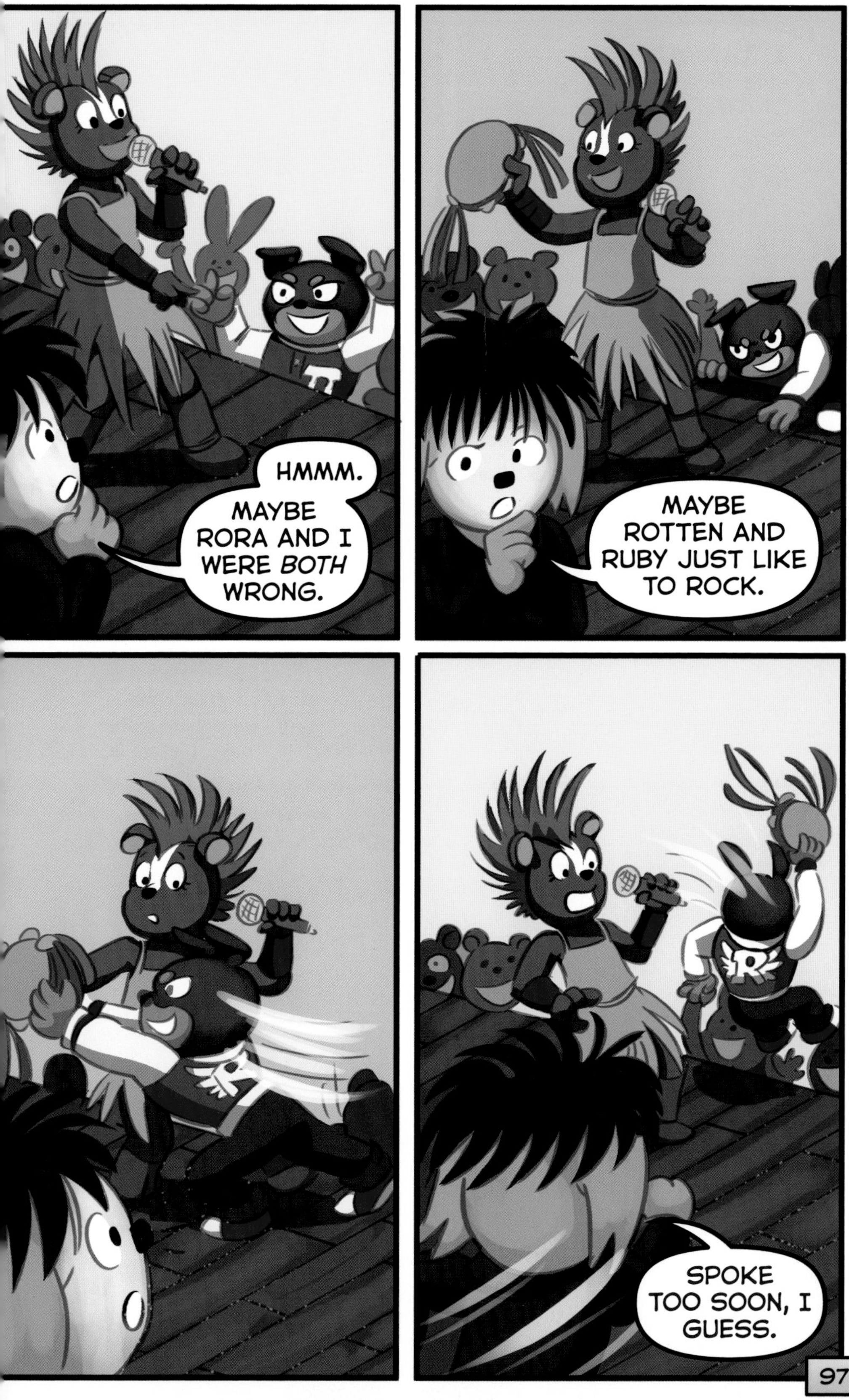
HMMM.
MAYBE RORA AND I WERE *BOTH* WRONG.
MAYBE ROTTEN AND RUBY JUST LIKE TO ROCK.
SPOKE TOO SOON, I GUESS.

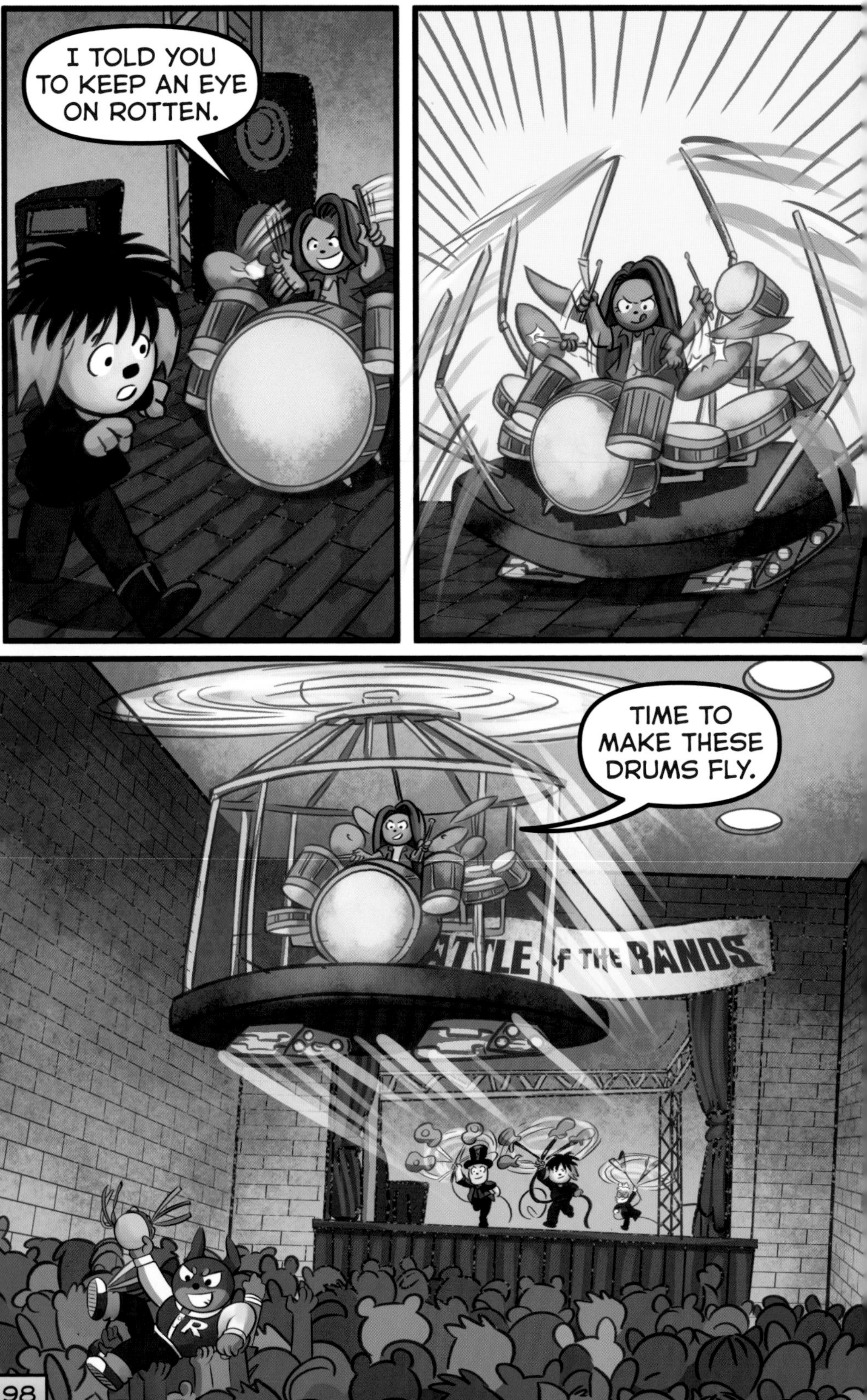
I TOLD YOU TO KEEP AN EYE ON ROTTEN.
TIME TO MAKE THESE DRUMS FLY.
LE OF THE BANDS

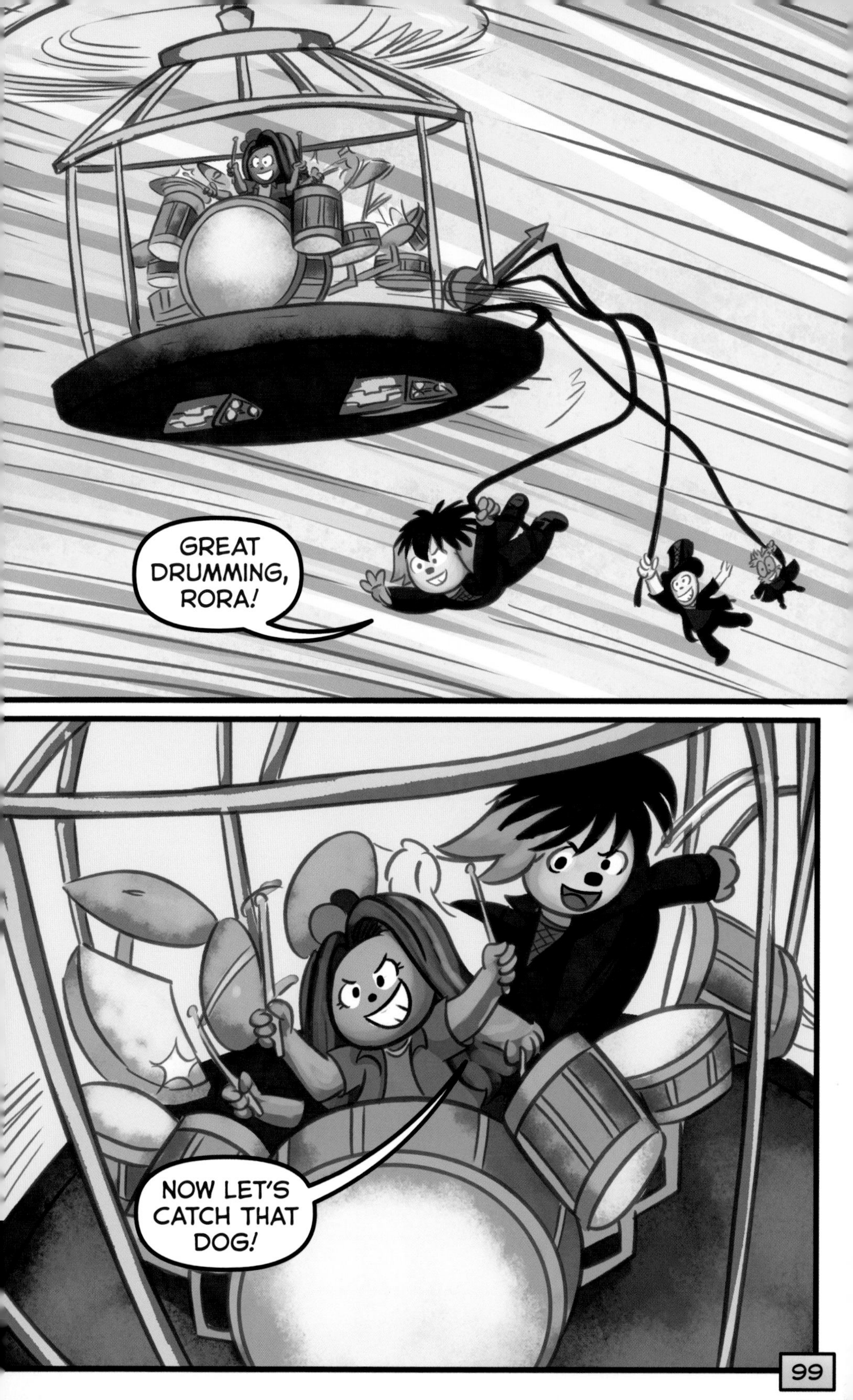
GREAT DRUMMING, RORA!
NOW LET'S CATCH THAT DOG!

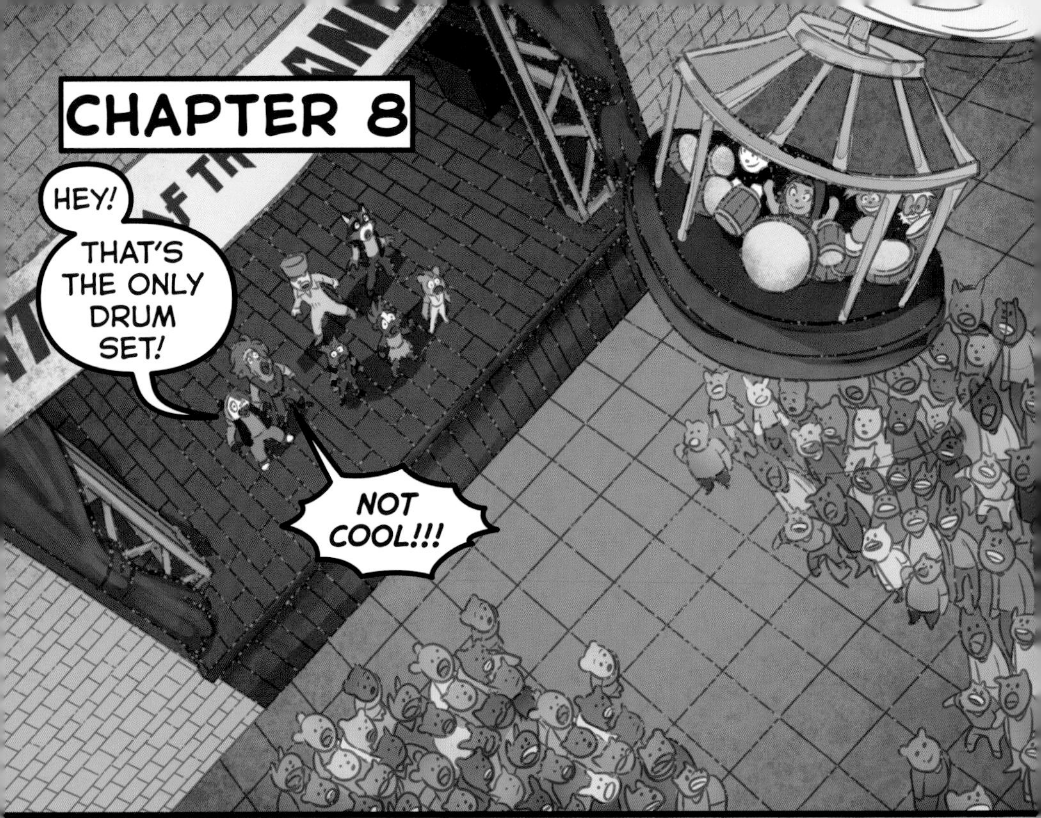
CHAPTER 8
HEY!
THAT'S THE ONLY DRUM SET!
NOT COOL!!!

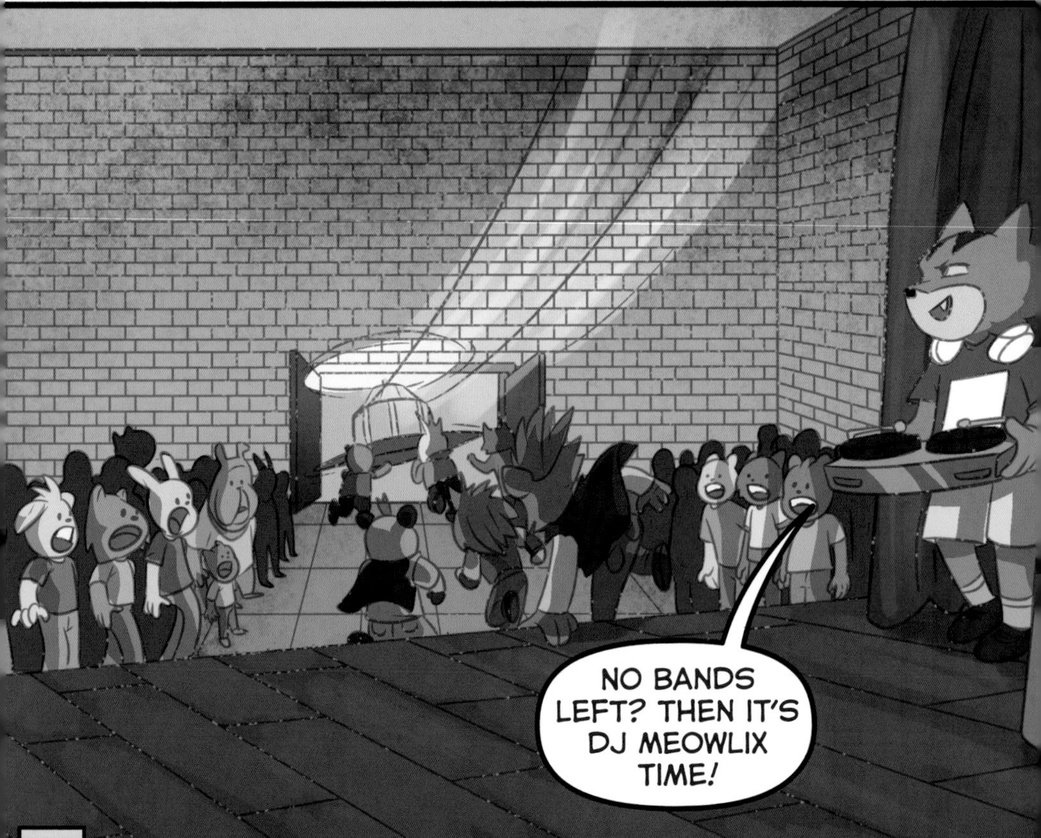
NO BANDS LEFT? THEN IT'S DJ MEOWLIX TIME!

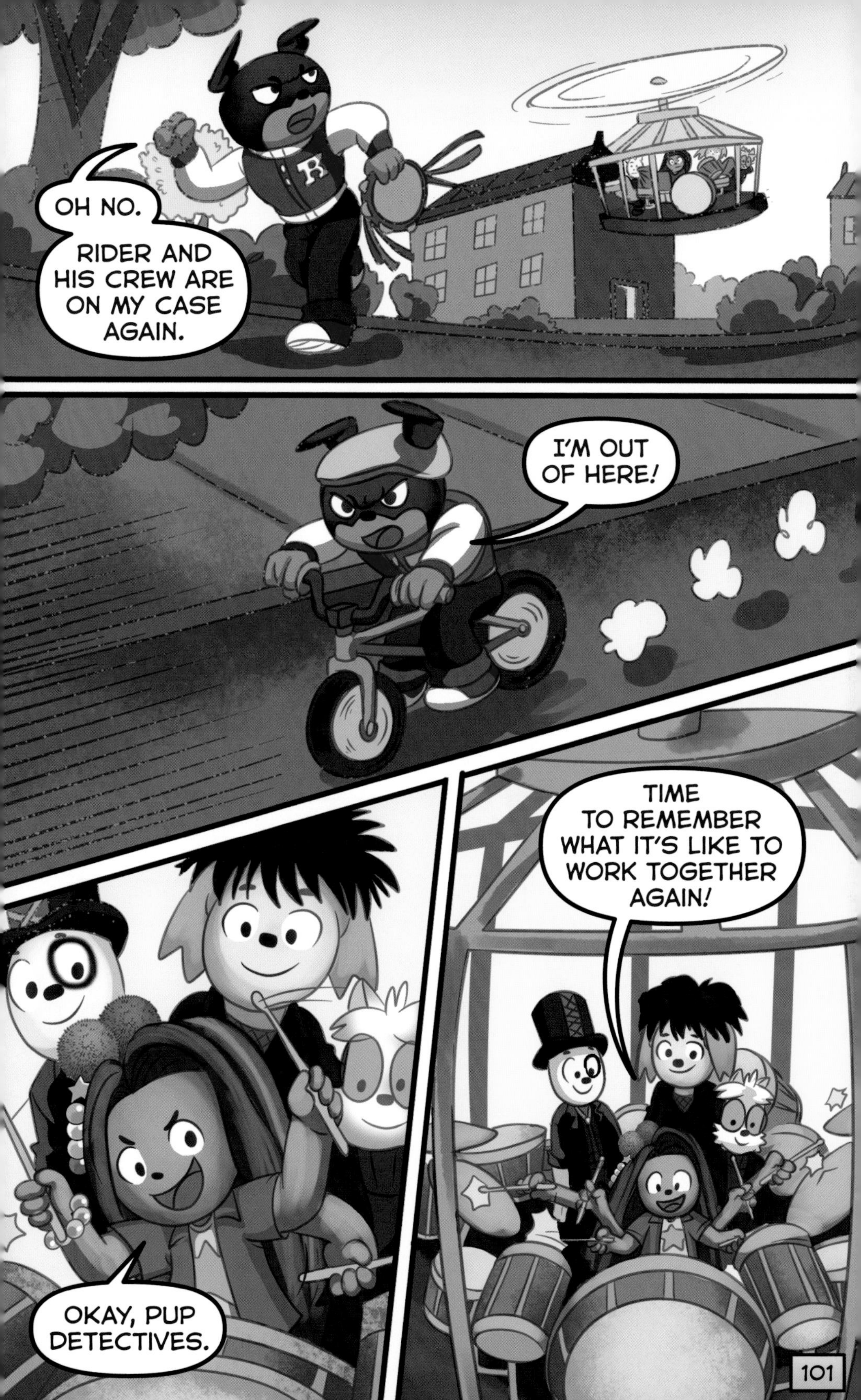
OH NO.
RIDER AND HIS CREW ARE ON MY CASE AGAIN.
I'M OUT OF HERE!
OKAY, PUP DETECTIVES.
TIME TO REMEMBER WHAT IT'S LIKE TO WORK TOGETHER AGAIN!

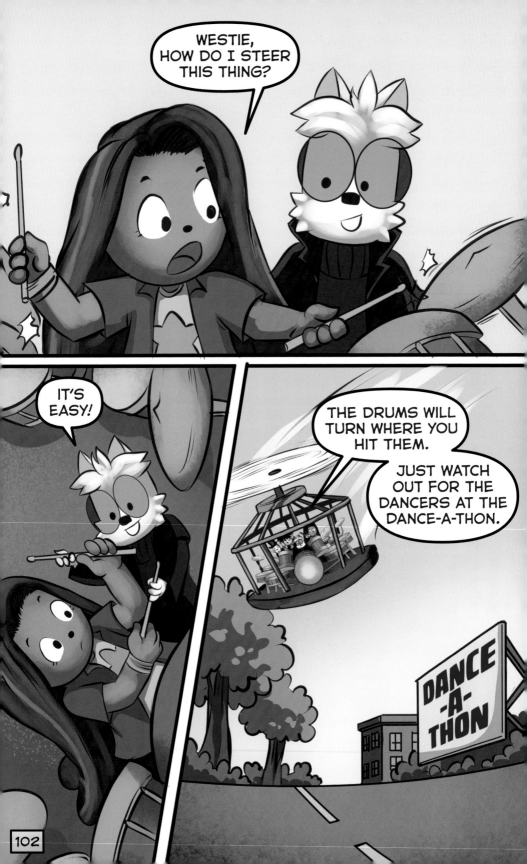

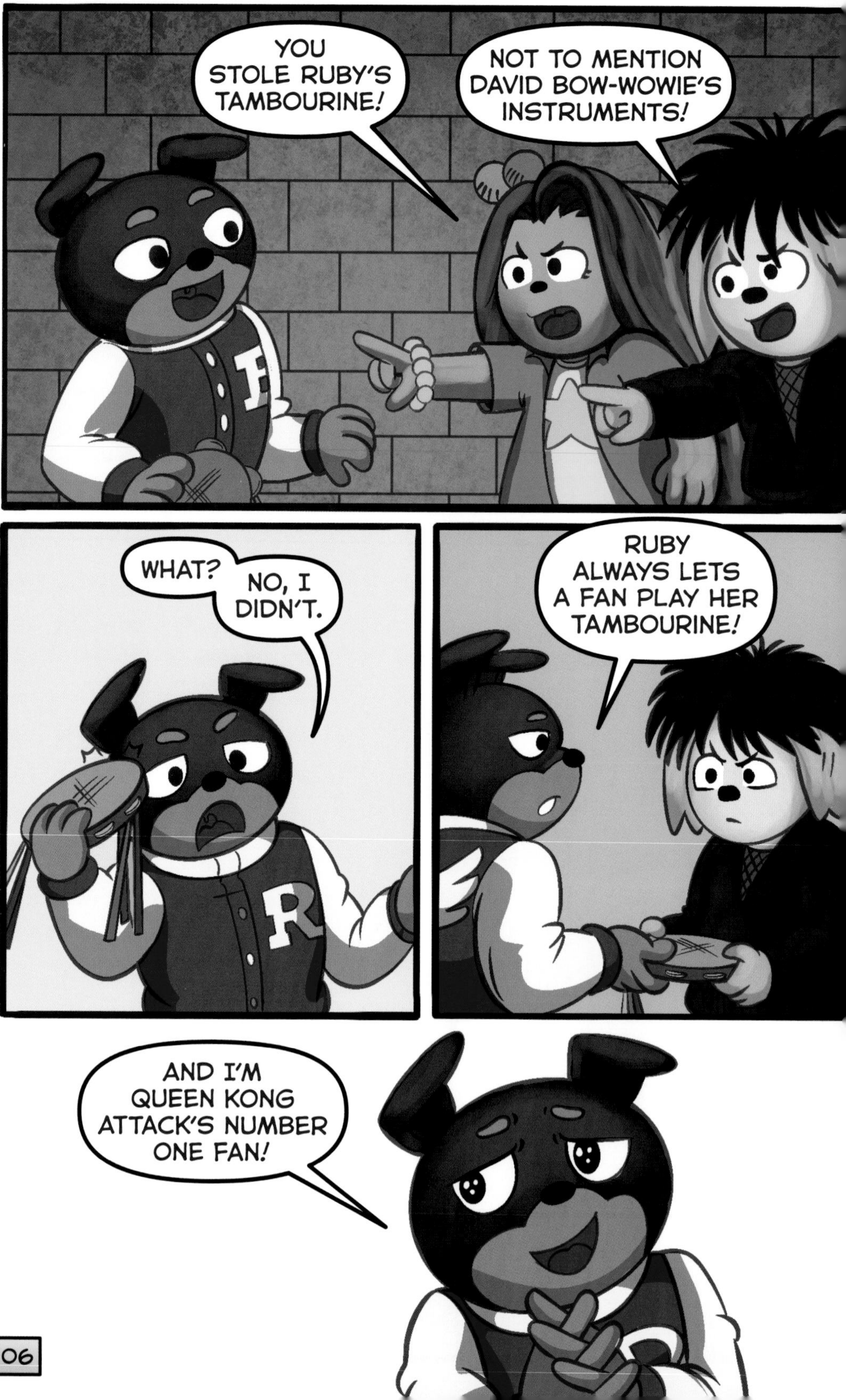
YOU STOLE RUBY'S TAMBOURINE!
NOT TO MENTION DAVID BOW-WOWIE'S INSTRUMENTS!
WHAT?
NO, I DIDN'T.
RUBY ALWAYS LETS A FAN PLAY HER TAMBOURINE!
AND I'M QUEEN KONG ATTACK'S NUMBER ONE FAN!

WELL, THIS ISN'T EVEN RUBY'S!

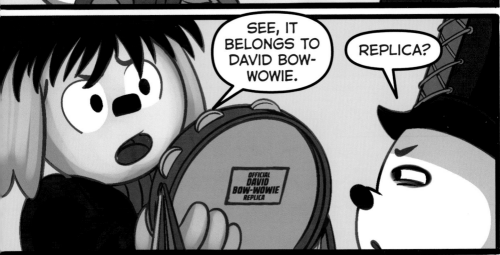

SEE, IT BELONGS TO DAVID BOW-WOWIE.

REPLICA?

OFFICIAL DAVID BOW-WOWIE REPLICA

OH NO! WHAT'S A REPLICA?

IS IT A GHOST? A GOBLIN? A GHOST GOBLIN?

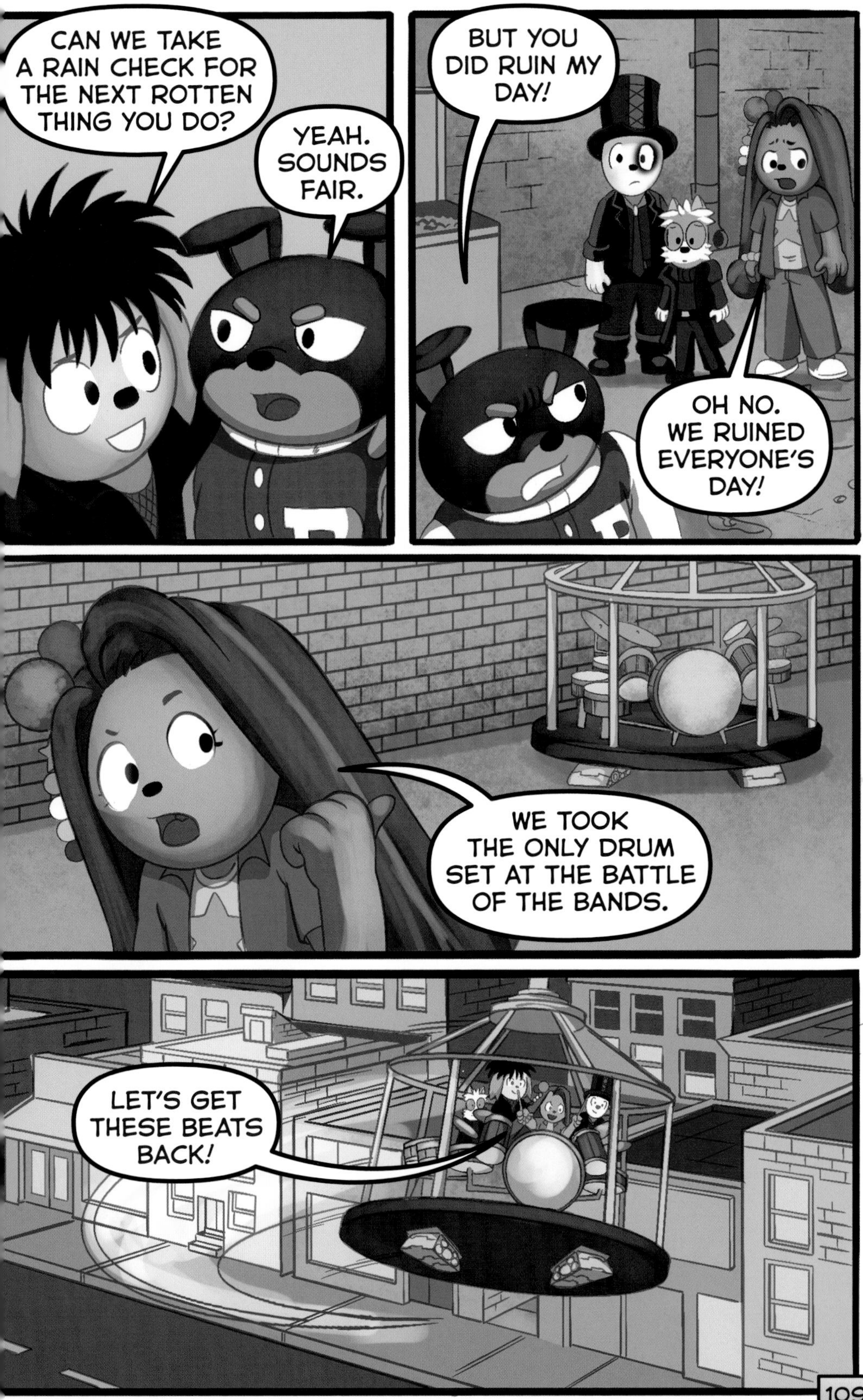
CAN WE TAKE A RAIN CHECK FOR THE NEXT ROTTEN THING YOU DO?
YEAH. SOUNDS FAIR.
BUT YOU DID RUIN MY DAY!
OH NO. WE RUINED EVERYONE'S DAY!
WE TOOK THE ONLY DRUM SET AT THE BATTLE OF THE BANDS.
LET'S GET THESE BEATS BACK!

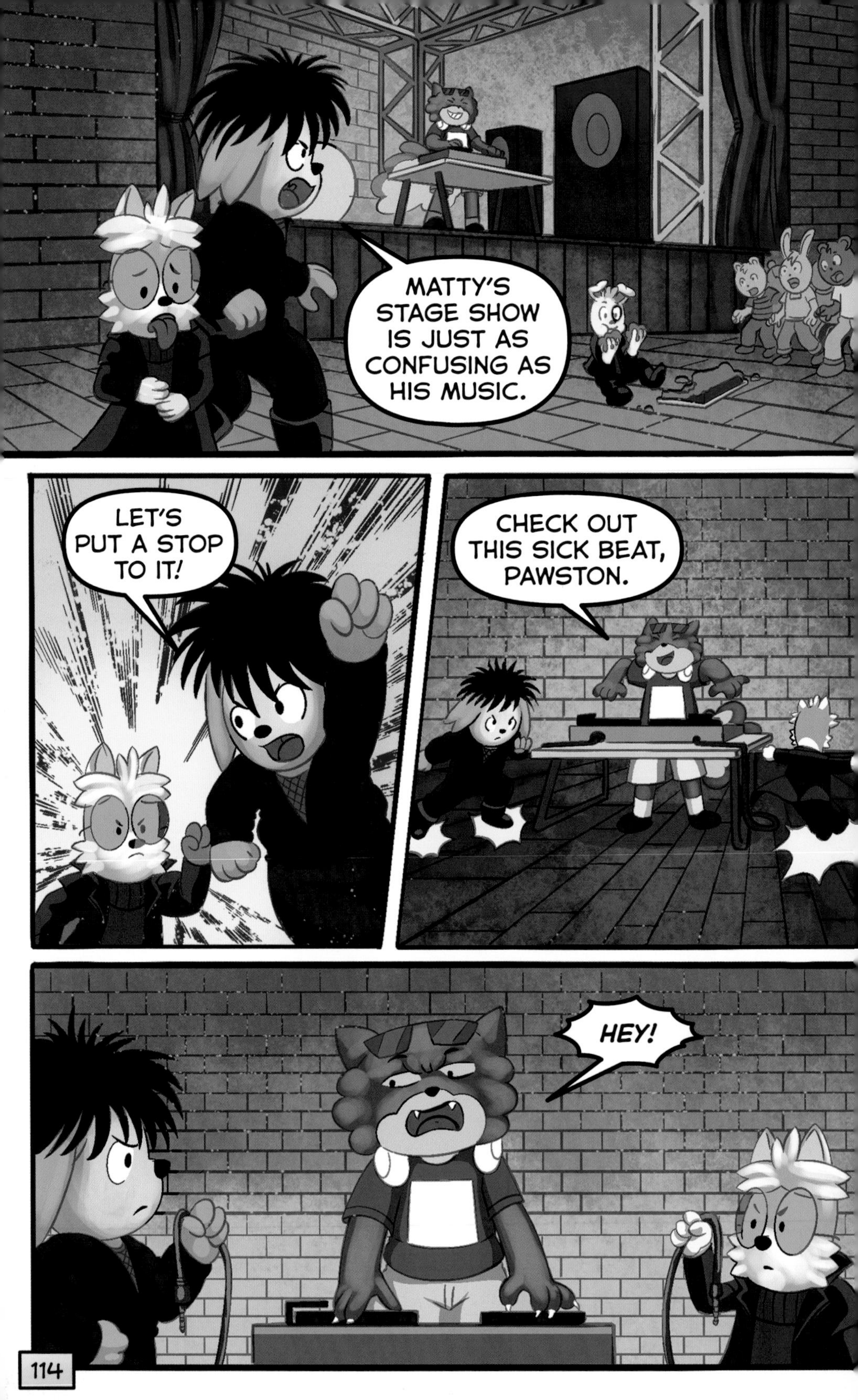
MATTY'S STAGE SHOW IS JUST AS CONFUSING AS HIS MUSIC.
LET'S PUT A STOP TO IT!
CHECK OUT THIS SICK BEAT, PAWSTON.
HEY!

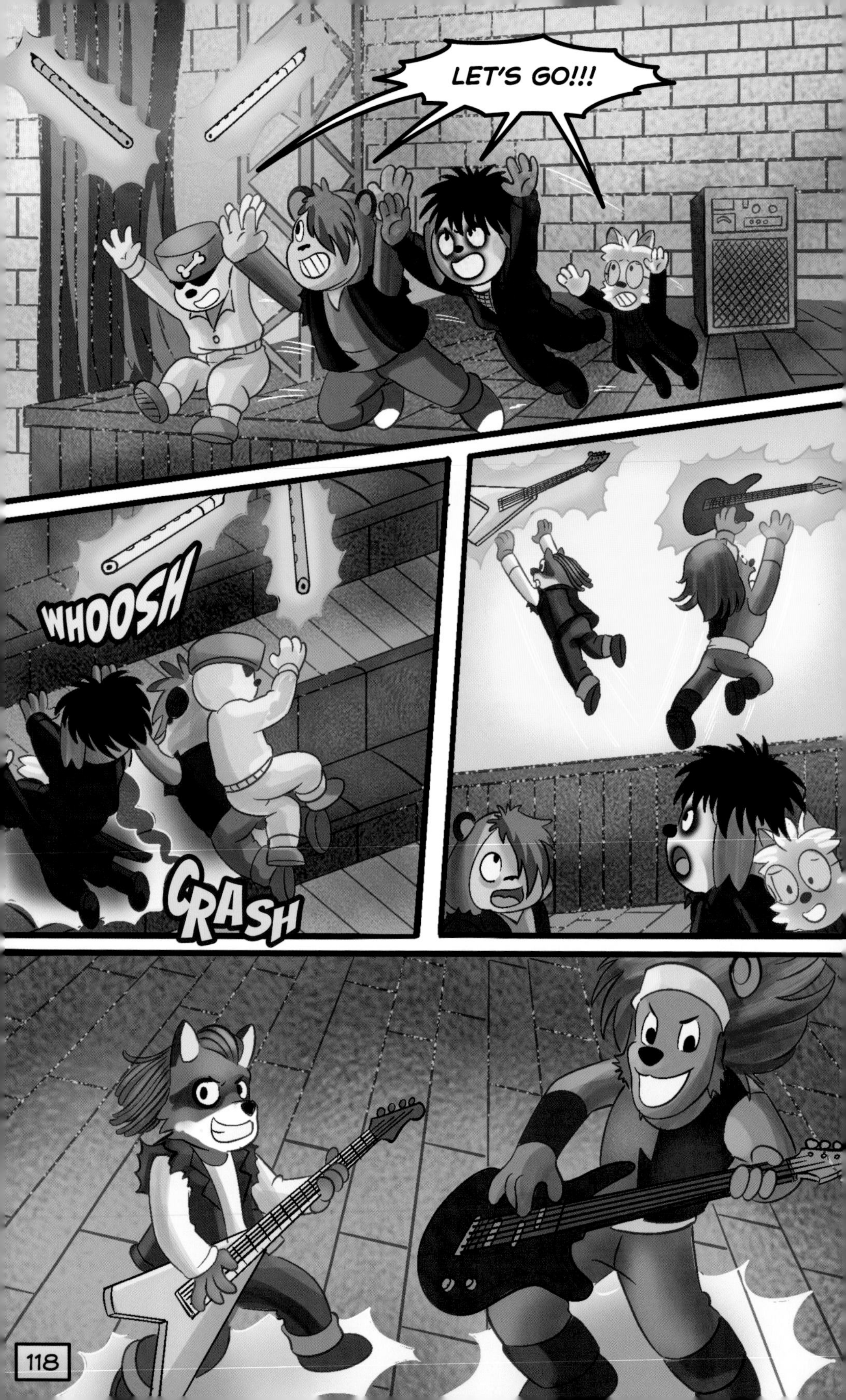
LET'S GO!!!
WHOOSH
CRASH

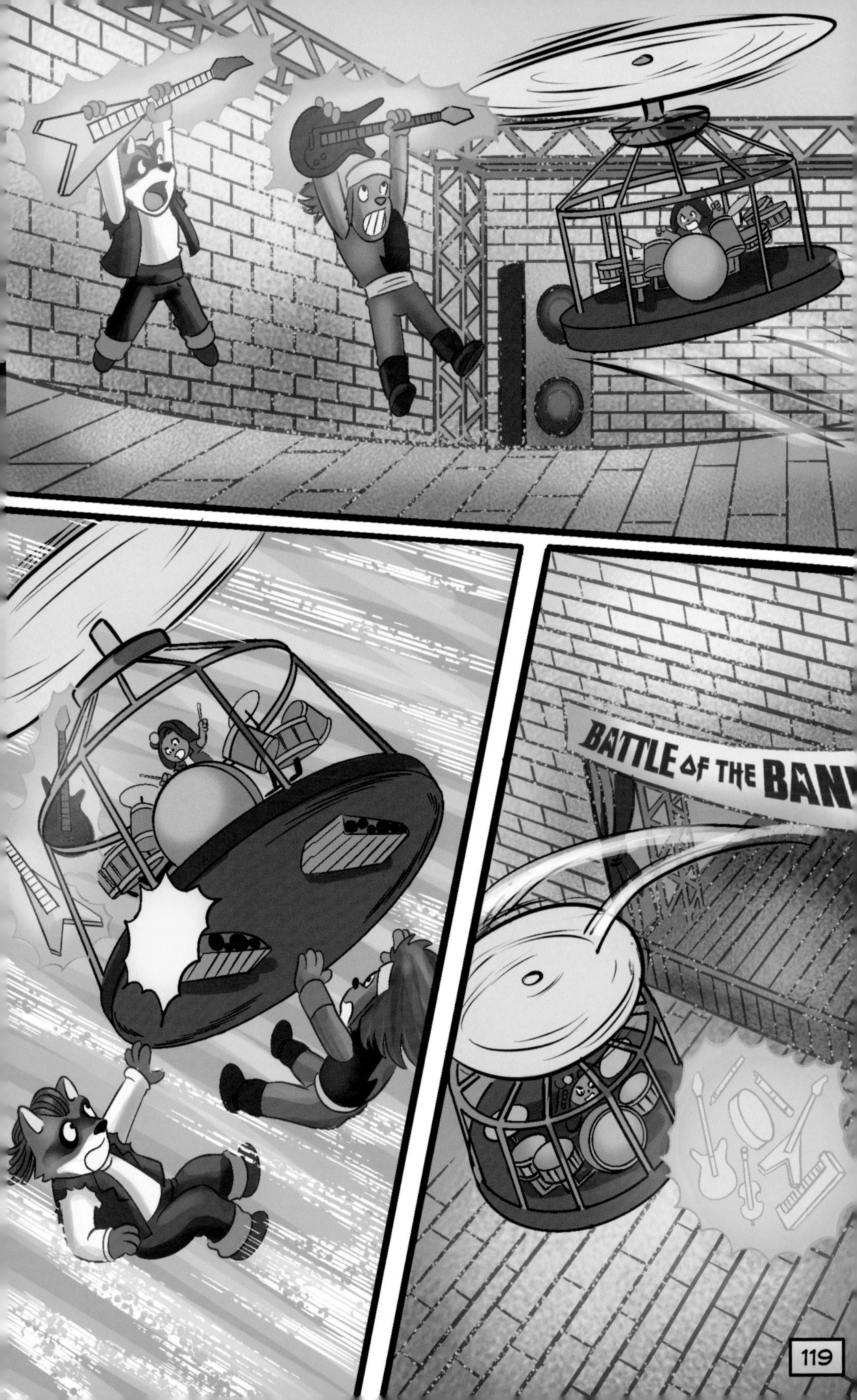
BATTLE OF THE BAN

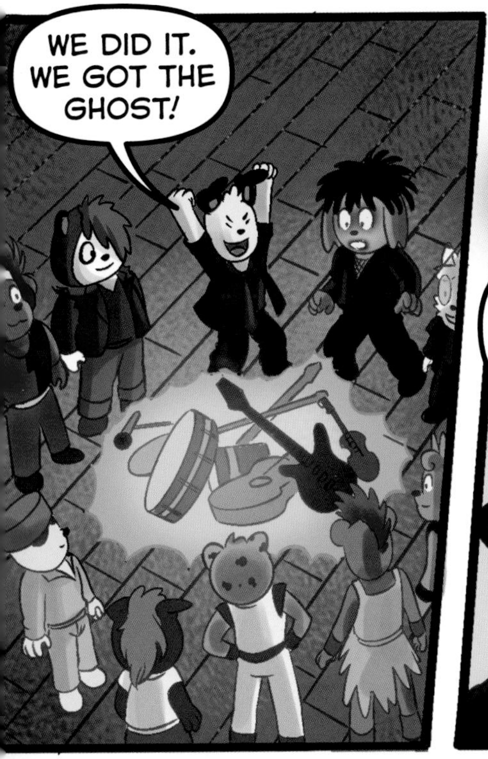
WE DID IT. WE GOT THE GHOST!

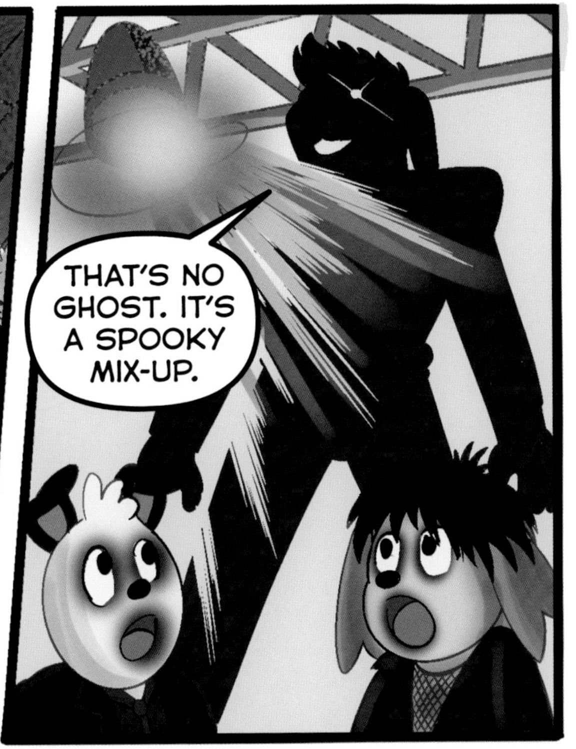
THAT'S NO GHOST. IT'S A SPOOKY MIX-UP.

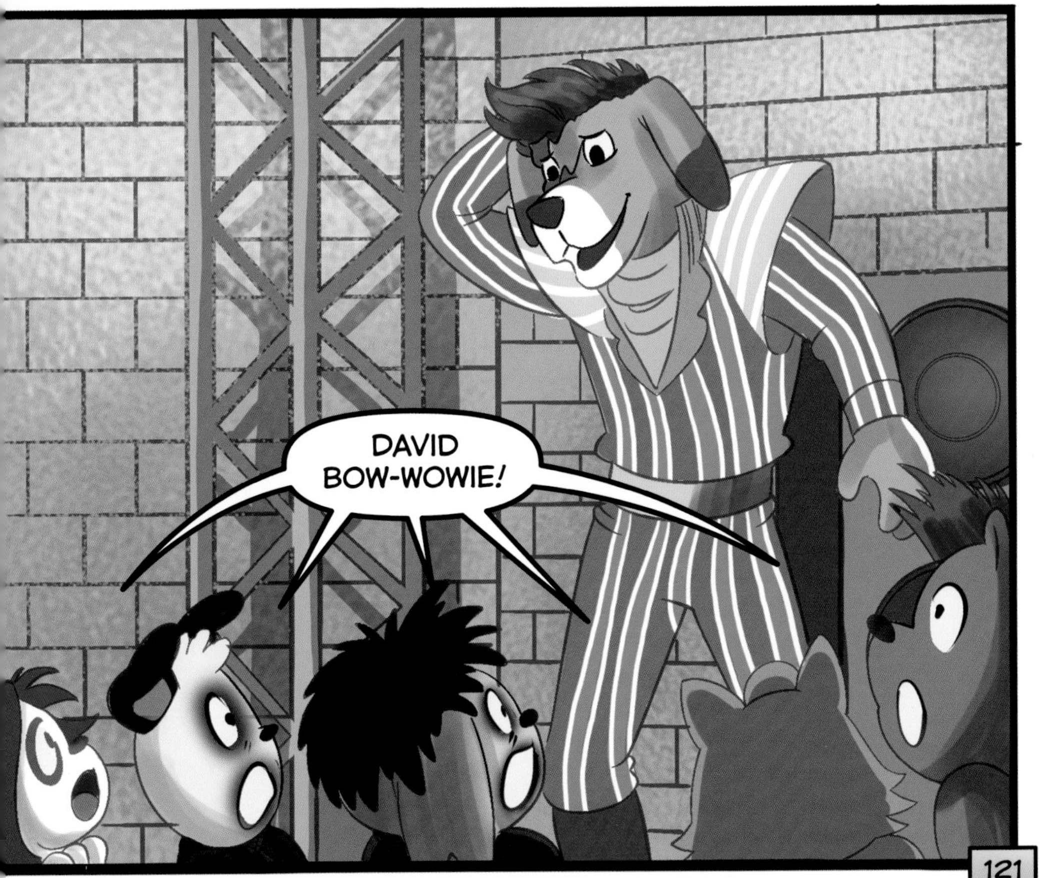
DAVID BOW-WOWIE!

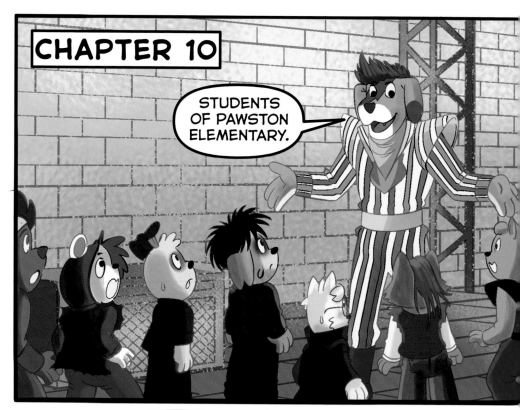

CHAPTER 10

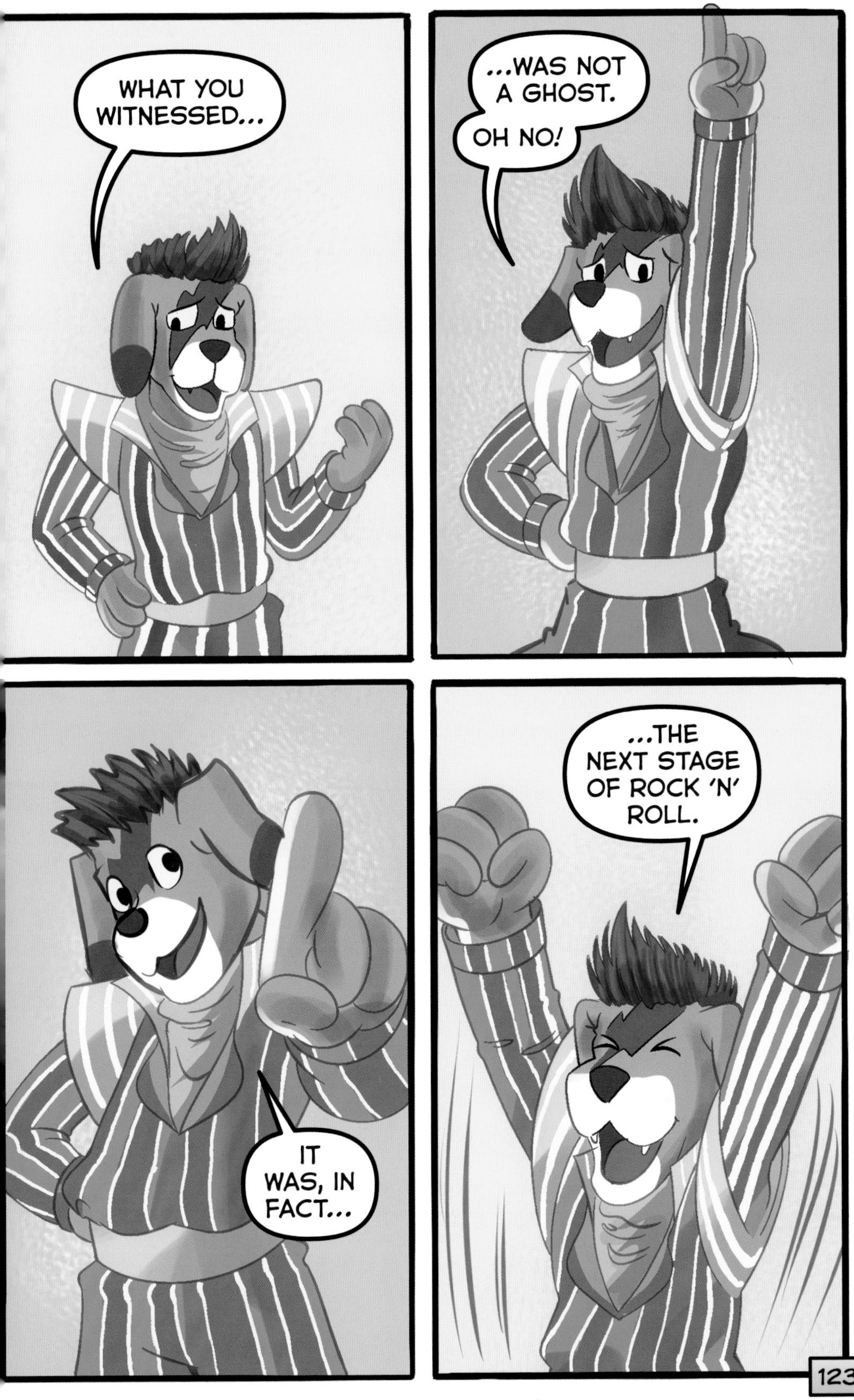
WHAT YOU WITNESSED...
...WAS NOT A GHOST.
OH NO!
IT WAS, IN FACT...
...THE NEXT STAGE OF ROCK 'N' ROLL.

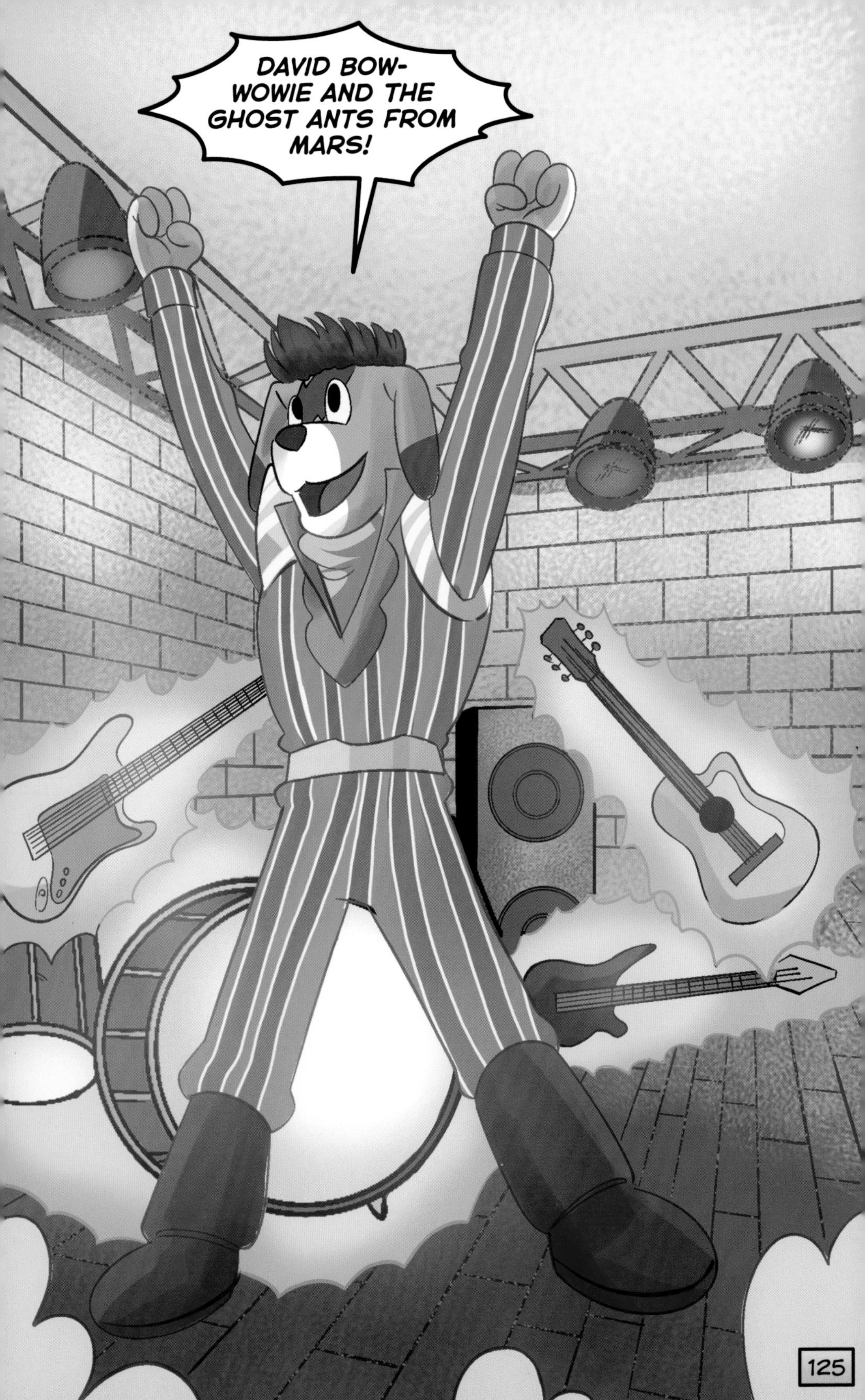
DAVID BOW-WOWIE AND THE GHOST ANTS FROM MARS!

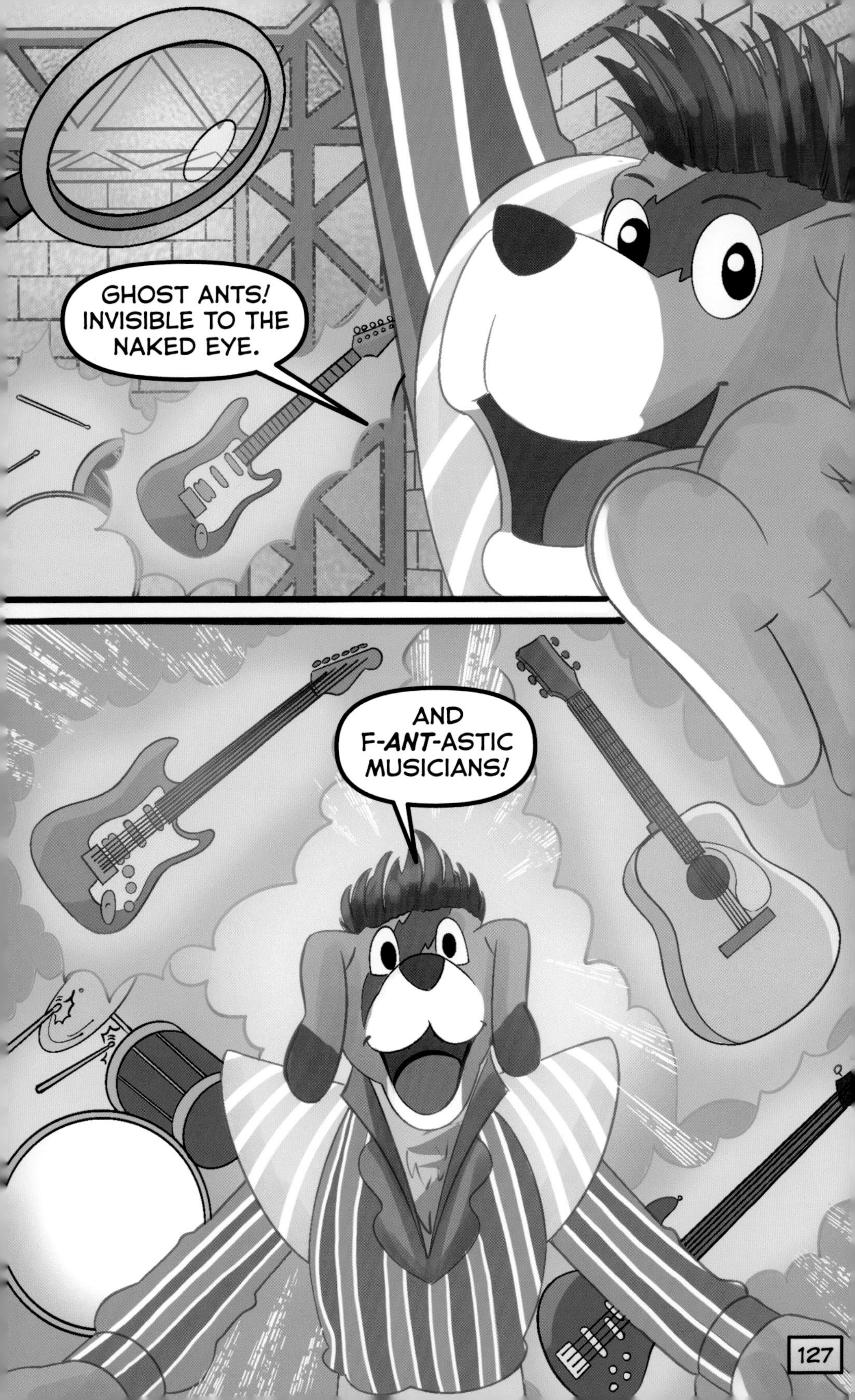
GHOST ANTS! INVISIBLE TO THE NAKED EYE.
AND F-ANT-ASTIC MUSICIANS!

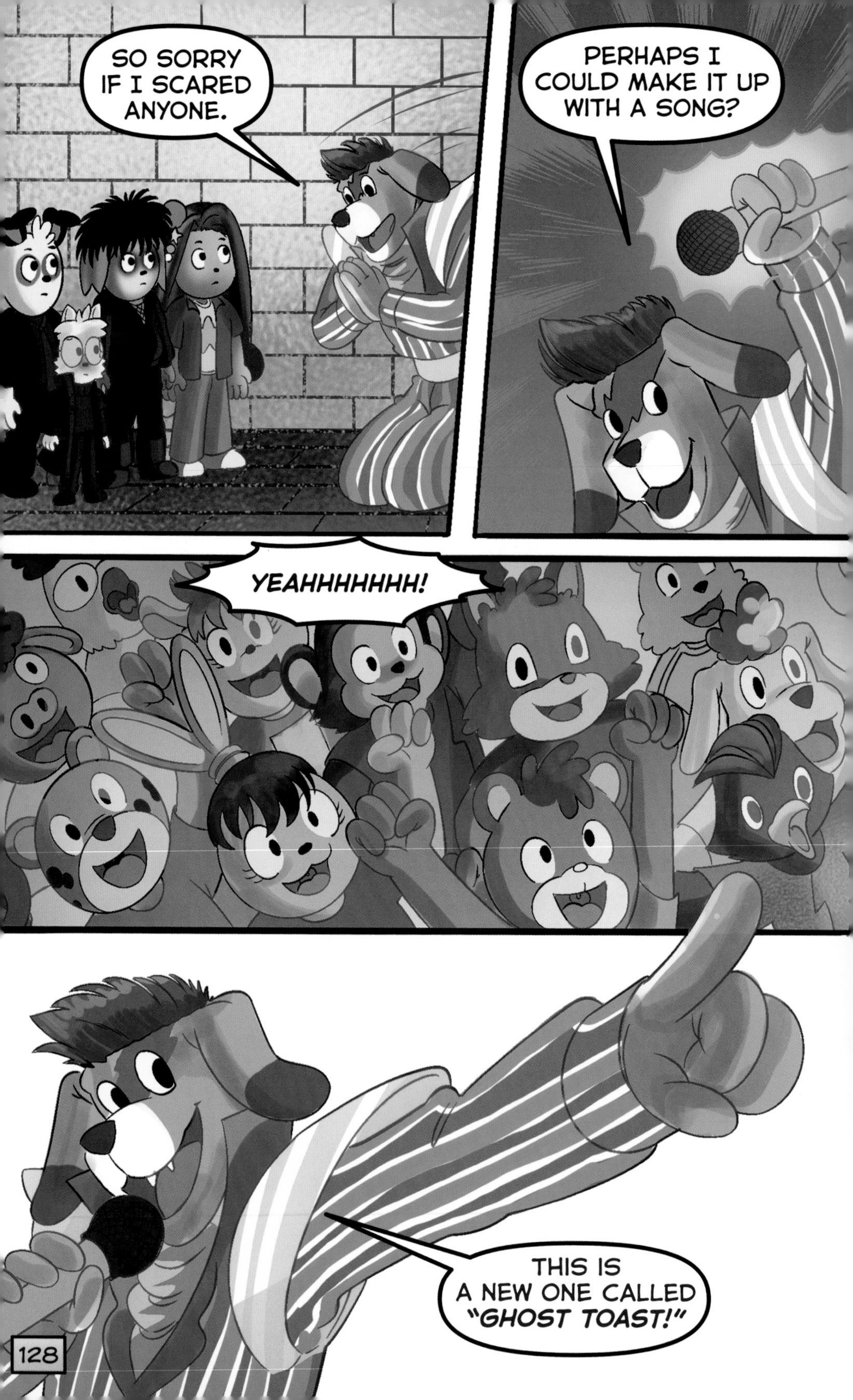
SO SORRY IF I SCARED ANYONE.
PERHAPS I COULD MAKE IT UP WITH A SONG?
YEAHHHHHHH!
THIS IS A NEW ONE CALLED "GHOST TOAST!"

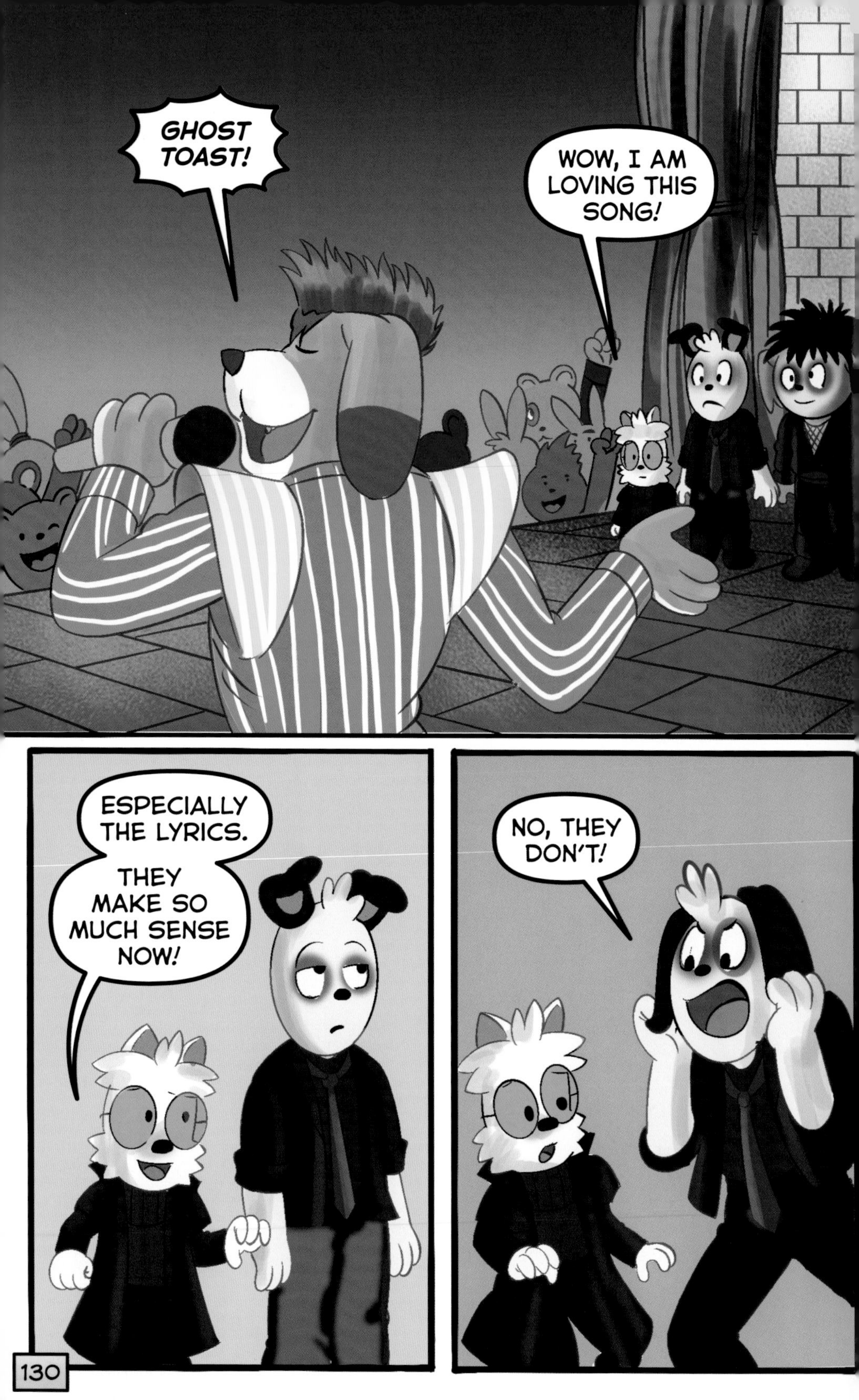
GHOST TOAST!
WOW, I AM LOVING THIS SONG!
ESPECIALLY THE LYRICS.
THEY MAKE SO MUCH SENSE NOW!
NO, THEY DON'T!

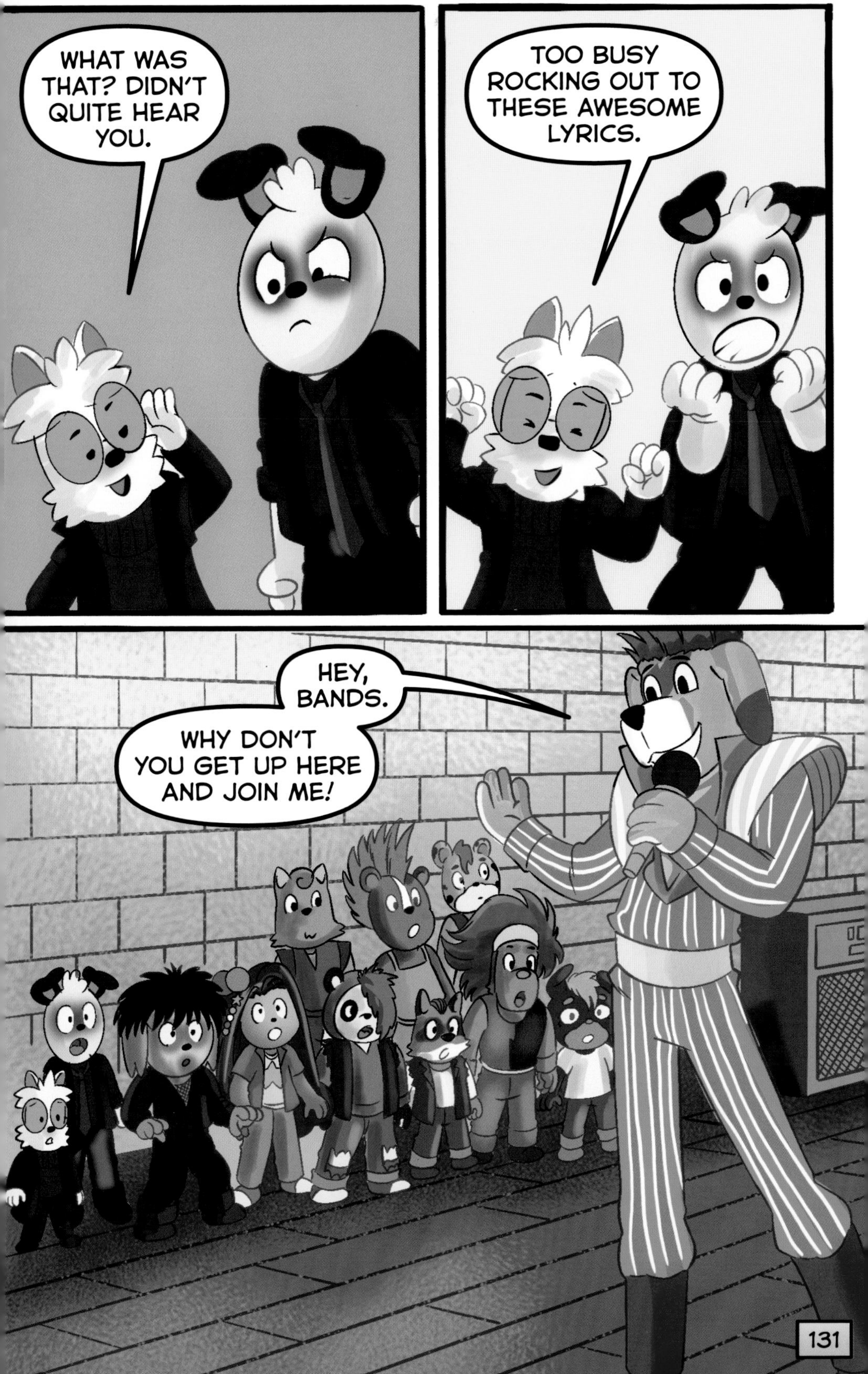
WHAT WAS THAT? DIDN'T QUITE HEAR YOU.
TOO BUSY ROCKING OUT TO THESE AWESOME LYRICS.
HEY, BANDS.
WHY DON'T YOU GET UP HERE AND JOIN ME!

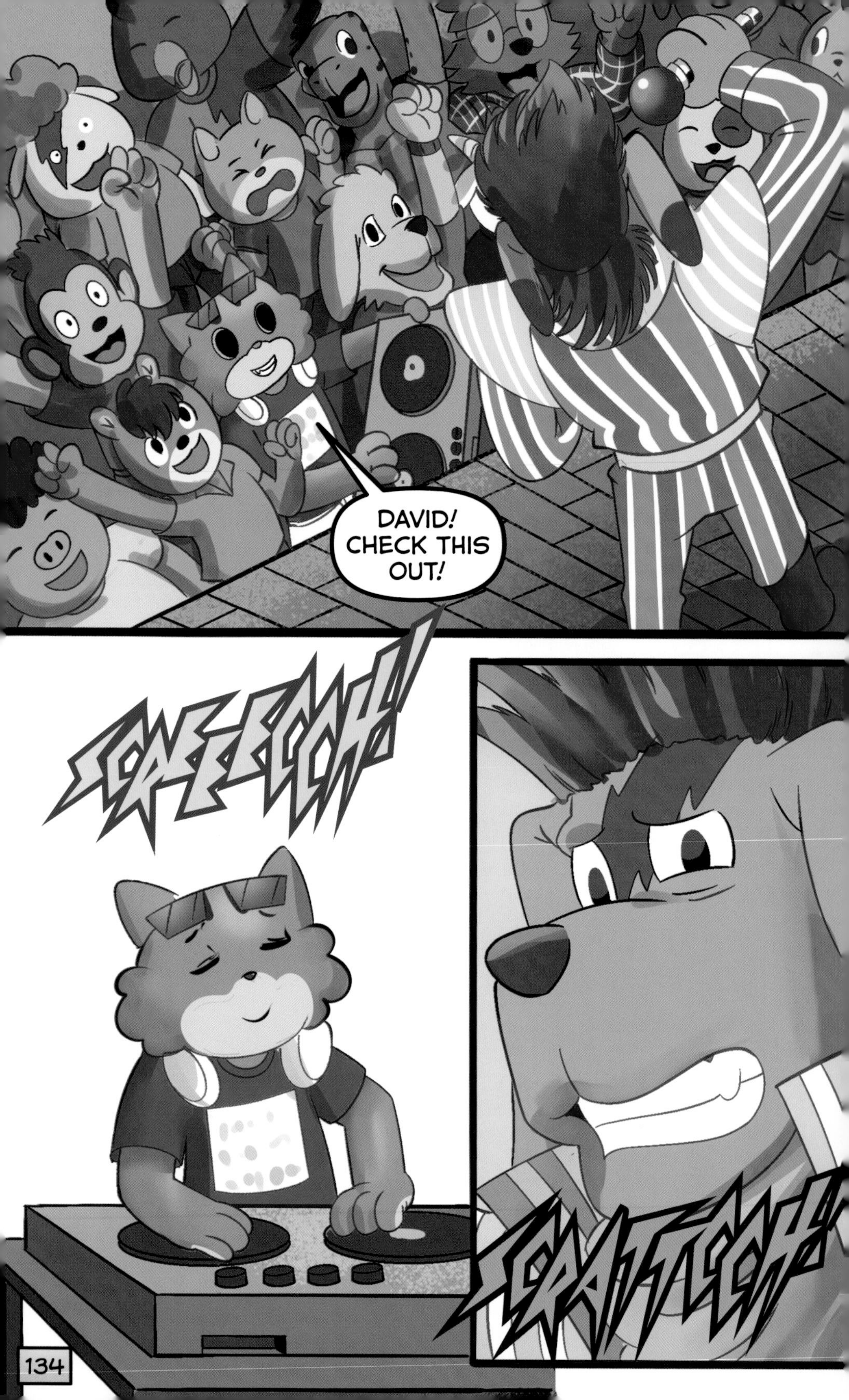
DAVID! CHECK THIS OUT!
SCREEECH!
SCRATCH!

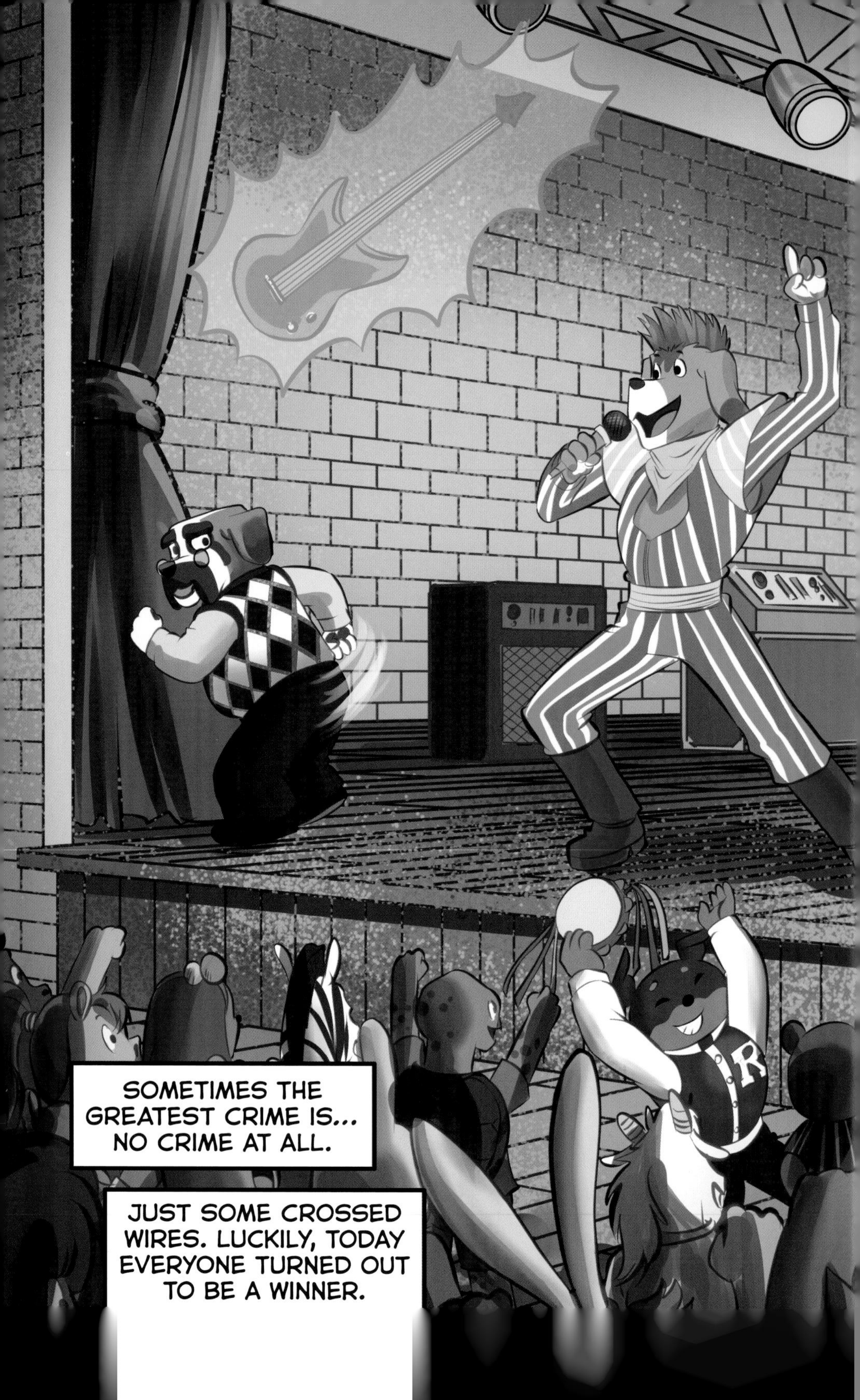
SOMETIMES THE GREATEST CRIME IS... NO CRIME AT ALL.
JUST SOME CROSSED WIRES. LUCKILY, TODAY EVERYONE TURNED OUT TO BE A WINNER.

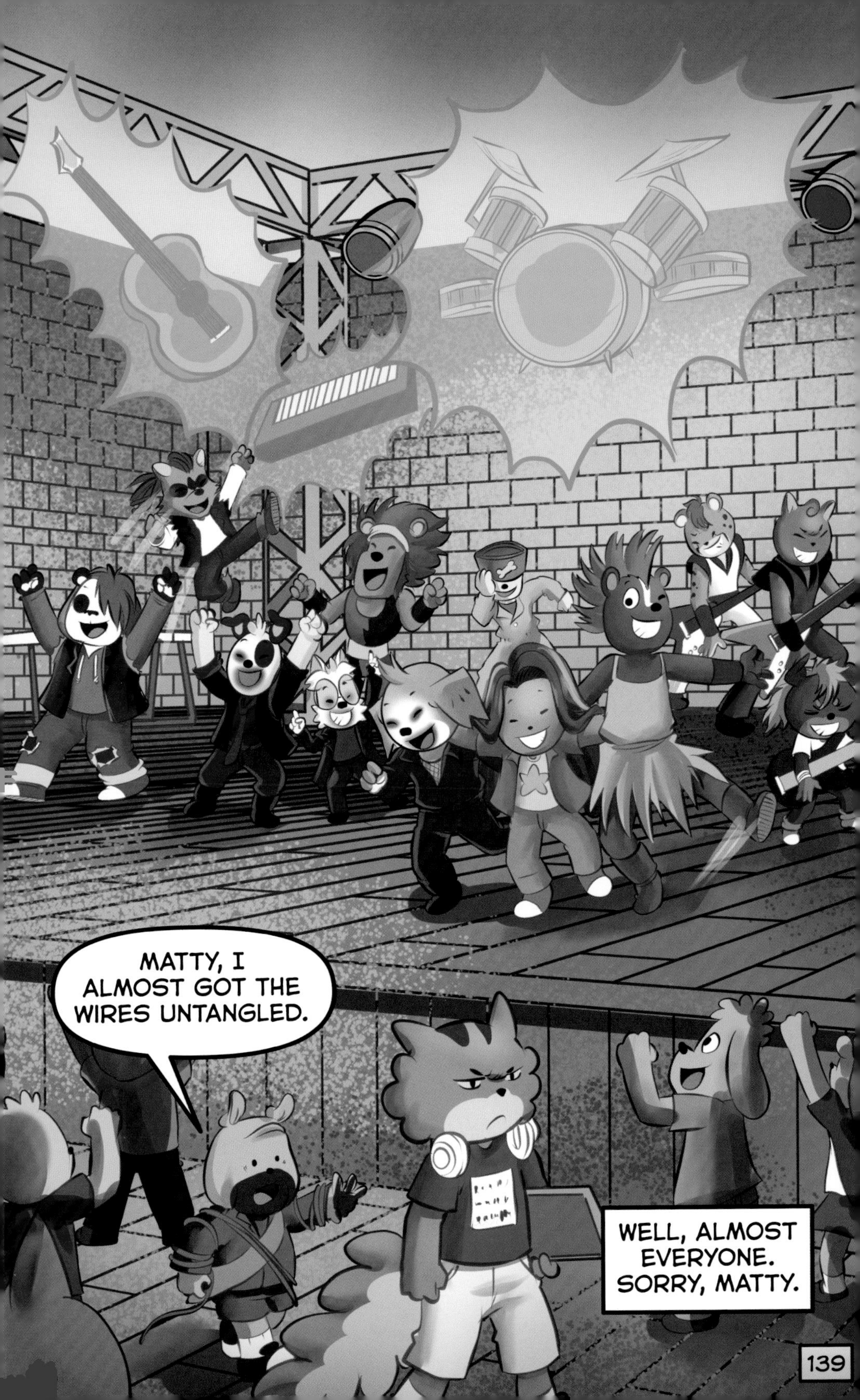
MATTY, I ALMOST GOT THE WIRES UNTANGLED.
WELL, ALMOST EVERYONE. SORRY, MATTY.

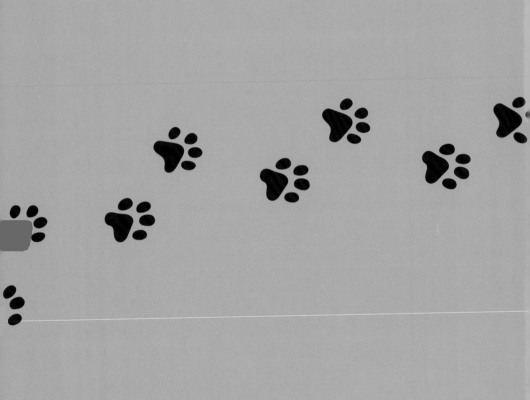

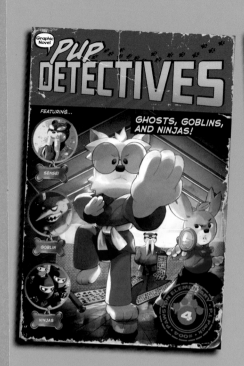

PUP DETECTIVES

FEATURING...

SENSEI

GOBLIN

NINJAS

GHOSTS, GOBLINS, AND NINJAS!

4

PUP DETECTIVES

FEATURING...

ZIGGY

FRENCHIE

MATTY MEOW

THE MISSING MAGIC WAND

5

PUP DETECTIVES

FEATURING...

PRINCIPAL

POPPA

RODERICK

MYSTERY MOUNTAIN GETAWAY

6

PUP DETECTIVES

FEATURING...

VICKY CROWN

BIG AL

MARTIN

THE BIG BAD WOOF

7